DISCOVERING MATTHEW

*A journey of acceptance and joy
in the world of autism*

VIVIENNE FREESTONE

Published by Vivienne Freestone

ISBN: 978-0-6453855-0-2 (paperback)

First edition, 2022

For book orders and enquiries, contact:
freestone8@bigpond.com

I dedicate this book to

Professor Jacqueline Roberts:

Chair of the Autism Centre of Excellence at Griffith University, former CEO of Autism NSW, Speech Pathologist, Mentor, Researcher and Educator of many.

Jacqui, thank you: your inspiration helped to start this journey.

The late and great Marcelle Van Gasselt:

Teacher, Mentor, Colleague and "Partner in Crime." Your teaching made a difference in the lives of so many in a rural area with minimal services. Your knowledge and humour brought us through so many tricky situations, to live to teach and try again!

Thanks Marcelle, from the bottom of my heart.

May you still be "checking the car" in heaven, dear friend!

To my husband David and my children, my children-in-law and my grandchildren:

You have all enriched my life, allowed me to practice my skills as a parent, grand-parent and as a therapist, and journeyed this path with me every step of the way.

Sometimes those dinners after work were a little dodgy but you all survived!

And you have taught me so much. Thank you for your love and support without which I would not have made these steps in this "life in Autism."

I love you all.

To all the families and children I have met and worked with:

You live this story every day. This is for you all, with love.

Finally, to my God: Everything begins and ends with You. Thank you in awe and adoration for always being there for me, no matter what.

For everyone who reads this: Ephphatha! Be open to hear.

DISCLAIMER

The following is a story, a fiction.

After working in this field for decades, there are many stories which reflect my experiences, but any resemblance to persons or situations - living or passed away - is purely coincidental.

Remember: If you have met ONE person with an Autism Spectrum Disorder, you have met ONE person with an Autism Spectrum Disorder, so every situation is unique!

CONTENTS

CHAPTER 1

WHAT THE HECK?
A TIME TO TEAR DOWN

"Matthew Luckmore, that behaviour is totally unacceptable. I am very disappointed in you. Get up and go to the office right now. I am calling Ms Montgomery and she will be waiting for you. Move!!"

Eyes on the floor he stood, shoulders slumped, shuffling sideways between the desks of classmates, mind racing. Matt thought "Avoid eye-contact. Don't look up. Don't look at <u>anyone</u>. Then it might all go away."

Reaching the doorway to 6ST, Matt glanced towards the playground and the distant oval bordered by bush. "Just 200 metres. I could do it in 52 seconds and disappear and run and run and run through the trees..." he thought to himself.

"OK Matthew – with me. Bring your school bag. We'll walk up to the office together." Ms Montgomery appeared at his side, and he knew it was too late to escape. Eyes still downcast Matt studied her shoes – red, with a little black bow and small square holes cut out all around the edges, highish heels, shiny and new, probably very fashionable although Matt really didn't know.

He did know that his Mum would never buy shoes like these; high, shiny, expensive.

Mum wore flat shoes from the Op Shop if she could get them, and boots; old, worn and comfy.

Matt's eyes followed Ms M's red shoes as his body traipsed behind her, dragging a backpack, trapped by the need to conform with the school rules, torn by the compulsion to run, to escape. "So, I'll focus on the shoes," he thought.

Ms M always wore fancy shoes. She was known for it, a hallmark of the principal who had risen to that exalted position at only 38 years of age, totally dedicated to her craft – "a calling" she liked to say, a calling to teach, to guide young lives, to organise their education so all their needs were met at a primary school where different cultures, economic status, geographic divides, and intellectual abilities all meant nothing.

"The individual must be catered for" Ms M often said at school assemblies. "We at Highcrest Primary pride ourselves on developing individual strengths and responding to individual needs, within the classroom and the wider school community."

Trudging along behind this dedicated educator, Matt wondered about HIS needs and HIS strengths. He was absolutely sure and certain that no-one at Highcrest Primary School knew the real Matthew John Luckmore, lately of "Treetops," Backridge Road, via Stockville. Yes, that was his new address written in black permanent marker on his school bag by an overanxious mother, worried he would forget a new address in a new town, a new life away from everything familiar.

No wonder no-one here understood Matthew Luckmore. He barely understood himself!

So many thoughts, ideas, and needs that went nowhere because no-one understood the crazy pictures in his head, the colours of his world, the way the letters on a page danced *like mad fairies with a fire cracker up their backsides*!! Yes, he liked that idea. He'd write that down in his special secret book when this endless day was over, when he was safe in his quiet space down the back behind the big tree near the soft-running creek, just where he wanted to be right now!

The walk to the office was over. Matt tripped slightly as he entered the carpeted centre of school administration. That distinctive odour – a little antiseptic, slightly soapy – made Matt suddenly feel sick, as if all the fear of all the children who had ever entered this door had collected together at the pit of his stomach, a tight ball that seemed to spread in hot waves towards his bladder, his hands hot and face sweating.

"Miss, Miss – I have to go to the toilet now," he blurted, the first words he had uttered since the incident in 6ST. Ms Montgomery looked down as Matt raised his eyes just enough to look at her shoulder, smartly-clad in black and red, some kind of draped woollen jumper, again something his Mum would never wear.

"Alright Matthew, go on. I'll wait in my office just across there." She pointed, *her long red nails morphing into bird-claws* as Matt darted across the corridor, slamming the door of the toilet next to sick-bay. Matt knew this place, this refuge within the antiseptic office world. He'd been here 6 times in the 3 ½ weeks since arriving at Highcrest Primary. The Sick Bay was a safe space as long as no one else was actually sick or faking illness as Matt did so effectively.

Thinking about this now, Matthew realised that his classroom teacher and the office staff did seem to be taking longer to give permission for him to leave the classroom or to stay in Sick Bay. He realised, as he relieved the pressure on his bladder, that he'd have to avoid Sick Bay for a few weeks and find another refuge temporarily. "Mix it around and they don't realise, just like at the last school," he pondered.

Matt finished – *blessed relief* – and turned on the tap, allowing the cold water to run smoothly over his fingers. He loved watching the sinewy stream flow across his skin in sliver torrents, imagining his whole body lying across the mossy rocks in the creek near home, flowing, flowing, all the tension going...

"Matthew Luckmore, are you quite finished in there?" Ms M sounded angry, a woman with things to do, for whom he was a nuisance, an interruption.

"Yes Miss, I'm coming now"' he mumbled, just loud enough for her to hear through the thin door as he wiped his hands. "No need to make her angrier" he thought, opening the door, eyes once again on the red shoes.

"In my office immediately." As he slid into the chair opposite her large Principal chair, behind the wide, immaculately tidy desk. Ms M sat too and cleared her throat.

"So, Matthew, you know why you are here. As a Year 6 student I am sure you are fully aware of the standard of behaviour we expect at Highcrest even allowing that you have only been here for 4 weeks."

Actually it's 3 ½ he wanted to correct her, but the words just kept flowing by his ears, noise pounding, their meaning disappearing as sentence after sentence ran into each other.

"Miss Spencer informs me that you were – ahem – *playing with yourself* under the desk and that the students nearby were extremely embarrassed and distressed by your behaviour." Ms M cleared her throat again, as if there was a hard object lodged near her tonsils. Matt knew about tonsils. His had been removed 4 years before after many doses of antibiotics, numerous ear infections, loads of sore throats and even chest infections, year after year... Still the jelly and ice cream in hospital after the operation had been great – all those red and green blobs floating on snowy white melting ice cream...

"Matthew, are you listening to me?"

He glanced quickly at her face, eyes sliding away as he noted her reddish skin-tone, wide eyes, slightly worried frown and tight mouth. "Oh oh, she might be getting angry again," Matt thought.

"Yes Ms Montgomery. I am listening," he said, hoping she believed his lie. He had no clue what she'd said after she cleared her throat.

"Well, what do you feel is an appropriate response to your behaviour Matthew?" Ms Montgomery paused, gazing at the young boy who confused her so much.

He was obviously intelligent but unwilling to comply with basic social behaviours; aware of the rules, in fact happy to point them out to others all the time, but apparently quite ready to break a basic rule of appropriate classroom behaviour. Matthew failed to respond, continuing to closely study the surface of her desk. Jane Montgomery sighed and shook her head.

"Do you realise that you will be suspended for 3 days from right now? I was going to call your mother to come and get you..."

"No Miss, please, Mum will be so mad and..." Matt blurted.

"Well as I was saying Matthew, I was going to call your mother, but as it is now 3.25 pm you can collect your bag and go to the bus lines immediately. And make sure your mother gets this note. She needs to call me tomorrow morning and set up a meeting to discuss your suspension. You need to discuss this with your mother tonight."

"Yes Miss." Matt would agree to anything so keen was he to grab his bag and run to the bus lines, sure he could be first today as the other students needed to wait until 3.30 for the dismissal bell. Shoving the note from Ms M into his backpack, he stood and almost ran out the door, remembering just in time to walk, apparently calmly, until he reached the school office exit.

Finally able to run, he made it to the bus line just before the first of the other students arrived, jostling and pushing as they released the pent-up energy of the day.

"Hey, Luckless Luckmore – get suspended did-cha?"- sneered Blake Barton, the "big guy" in 6ST. *Always on Matt's case, always with a word to push Matt's buttons.* Determined not *to take the bait*, Matt thought about what to do or say. Through his mind ran pictures of past situations just like this one, lots of them, at past schools. Nothing much had worked with bullies like Blake Barton, so Matt just turned away, ignoring him.

"Hey Luckless, I'm talking to you!" A hand pushed Matt's shoulder and his backpack slipped to the ground. "I'm fully aware of that" Matt replied, picking up his bag.

"Oh, you're 'fully aware of that' are you? Who do you think you are Luckless? Prince William or somethin'?"

"I'm Matthew Luckmore, not Prince anyone," Matt said, although such an obvious answer was a waste of his breath.

"Oh yeah! Wanna make something of it?" sneered Blake, pushing his face closer to Matthew's, threatening to punch Matt with a large red fist.

Matt took a half-step backwards, as another voice rang in his ear.

"Now Blake, what's going on here?" Miss Spencer approached the bus lines, smiling and talking, as Blake quickly hid his clenched fist and backed away.

"I was just asking Matthew if he was OK Miss, seeing as he didn't come back to class."

"Mmm. I'm glad to see your concern for others Blake. Step into line now, the bus is coming," said Miss Spencer, Sarah to her friends. A first-year teacher who had graduated near to the top of her university year, she prided herself on her High Distinction record, academic brilliance, universal commendations as a student with a "brilliant future as an educator" from every lecturer, backed up by every supervising teacher during her practical teaching experiences. Miss Spencer felt she knew how to handle Year 6. It was *a big ask* for a first-year teacher but because of the sudden retirement of the ever-reliable Mr Whitting after a heart turn in Week 2 of the first term, Ms Montgomery had had to fill the vacancy quickly.

Miss Spencer was perfect – smart, keen, a hard worker and a woman. The fact that Sarah had grown up in the area and was interested in returning to a rural teaching job, and that her University record and references were so positive, had allayed any concerns about her inexperience that interview panel members may have had.

Miss Spencer smiled as Blake moved into the line, with 2 other students making room for him. *They knew what was good for them.*

Matthew looked towards the bus, now pulling up 2 metres away. He could be first on, get the front seat near the driver, Mr Maddison, who kindly allowed Matthew to discuss bus routes and timetables for the 36 minutes it usually took to get up Backridge Road to the front gate of "Treetops."

"Matthew come here please."

Miss Spencer had to be kidding. The bus was almost here, he was almost safe.

"Matthew, now."

Matt was torn – he could jump on the bus, now stopped in front of him, and risk upsetting Miss Spencer again, but he was already in trouble and Mum would be mad enough about that.

He moved one reluctant step towards his teacher, devastated by missing the opportunity to get his precious front seat. Miss Spencer smiled tightly at him then put a hand out and summoned him.

"Over here please. I want to speak to you before you go home."

He complied, resentfully, still upset and angry. She lowered her voice as he approached.

"Matthew, I'm sure you are fully aware that what you were doing was not OK in a public place, in the classroom, especially with girls around. Skye and Beccy were very embarrassed. I simply can't have that behaviour in my classroom. I hope you will think about that and when you return next week, we will have no more of that behaviour again."

Matt raised his eyes to look at her ear – silvery earrings glittered reflecting multicolours into the grey afternoon. All the other kids on his bus had boarded now – he had to go, to get on and endure 36 minutes in the middle seats, 36 minutes of teasing and people touching him. To end this conversation he replied, "Certainly Miss Spencer. I am very sorry. It won't happen again," not entirely sure what he was promising. However, Miss Spencer appeared satisfied and released him to board the bus.

Climbing the 3 steps, Matt cringed as he heard Blake Barton's loud voice booming out from the rear seats. "Back here Luckless. I've saved you a seat."

"It's OK Matthew," Mr Maddison said quietly, "I kept the front seat for you. You look like you've had a hard day."

Matt looked up full at the face of his friendly driver, managing eye contact for the first time that day. He wanted to cry as he realised he could trust this quiet man he barely knew. Slumping into his seat with evident relief, Matt knew he had found his first friend since arriving in Highcrest.

CHAPTER 2

SOMETHING NEW

A TIME TO SCATTER STONES

The dirt driveway was more like a goat track, erosion having formed two deep wheel ruts with a high middle path between them.

Mum's old 4WD ute just made it, scraping slightly when heavy rain caused a deeper indent to appear as water pooled temporarily on the track.

Matt tramped towards home. It was only about ½ a kilometre from Backridge Road where the school bus dropped him off, but it was a brief period of calm; repetitive movement before the sights and sounds of his new home overwhelmed him again.

Keeping each foot in the left wheel rut, one in front of the other, careful not to walk in the puddling water and wreck his brand-new white school sports shoes, Matthew kept his head down, concentrating.

"Hey Matt! Wait up! I'm here," his sister's voice rang out, high-pitched and annoying. Matt hadn't realised that she was on the early bus. Sometimes Breeanna caught a later bus if she had a late class. A bright student, she was young for Year 10, having been accelerated at her previous school and in spite of all the upsets at home in the past year, Bree continued to *breeze through life;* school, sports, social events, you name it and Breeanna found it easy! "Breezy Bree" his mum called her; life seemed to come easy for his sister.

In fact, since they had left Dad, Bree seemed even more relaxed. She had coped well with the move from the city, making friends quickly with 2 local girls. It was like they had always known each other, constantly on the phone and the Net, as if a single waking moment apart was too long.

Matt couldn't work it out. He'd made 0 friends as yet, zero! At his old school in the city, a big mega-primary school with 718 students, there were 4 Year 5 classes, and 123 Year 5 students, of whom 56 were boys. That gave Matt a fairly good chance of finding someone to connect with, and he had!

Not that Benjamin White was a "friend." In Matthew's opinion, "friends" held hands and giggled, chatting all the time about nothing, just like his sister and her large group of city friends.

Even at Highcrest Community Secondary school, Breeanna's group of 3 were always hugging and constantly touching, especially if they were apart for as long as one lesson!

Matt couldn't handle all that touchy stuff. He and Benjamin had shaken hands at the end of Matt's last day at the school, wished each other well and promised to meet online for one of the nightly computer games they played together.

Benjamin was a great colleague, interested in the same things as Matthew, namely computer games, numbers and statistics and handball, the one game Matt and Ben could play with a couple of others, keeping to strict (and complicated) rules and minimizing the social issues that arose in other playground games.

Matt missed Benjamin more than he had expected to, but had emailed him a few times, although the dial-up internet at the farm was so slow that their online gaming was impossible now.

Mum had promised to get better internet connection as soon as she could afford it, but her part-time job cleaning caravans at the big park near Highcrest Town Beach was only just paying the bills. There was no money for luxuries like Broadband connection.

Even when Dad remembered to put money in the bank for them, Mum always shrugged and said "Just enough for the electricity," or "Finally, we can clear the credit card bill." Then she would click on to B-Pay before Matt had time to suggest looking into Broadband connection.

Matt looked slowly back towards Breeanna just as she caught up and punched his arm hard. He didn't mind; he had seen it coming and strong touch was something he understood. If she'd patted his head, or brushed past him from behind like the kids did in the school corridors, that would be different. Sometimes soft touch actually hurt, especially if he didn't see it coming and expect it.

"Hi Matt, how was your day?" Bree spoke quickly, not waiting for his answer.

"Hi Bree," Matt greeted his sister, looking up the driveway to where his mother stood on the verandah waiting for her two "babies" to wander along.

She always said that – *"My two precious babies"* – even though she knew he hated it. He was NOT a baby, not even close. He was Matthew John Luckmore, 12 years old, computer expert and mathematics master!

Bree called out "Hi Mum. Darcy and Tilly are coming over soon to watch a DVD for school."

As they neared the steps up to the verandah that encircled the old farmhouse, Breeanna brandished a DVD case. "Hope that's OK" she finished, pushing open the front door and disappearing down the long central hallway to her room.

"Won't see her until the girls arrive, I suppose" said Jeannie, reaching to give Matt a hug of welcome.

"Good day Matty?"

He always endured Mum's hugs, and tried to stop his body stiffening in her embrace. He knew it upset her if he withdrew from her, but did not understand why.

"OK. Got a note from Ms Montgomery for you" he replied, handing over the envelope addressed to his mother. He pushed past her, heading for his room. At least in this big, rambling old house he got his own bedroom. In the city, he and Bree had shared a bedroom for nearly a year, the

2-bedroom unit being as much as Mum could afford on the Centrelink payment.

Mum had moved them out of their house just before Christmas, 18 months ago. They just left without a real farewell, saying they'd see Dad on Christmas Day, but then he hadn't turned up as arranged. They had organised a meeting at the local park, a picnic Christmas lunch. Outdoors, to make it easier for everyone, with lots of space to keep apart from one another. But Dad hadn't shown up.

Matt knew his Mum and Dad had 'separated', but he didn't know why he had to leave the only home he had ever known with all the familiar smells and shapes and colours.

Mum had rented a unit in the next suburb, the same distance from school on the bus route. She had said it was just for a short time, while she 'worked things out'. That year had been hard on everyone, but Matt and Bree didn't talk about it. Bree spent hours on her phone talking to her friends, and he knew she told them all about it. He'd heard her crying and saying it wasn't fair of Dad, it wasn't fair of Mum, to do this to her.

Again, Matt didn't understand. Mum and Dad hadn't done anything to Breeanna, or for that matter to him. They had just 'separated' – it was just that.

Dad was in their house; they were in the Unit – separated.

One time, Mum said that Dad never talked to her, that he didn't show her that he loved her and she wanted more than that.

And on one access visit, Matt asked Dad exactly what Mum wanted. Dad didn't say much, just that he needed to work a lot, to earn money at the big software company he worked for. He didn't understand what it was that Jeannie wanted either, but he thought that it – 'the separation' – was all for the best if she was happier that way.

When Mum had decided to try living in the country for a year, Matthew realised that Dad and Mum were going to stay 'separated', this time by a much bigger distance. Breeanna complained and whined that she'd miss her friends and going shopping at the mall, but when she'd realised that she'd be living near the beach where "High Bay" was filmed, she suddenly stopped complaining and got very excited. "I might get to see Travis Rawson or Brayden Lestrange," gushing over the two male stars of the most popular teen soap opera ever made in this country!

On arriving in Highcrest, Breeanna had taken every opportunity to go to the beach in the 3 weeks before the school term began, hoping to spot her T.V. idols in person. Even now, with school back, she and her trio of friends spent all weekend hanging out at "the Highrise," the local surf spot just out of town. Without a television star in sight, Breeanna had *fallen for* Jonno Freeman the local surf champion and school sports captain of Highcrest High. Mum wasn't happy, especially as Jonno had a reputation around town as a 'bad boy' who got into a lot of trouble, and he was nearly 18!

As far as Matthew was concerned, the move to the country was an improvement on the immediate past at least. Lying on his stomach on his large soft bed, he gazed through the window that overlooked the backyard, past the old post and rail fence towards the creek. Could he try getting through the kitchen and escaping to his special place without talking to his mother? He didn't want to talk about his day.

Matt knew that trying to understand all that had happened was impossible. It all just gave him a headache. He wished again that they had brought the old trampoline from Dad's house, but Mum had said she'd buy him a new one soon, and to be honest the old tramp was almost worn out after he had literally jumped on it for hours on end, every afternoon for the first few years of school. It had been by far the best way to calm himself; to let go of the stress of school; to come to a good, quiet place inside himself.

His mother's voice broke the silence "Matt, can you come here please?"

"Oh, oh" he thought, but he obeyed, slowly leaving his own space to face up to a lecture. Mum looked worried as he entered the kitchen. She had 3 wrinkles on her forehead and tight lines between her eyebrows. Her mouth was not curved, just a straight pink line across her familiar face. She looked up at him as he approached and smiled briefly. Jeannie knew not to look into his eyes if she wanted him to listen, so she looked at the badge on his pale blue school shirt, the badge that said "Highcrest Primary School: striving for excellence for all."

"Well Matt. Can you tell me what this is all about?" she indicated Mrs Montgomery's note lying open on the old wooden kitchen table.

Matthew suddenly felt hot and a bit sick, and his breathing accelerated. "Oh no! Here we go again!."

CHAPTER 3

DREADED SCHOOL
A TIME TO GATHER STONES TOGETHER

Matt stretched and turned over in his bed. The 5 blankets were heavy, almost suffocating according to his mum, but he liked the weight they provided. He felt his knee joints moving, his ankle joints flexing, his hip joints adjusting to the weight. His elbows and shoulders tensed; a school day!

"No wait." Matt realised he didn't have to go. He had today and the next 2 school days to do whatever ..... yay!

As he flopped back into his bed, relaxing, Jeannie called out to both the children "Come on, breakfast. I'm taking you to school Bree. Matt, get dressed, you're coming with me today."

"Nooooo," Matt groaned. Surely he was old enough, sensible enough, to stay home alone. Why not? He knew all the rules for home and for school, plus all his Mum's new rules about the new place, the farm, with all its hazards:

1. Keep away from the creek unless you tell me first.

2. Don't go to the machinery shed without me.

3. No riding the quad bike without a helmet.

4. No driving the farm truck in the paddock without Mum.

Matt knew he could ride that bike better than most people could drive a car.

In fact, he'd had that argument with his Mum – if he was safe on the "quaddie" he should be able to drive the old farm truck by himself. After all, Mum had taught Bree and Matt to drive it, he could just reach the pedals and didn't crunch the gears anymore. Mum had said he was a better driver than most adults.

Logic said he should be able to drive, even get his L plates, and drive on the roads, so he'd argued for what seemed like hours until Jeannie, with a brainwave of literal thinking of her own, shut him up completely with "Look Matt. It's against the law. No driving on the roads until you're 16."

"Fair enough," thought Matt. She only had to explain that fact, and that was that.

Wandering into the kitchen after getting dressed, Matthew realised that Jeannie was not going to stand for any arguments today.

His Mum was dressed up in what she called her *"Sunday best"*; a neat suit, with medium heeled shoes, all black, with a white tailored shirt. It was the outfit she'd worn to job interviews, all so far unsuccessful except for the cleaning job at the Caravan Park.

Jeannie had laughed when she talked about her frustration at the last failed interview for office work at the Real Estate Agency. "Over qualified," she'd heard once again and in frustration dropped in to the Ocean Breeze Caravan Park on her way home, desperate for any work they had!

Old Charlie had offered her 3 shifts a week cleaning cabins and vans. "Me wife Shirl has a bad case of rheumatoid, so we need some extra help. But don't turn up in the suit and high heels love!," he'd chuckled.

"The best-dressed cleaner ever!" Jeannie had laughed as she told Bree and Matt over dinner that night, and for a moment Matt had frowned.

Surely she didn't have to wear her "Sunday best" to clean up other people's mess? Then he realised she was joking by the smile that reached her eyes.

Mum was glad to have work – any work – and she DID keep her suit and white shirt for special occasions, like the meeting with the Principal of Highcrest Primary, at 9am today. Matt realised that he could not avoid this, another frown worrying his forehead.

"Get a move on Matthew. Eat your Weetbix, then we'll go." Matt poured some OJ into his bowl then crumbled 2 Weetbix in next, following his usual routine; no milk, orange juice instead, Weetbix crumbled one at a time, wait until they're soft and squishy then eat as fast as possible.

It wasn't that Matthew couldn't eat other things for breakfast, he just didn't want to. This combination was fine, every day without fail. And Jeannie made sure that the OJ and Weetbix never ran out; it just wasn't worth the fuss of changing a winning breakfast formula.

Matt ate, with Jeannie tapping her foot by the door, Bree languidly brushing her hair. "Come ON you 2. It's 8.25, and we'll be late for Principal Montgomery if we don't leave NOW!"

<hr/>

Usually, Matt enjoyed the 26-minute drive in to Highcrest, 10 minutes shorter by car than bus, without all the pick-ups or drop-offs.

The farm house was perched on 100 acres of river flats, up- stream from Highcrest on the Brooklee River. The creek that ran past their house was the Brooklee Creek, a small feeder stream to the bigger river at the bottom of the river flat beyond their front gate. It was green scenic country, the river meandering slowly at this point down towards the river mouth at Highcrest Point, one end of a small heart-shaped bay.

There, too, was the Town Beach complete with its all-weather anchorage. In the harbour, a few small pleasure yachts and three elderly fishing trawlers strained at their anchor chains.

Sometimes, when the fishing had been good, Matt couldn't stand to go to the bay to wander near the wharf – the fishy smell was too overpowering for him and he had to turn away, to find a fresh sea breeze.

Today the boats lay idle, nets spread on their decks. It had been too rough *out wide*, the sea swell too big for fishing in these small boats.

Once, Highcrest had been known as the "gateway to the Southern Fisheries," home base for a large trawler fleet and a busy fish cannery. Now, the cannery stood silent, closed and derelict, testimony to overseas competition (that took some 50 jobs), and to overseas processing. The government's buy-back of fishing licences had not helped.

Matt was quietly glad that the cannery was closed, and that fish numbers were being replenished by the declaration of a fish-friendly Marine Park – at least he didn't have to worry about the cannery smell drifting over the school every day as the on-shore breeze gathered strength around 11 am.

He didn't like fish to eat, and he hated its smell when it was cooking, so he was pleased the fish were staying in the ocean where they belonged, free to swim and not to smell badly when he passed by!

Mum stopped the ute briefly to drop Breeanna at the Secondary school "drop zone."

Bree was barely out of the car when one of her friends ran up and gave her a huge hug. Matthew looked away, confused by the showy affection.

Girls! They only saw each other yesterday!

Too soon, Jeannie parked the ute opposite the Primary School gate. "Time to *face the music* Matt," she joked.

Feeling hot and a bit sick in his stomach, Matt looked around. There was no music, not even a kid with an iPod in sight. Jeannie recognised his confusion – "Just an expression mate. Come on, let's go and see Ms Montgomery."

She climbed out and waited while Matt carefully held up the door handle as he closed the door, making sure it was locked. The old car, the one Mum had sold to pay the bond on the farm house and some other bills, *had boasted* central locking. Matt missed that car, with its great stereo and comfortable seats. He could relax in that car, unlike the ute with its jarring suspension and hard bench seat.

Sometimes he really wished life could go back to what it had been before. Before "the separation," before Dad became a stranger living 5 ½ hours' drive away.

———≈≈≈≈≈———

"Matt, stop dreaming. Ms Montgomery's waiting for us." Jeannie grabbed his wrist. Even as she was rushing Mum remembered he hated to have his hand held, and pulled him gently across the carpark to the office door.

This time, as he waited on the green vinyl armchair, Matt was ready. With his Mum to rely on, he was calmer than he had been yesterday.

Quite suddenly Ms Montgomery appeared, not from the direction of her office, but from the photocopying room in the other direction. Brandishing a fistful of copied documents, she spoke rapidly.

Matt didn't catch what she said at first, as the words seemed to collide with each other. But he did understand when she said "I'd like to speak to you alone Mrs Luckmore, so come on in. Matthew, you can wait right here."

Catching the eye of her ever-reliable School Administration officer she continued "Mrs Arnold will *keep an eye* on you."

Matthew breathed a sigh of relief. He could wait here quietly, alone, watching the rainbow of colours in the dust particles reflected in a shaft of light that beamed through the office window. He started to complete Algebra problems in his head.

Mrs Arnold glanced his way from time to time, reassured that this self-involved young lad would need very little of her precious time.

As the door to the principal's office closed, Jeannie looked back to see Matt staring into the middle distance. She knew that look – that spaced out "I'm not here" look that Matt had perfected when wanting to opt-out.

She sighed, turned and squared her shoulders, thinking "I can handle this," knowing she couldn't really, not after all that had happened at other schools, at other times.

"Now Mrs Luckmore, you are aware of why I asked you to come in today. The note I sent explained what happened in the classroom yesterday and I..." began the principal.

"I disagree – with er... the greatest respect Ms Montgomery."

Jeannie interrupted, deciding to *go on the front foot* with this authority figure.

"You wrote down what Miss Spencer said happened. No-one asked Matt what happened, what *his take on it* was."

She sighed again – it was going to be like all the other times, when Matt was to blame without anyone even trying to understand. Tears welled in her eyes and she cleared her throat, struggling to *buy some time.*

Ms Montgomery seemed ready *to jump right in*, ready to defend her teacher and her school's processes, but her expression changed as she observed Jeannie's face, her slumped shoulders, the tears threatening to fall. She seemed to realise there was more to the story; a lot more.

Pushing a tissue box across her desk, she quietly said "Just tell me about it. From the beginning."

※※※※

"Time to go Matt!" Matt's calm concentration was broken as his mother approached. "Thanks for *keeping an eye on him,* Mrs Arnold." Jeannie nodded to the older woman.

"He was no trouble at all, just sat there staring into space," she replied, and went back to her computer screen. A School Administration Officer's day is constantly busy and Joan Arnold was secretly relieved that this odd young boy had not caused her one second of concern in the last hour!

As the Luckmores left the building, Ms Montgomery stood at her office door, arms crossed, watching them go.

Matt looked back and she smiled, a kind-of sad smile that didn't reach her eyes. Matt quickly looked away – that was just too confusing, when a facial expression didn't match the rest of a person's body language he didn't even try to understand.

"What happened Mum? I don't have to go back to school today do I?" he asked, anxiously.

Jeannie shook her head and hurried across the carpark. "We'll talk at home. I need to have a quiet think as I drive," she replied, unlocking his door before walking around to the driver's side. Matt climbed into the ute, trusting his mum and relieved to be going home again.

Tossing her bag on the seat, Jeannie backed carefully out, pulled onto the road and turned towards home. Matt gazed out the window, apparently content. Sometimes he was so much *in a world of his own* she thought, and blinked away more tears.

What Ms Montgomery had said was hardly surprising really. Considering what Jeannie had finally shared with her, the principal had every right to be a bit upset, even angry.

"Why didn't you tell us about Matthew's Autism Spectrum Disorder diagnosis when you enrolled him?" she had asked.

"If you have a report to back it up, we may possibly be able to get some funding to help Matthew in class." An aide to assist the teacher, *an extra pair of hands* that meant Matt might get some 1 on 1 help, because of his "special needs."

Jeannie had gasped and tried to respond, but Ms M spoke rapidly.

"Of course, it all has to go through District Office, and at this stage of the year there won't be much money that has not already been allocated, but if you bring in the report, we'll fill in the paperwork and see what can be done. Rest assured, it's all about the best outcomes for Matthew." She paused for breath just long enough for Jeannie to jump in.

"I'm sorry. I don't have any reports to give you. You see we left the last school in such a rush and with the separation lots of documents got lost." She paused, breathing fast – she just had to admit it – "and I couldn't face getting it all in writing. I know Matt's unusual, but I've had a really hard time facing a diagnosis of Autism." Her voice broke, and suddenly the tears flowed.

Somewhere, sometime she had to let it out – all the confusion, all the fear, all the pain – but NOT here, NOT in front of this power-dressing Principal! She shut her eyes and gulped to try to swallow the tears, but it didn't help.

Suddenly an arm circled her shoulders and Jeannie leaned in towards Ms M who was speaking again, her voice softer, slower, kinder.

"Jeannie, it's OK. Just have a cry. I know it's hard." As Jeannie slowly calmed, Ms M continued "I can follow it up for you, contact the Department of Health and request a copy of the report they did, if you give me permission. We can work it out. And you are welcome to talk with our School Counsellor – Matt too when he's ready."

Jane Montgomery had seen this before; this reluctance to label children as "different"; this unwillingness to acknowledge their additional needs, especially when the child was so bright and capable in many ways. And she also realised that Miss Spencer, enthusiastic but inexperienced, needed more support too. "We'll organise a round-table meeting with Miss Spencer so she can understand that Matthew needs to be handled differently. He needs more help to fit in with the other students. And they need help to understand Matthew."

Jeannie sniffed and blew her nose into a tissue. One deep shuddering breath and she felt able to look at Jane Montgomery, now seated again across the desk.

"He doesn't know," she started, "I haven't known how to tell him." Jeannie gulped again as tears threatened to flow once more.

"That's OK Jeannie. I understand that it's difficult to know how to tell him, what to say. That's one reason why it would be good for you to speak with our Counsellor. I know she's advised parents about this before." Jane paused, thinking hard.

"Does Matt like horses?" she asked suddenly. Jeannie had to smile – where had that come from?

"Yes, he's always asking me for a horse now we live in the country, but I can't afford one," she replied, looking down. The last thing she wanted to get into was her financial situation, not after all this!

"Look, I know a lady who runs riding lessons and she takes children with different needs. She's terrific with them, and I wonder if Matt would like to try that, just to get him into an activity with other people. She even lives out your way. Here, I'll give you her number."

Jane was scribbling a number on a post-it note, and handing it over the desk. Jeannie took it doubtfully, thinking about the cost, but also appreciating that Jane was trying hard to "problem solve" for her son. She really did care, and beneath the busy, bossy exterior was a genuine person!

As she left the office, Jeannie felt lighter than she had for months. This felt right; confiding in Ms Montgomery, setting up a School Counsellor's appointment, even getting the number of the horse lady!

She breathed a sigh of relief, smiling as she watched Matt, still staring into space. "Time to go Matt" she said, thinking that maybe, this time, this new start might just work.

CHAPTER 4

HOME AGAIN
A TIME TO LOOK BACK

The drive home felt easy. The road hugging the river bends flowed beneath the ute's wheels as Jeannie hummed an old song to herself. Golden, late morning light reflected brightly through the stands of river gums as Matt sat quietly beside her.

Matt was thinking; analysing, working it out. His Mum seemed to be happy, happier than she had seemed in a long time.

He was aware of his Mum's emotions, although he often could not name them or describe them in words. He just knew if she was upset or if all was right in her world.

Matt KNEW, like a sensation deep inside, because she was his closest "trust" person.

And he needed Mum to cope, to be OK, because if she wasn't OK, neither was he.

So right now, heading home to the farm, the world looked good.

No school for 4 days and 20 ¼ hours (including the weekend).

At the farm entrance, Mum stopped the ute allowing Matt time to get out and undo the chain, then swing the old rusty gate wide to allow the ute to roll up the track to the house. As he pushed the gate shut, Matt glanced towards the farm house and caught a glimpse of dark blue.

Matt looked again, unable to immediately process what he was seeing. Shoving the rusty iron ring over the gate's bolt to ensure it was closed, he turned and looked again; he knew that car, a 2019 Pajero 4WD, and he knew who drove it, but it wasn't supposed to be here, at the farm.

As Matt hopped back into the car, he noticed that his mother's face looked pale, and a worried frown had appeared, which rapidly changed into a thin-lipped smile as she realised that he was looking at her.

"Looks like Dad's come to pay us a visit." She looked directly at Matthew, who shifted his eyes down to regard the dusty floor mat, and tried to keep his face blank. In his experience, when you didn't know what to feel it was best to show no emotion at all – zero, 00000, nothing.

Right now, he had no clue how he should feel or how he was feeling, it was all just too confusing.

Here was his father, come all the way from the city, without warning, something he had never done before even when Mum, Matthew and Breanna had only been living in the next suburb.

His Dad, Michael, who loved his work and the flow of his usual routines, coming all the way here – was something wrong?

Matt couldn't process this new event at all. Even Jeannie looked confused but as usual she went into reassurance mode and said "He didn't call me but I'm sure it's all OK Matt. Let's just wait and see."

The ute pulled up in a small cloud of red-brown dust, as Michael rose stiffly from the old arm chair that seemed permanently attached to the corner of the verandah.

Even that was odd – it was Mum's favourite chair, where she normally sat and waited for her "precious babies" to wander up the track from the school bus, reading or knitting one of those horrible, itchy woollen jumpers Matt got every year for his winter birthday.

As he got out of the car, Matt heard his father's quiet voice. He sounded unsure. Matthew realised he had almost forgotten what his father's voice sounded like. "Hello Jeannie. Hello Matthew," Michael said.

Matt's eyes brimmed and he pushed past his father, unsure how to react, needing the sanctuary of his own space, his bedroom. Down the corridor he went, slamming the bedroom door, looking frantically around as he realised that even this space was not removed enough from the turmoil inside him that he didn't understand. Matt took 5 deep breaths, trying to slow himself.

Escape – and only one place to go!

Opening his bedroom door, he looked quickly around and seeing no one, tiptoed out, quietly closing the door behind him. As he walked silently to the back door, he could hear his mother's voice at the front of the house, and knew his parents were still on the front verandah, taking their time to adjust to each other again.

Matt let himself out the back door, making doubly sure he didn't slam the screen-door. Usually it banged loudly, making it easy to follow one of Mum's rules "Keep away from the creek unless you tell me first."

When he went down to the creek the door always banged, always 'told' her where he was headed more effectively than any words he could say.

Mum would call out "OK Matt. You're going down to the creek. Be careful and see you soon," and Matt knew it was OK, that Mum would call or even come and find him when she wanted him to come back. And she always called out his name so he had time to leave his special place, and meet her on the creek bank, both of them pretending that's where he'd been all along.

But today she'd think he was in his room, quietly reading a computer magazine.

He needed more space today, more air around him to be able to breathe, more freedom to 'be' by himself, away from the confusion of emotions.

The secret spot was cool, slightly damp and smelt of old leaves. Sometimes Matt imagined that a possum might crawl in here to sleep in the daytime, or a black wallaby might hop up to investigate the cool hollow, but all he usually saw were spiders.

Matt actually liked spiders and he knew which ones were dangerous, which ones to keep away from. There were only garden spiders in his spot, one web looking quite deserted. No nasties, like red backs or funnel webs.

He checked carefully every time he arrived, flashing the light from his pocket torch into the dark corners of the old hollow tree, the recesses where spiders loved to hide.

But today it seemed Matt was quite alone. Not even 6 legged arachnids to think about, and that suited Matt fine.

His brain was rushing, his body was hot and uncomfortable, undies itching, scalp prickling, the label on his new t-shirt rubbing his skin. He could smell the new soap powder Mum had used to wash his shorts, new because the reliable brand she had always used in the city had run out and the local Highcrest supermarket did not stock the brand she wanted, the brand Matt knew and tolerated his clothes being washed in.

Suddenly all Matt's senses seemed to fire at once. He didn't know if he was seeing with his eyes or his ears, hearing with his ears or his mouth, feeling everything at once with every sense he had.

He had to strip off, had to be free!

Pulling off his t-shirt, his old singlet, his undies, kicking off his thongs, all in world-record time, he stumbled into the creek, at once relieved and shocked by the cold of the clear water.

He lay down, fully stretched out on his back, the meandering stream settling and soothing, quiet, with only the birds as witnesses.

Matt stayed there, completely still, for the longest time, feeling his body slow, colder and colder until he was freezing, but calm too.

Matthew at 12, nearly 13, was an outsider in this world.

He knew he didn't fit in, and most of the time he didn't care.

If others thought him strange, or called him a "retard" or a "weirdo" – or worse names, like the one based on a 4-letter word and the unfortunate connection to his surname, Luckmore – then that was their problem!

He didn't have to try to understand them. It was usually enough to ignore it all, to revert to thinking about numbers or interesting facts.

He didn't need other people, including friends.

One hot tear slipped down Matt's cheek, merging with the cold water, running away down the creek, like a part of Matthew was escaping him, going to live in a wider world down to the Brooklee River and out past Highcrest Point and the Town Bay with its 3 fishing boats, out into the deep ocean, leaving the surfers at The Highrise behind, free of cares, free of confusion, free of fear.

The tear had gone.

Suddenly Matt realised how cold he had become. Even his brain felt cold, numb – and that was OK too, but he knew he needed to get warm again or hypothermia could set in.

He'd read about it in Australian Geographic magazine. Back issues were stacked in a bookshelf in his room, courtesy of a previous tenant.

Or they may have belonged to the elderly couple who had farmed here for years before dying in the local nursing home within 4 months of moving there.

The old man, Mum had told him, had died first, missing his land, his place, his animals; then the old lady soon after, missing her mate, giving up on a life that had shrunk to the size of a single bed, a large impersonal vinyl armchair, and a flickering TV full of someone else's "reality."

Matthew knew these things as facts, because the Real Estate agent had told Mum when they first arrived, handing her the keys to their new life, rusty old door keys plus brand-new silvery keys to new locks placed there by the new owner, the absent, city-based son of the old couple.

The son – Rodney was his name – lived hours away and had no interest in the area, his aging farm, or his inheritance. The real estate bloke had said he had become *"citified,"* whatever that meant, and he would probably sell the farm as soon as probate was finalised to just *"take the money and run!"*

Matthew didn't really understand that expression. He had a mental picture of Rodney, who was apparently very overweight, running up the main highway towards the city with $100 notes in both hands! Ha! That would be funny!!!

Matt wished his Mum had the money to buy the place, so familiar had it become, so quiet and peaceful, that he couldn't imagine being anywhere else now.

But he knew it was impossible – there was no money!

Mum would not force his father to sell their old house; she said she knew how much he needed his own familiar place.

Now Matthew dragged his cold body from the water, slapping his arms to get the blood flowing again as he struggled to pull on his clothing.

It was always hard to get dressed again when you were wet. That was exactly why he hated swimming lessons at the public pool; well, that and all the stupid kids splashing and yelling everywhere.

Thinking hard as his brain warmed up too, Matt revisited what his mother had said.

If his father needed his own place so much, why was he here, in their place?

Why had he come, especially without warning?

As he crouched down in front of the hollow gum, the sun's rays warming and drying him out, Matt decided not to think about the "whys."

He couldn't explain them, so he had to stop thinking about them.

A black ant carried a dead ladybird past his foot. Twice the size of the ant's body, the ladybird glistened red and black in the sun. She had 4 spots on her back. The ant had

4 legs, plus 2 feelers. Matt added the numbers, calming and warming in the sun.

———≈≈≈≈≈———

"Michael!" said Jeannie, hot tears stinging unwanted at the back of her eyes. She coughed, taking the opportunity to turn slightly away from him and quickly wipe her eyes with the back of her hand. Turning back towards him she smiled briefly and continued "I wasn't expecting to see you here."

Michael looked back steadily at his wife. She was still his wife; they had never bothered to divorce, both deciding it was not necessary.

He knew Jeannie had seen a solicitor here in Highcrest, a local country lawyer who "specialised" in everything as one had to in small towns.

She had told him about it over the phone: "He was very kind Michael. He told me we should wait, maybe get some counselling before we do anything else. He seemed to think we should have a parenting plan so you could see the kids at set times, but I explained that we couldn't get to the city very often because of the petrol cost, and you were really busy with work even on weekends. So David, the solicitor, he just looked at me over his gold-rimmed glasses and told me to go away and talk to you again. He didn't even charge me a fee this time; he said he'd count it as a 'no fee initial consultation'."

Jeannie had conveyed the information, Michael had listened, and they had decided – nothing.

Now here he was, having left the city early, before 7 am, after a sleepless night.

He had worried about taking a day off "sick." Michael had 15 years of built-up long-service leave, all his sick days and 38 weeks of annual leave accrued. His pay-master was always going on at him to take his leave, but he had only ever taken a few days here and there, preferring the routine and challenge of his workplace.

Consequently, he had risen steadily in the company ranks.

Now his title was "Computer Analytics Manager," and he was earning a 6-figure salary that also accrued in his bank account; his focus was never on the money.

Most of his bills were paid direct from his account. He spent money on food, the odd bottle of wine, an occasional DVD to watch alone – BBC documentaries, old comedies where the humour was out-there and slap-stick, and AFL football.

Michael liked to run too. He ran daily at 6.15am rain or shine, out along the nearby track, around the local oval, back behind the shops, arriving home for a shower at 7.10am, taking precisely 55 minutes. It was enough.

Then he took a shower, ate a quick bowl of Weetbix (always Weetbix, with hot water), then was in the car by 7.45am to hear the ABC radio news.

Fortunately, his commute across town was only 21 minutes on a good day, so after parking in the company carpark, in his own designated car-parking space, he was always at his desk by 8.10am. People said they could *set their watches* by him!

Michael liked the thought of walking through the office and everyone setting their time-pieces as he passed!

So, what had possessed him to leave a message on the Department secretary's answering machine to say he was unwell and wouldn't be in until Monday?

Even to his own ears his words sounded false, hollow.

Michael knew he was a terrible liar. He had not had enough practice in his black and white world, where the grey areas of untruth never played a part.

Michael had felt panicky as he drove through the southern outskirts of the city, down along the escarpment, past the industrial smoke-stacks of the port where 23 container ships lined up out to sea waiting their turn to disgorge their contents.

His anxiety slowly abated as he decided to stay by the coast, avoiding the inland villages, the weekend tourist-drive meccas complete with never-to-be-finished roadworks.

The coast was spectacular; rocky, with blue ocean, shores of golden sand, green hills beyond. For short periods as he drove, he was able to forget this madness of visiting his wife and children.

Thoughts of his past life came unbidden. Years of living in a small town close to this coast, but different, further north. Years of aloneness, years of not fitting in, until Jeannie convinced him to try the Church group.

He'd enjoyed that with her for a while, before leaving the small town to go to university.

They had been years of being told he was destined to be something great; so bright, a genius even! Mum and Dad had agreed on that, and so had his teachers.

He was exceptional, apparently.

Then his parents were both *gone in a flash*, in a head-on car accident with a semi-trailer on Highway Number 1, while Michael was away at Uni; he was orphaned at 20.

Michael remembered coming back to home from his austere university room, but no home existed any more, with Mum and Dad gone.

Only Jeannie! Bright, bubbly, clever Jeannie who greeted him with a hug he didn't have to withdraw from. Who organised him to stay with her family, not in the empty house, so changed now without his parents there to fill it.

Jeannie, who he'd always known, the closest thing he had to a "sister" for an only child like Michael. She was there to support him through the funeral, packing the house up, selling things or giving them away, then finally saying good-bye to the house which sold quickly through Jeannie's boss at the Real Estate office.

"Properties like these are in demand Michael. People want to escape for a tree-change, so small acreages near the sea are *like diamonds*! You'll see."

And Michael did see; he saw his past nearly erased, and it was too much for his confused brain to deal with. The only thing he could do was to put that "chunk" away, to be understood later, and to go back to Uni, richer in dollars but poorer by far.

Michael's graduation 3 years later would have been a hollow day to endure in memory of his parents, had it not been for Jeannie.

Jeannie, who had called and visited from home when she could, now arrived with her Mum and Dad to be his guests at the Graduation ceremony and drinks on the Uni lawn.

They clapped as Michael was awarded his degree with Honours, cheered as his name was called for the University Medal, and toasted his achievements as other students and Uni staff patted Michael on the back at the drinks party.

Michael had just wanted to leave and cringed every time he was touched, but he understood the need to remain, to honour his parents and to smile!

Even so, he couldn't have done it without her, without Jeannie by his side.

He had been offered a job in his faculty, but he thought it the 'easy' way out, leading to a PhD and an ongoing lecturing post.

Instead, he took a job with a leading software company who *headhunted* the brightest new graduates, with offers that he would be Head of his own Department after 2 years, with freedom to program as he saw fit (within the Company's objectives of course) and an attractive salary package.

Mum and Dad would have been proud!

Throwing his energies into the new job, Michael worked horrendous hours and came home exhausted to a silent, empty rental flat.

After 18 months, he had an epiphany!

Weekly phone calls with Jeannie were not enough – she was his "constant," and life was hollow without her.

He'd *taken his heart in his hands* and visited; a *spur of the moment* thing, just like this visit was.

He'd knocked on her door, praying she would answer, then there she was.

His courage nearly failed him, but he knew he needed her like he needed oxygen. He asked her to come, to share his city life, to continue her accounting studies in the city, and (with a very deep breath, struggling to maintain eye-contact) he asked her to marry him!

And to his everlasting surprise she said "Yes!"

For Jeannie, marriage came first. As quickly as possible, in the beautiful stone church she and her family attended, Jeannie walked up the aisle, dressed in shining white, steadily holding on to her father's arm, her Mum *crying buckets* in the front pew.

A small wedding lunch at the local park followed, catered by the local CWA ladies. It was all freshly made food, fresh air and a fresh start.

Michael imagined his parents looking down, pleased.

And so it went, moving to the city with Jeannie, excitedly setting up their new home. Jeannie finished her studies full-time in one year, also graduating with honours, and moved on to a good job with a small accounting firm in the suburb they lived in. Michael was *like a pig in mud,* so pleased and proud of his lovely wife.

Soon, there were children.

Michael had wanted to be a father, to build a family in the hollow cavity that was his history, to be a Dad like his own father, a quiet but loving man who had provided well and was always there.

But it did confuse him – all those wakeful nights, nappies, small bodies in his bed; small needy bodies, who required washing and changing and feeding and burping! Not to mention the smells!!

Jeannie was *in her element*, enjoying breast-feeding, constantly tired, but happy.

He remembered the children growing through preschool to primary school.

They were great years, busy years!

But somehow though, somehow in that busy-ness, he had lost Jeannie.

She became too busy with the children, with a part-time job, with the house and garden. Too busy to be his "constant."

And he was busy too – busy at work, busy providing, busy meeting deadlines – too busy to be the Dad his own father had been and unsure how to make it right.

So, over time, he withdrew from his family to the safety of numbers and computers. They, at least, did not judge. The numbers were never disappointed in him, or expected more than he was able to give.

Knowing that Jeannie was unhappy, and knowing how to fix things, were 2 very different things.

Now here he was, and here they were, 'separated' by distance both physical and emotional. But together today, together again even briefly, his journey to reach them finished.

What would happen? Now he was here, Michael was scared but determined to see this through.

———✦———

Jeannie was also confused by Michael's sudden appearance.

She ran her hand through her hair and gestured inside, holding open the front screen door.

"Come in to the kitchen Michael," she managed, trying to offer a small smile of welcome.

A cup of tea usually helped. Jeannie let the screen slam shut, welcoming the cool of the dark hallway, taking her time to walk the short distance to the kitchen door where Michael hovered, unsure.

It felt like a walk back in time, to sit around a kitchen table with her husband – sorry, her estranged husband.

Entering the kitchen, she grabbed the kettle and filled it quickly, turning on the gas and lighting it with a match. She busied herself with cups, teapot, a tea strainer, loose leaf tea being her favourite.

She opened the fridge for milk. She knew Michael's taste – a splash of milk in the cup, then the tea, brewed for 2 minutes maximum.

Longer than 2 minutes was scientifically proven to make tea bitter, so one needed sugar. He had told her often in the early days of their marriage as she had learned his habits, his preferences, his quirks, back when they didn't worry her and she thought them funny and endearing.

Making the tea was automatic, enabling Jeannie to recall hurried conversations over a quick cuppa, 5 minutes together before the day really began, 5 minutes at night before sleep claimed them both, 5 minutes to connect and talk. It had only been enough time to discuss family arrangements, the kids' schedules, who was dropping off whom.

Admittedly it was mostly about Breanna. She was always visiting friends, going shopping at the mall, attending a sports practice or a music lesson after school.

It was usually Jeannie's job to *juggle* running the kids around. No not usually, it was always Jeannie's job.

She had kept Michael informed during their brief chats, just in case.

In case of what, she hadn't ever worked out. Her illness or death maybe, when he would have had to become involved?

Well, it didn't work out that way – he did care, but not enough, not enough to see her struggling to *keep all the balls in the air*, and not enough to work on retrieving their marriage when she could not.

Perhaps if he'd just talked to her more, taken her in his arms and held her just as he had done "B.C."

Before children, they had talked about work, about the house, about family and friends. It had been enough.

Jeannie knew Michael wasn't good at emotional stuff, but he had listened and tried to respond when she brought something up that was worrying her.

He loved her – she knew that – and he showed it with small presents (not cut flowers, he said they died too soon), and an occasional night out.

He called her his "constant one," which was lovely – at first.

Later, as she lacked the energy to initiate a conversation, Michael withdrew into his work, and the only "constant" seemed to be tiredness.

The distance between them grew, imperceptibly at first, then it became more obvious.

Michael was always at work. Oh, she knew it was work not another woman.

What a laugh!

She had believed that Michael would always be a one-woman-man, his heart only for her. But when she had most needed his support and attention, he seemed to have no answers, no idea how to help, and she was too tired to make a fuss!

She could not be there, be his "constant" for a minute more.

She had had to leave.

Her Mum and Dad saw the separation coming and tried to provide support from a distance, but Jeannie found she couldn't share her failure with them.

For Jeannie knew she had failed. She could not be "Superwoman" anymore.

She could not be Michael's all, Breanna's all, Matthew's all – and where was Jeannie in all this? Gone, swallowed up by the busy-ness of existence, the demands of mothering, of a job she had ceased to enjoy, of kids and of a husband who had become increasingly remote.

Jeannie knew the tipping point, the point at which it was time to tear it all down.

It was Mrs Greenacre, lovely solid Mrs Greenacre who "got" Matthew, who seemed to understand, who didn't judge her at all.

Mrs Greenacre had called Jeannie in for a parent-teacher interview, *out of the blue* on a Monday afternoon.

Technically, Mrs Greenacre invited both Michael and Jeannie but as always Michael was working and vowed that he trusted her judgement completely.

Jeannie had organised an early finish that day at work, set up for Bree to go to a friend's place after school, brought food for Matthew and rushed off to the school arriving 3 minutes late.

Matthew was waiting, looking crankily at the big clock on the wall – he hated to be late.

Fortunately, Mrs Greenacre met them at the office, handing Matthew 2 dinosaur books and a series of kaleidoscope pictures to keep him occupied. He was happy and secure in a familiar space with his favourite teacher and his "constant" mum just metres away.

Jeannie had sunk gratefully into a chair and had taken a breath, waiting to hear the latest "Matthew" story and how Mrs Greenacre had dealt with it and made Matthew calm again. This was certainly not the first time Jeannie had sat in this very chair! But always Mrs Greenacre had made it right, taken the pressure off and helped them all to move forward.

Mrs Greenacre had sat down too, a thoughtful look on her face.

Jeannie thought she noticed something there, behind her smile, something that Jeannie dreaded hearing today, or any day.

"Jeannie" Mrs Greenacre had started – and it was always her first name not the more formal "Mrs Luckmore"; non-threatening, making Jeannie feel comfortable.

"I called you in because I have some news and I wanted to tell you myself, before the car-park gossip reached you," she had smiled, a little sadly.

"As you know, our plan was for me to teach Matthew again next year in Year 6. The school will probably have a Year 5/6 composite and we had decided that would work well for Matthew to be with younger children more his "social" age, with virtually an individualised program as he's had this year, with lots of extension in Maths and Computing."

Mrs Greenacre continued to smile, however Jeannie could hear the 'but' coming, and had leaned forward in the chair, her fingers clenching around the front of the seat.

"The thing is," Mrs Greenacre had continued. "I'm not too well, and I need to have some quite major surgery. The doctors assure me that I will get better eventually, but I need to take a whole year off to recover."

She looked at Jeannie's stricken face, her eyes bright with emotion.

"But you're the only one who understands Matty," Jeannie burst out.

"What will he do in Year 6? What will I do?" she almost wailed; her despair barely controlled.

"Jeannie, Mr Hawser has assured me that he will make every effort to find an experienced teacher as my replacement. And Mrs Thomas, the Special Education teacher, has offered to help settle Matthew into his new class."

"But Mrs Thomas doesn't know Matty. And he doesn't like her! He says she talks to him like he's stupid!"

Jeannie had known it wasn't any good, but she couldn't seem to stop.

She stood up and paced across the room. "I can't deal with this by myself, I just can't" she had mumbled.

"I'm so sorry Jeannie, but it can't be helped I'm afraid." Mrs Green *looked as sad as Jeannie felt.*

Jeannie had glanced up at her, and gulped. Her body seemed to hunch over and her words had come out in gasps.

"I know, and I'm so sorry you're sick. How selfish of me! I really am thankful for everything you've done for Matthew, for making school alright for him. It's just that – I don't know how it will work. I just thought next year was settled, one less thing to worry about."

Suddenly, Jeannie had stopped, her hand flying to her open mouth.

"I need to leave; I need to go <u>now</u>. Thank you. So sorry. Thanks."

She had spoken rapidly, opening the door and virtually running, pulling Matthew to his feet and pushing him, protesting, out the office door to the car.

After that, inevitably the downward spiral began.

With only a month until the end of school, and 5 ½ weeks until Christmas, Jeannie had snapped.

She had taken Matty home, packed some cases, and walked out the door before Michael arrived home at 6.40 pm as usual.

Collecting Breeanna, she drove to a motel via MacDonald's – take-away food, a movie on demand, and bed.

The kids had thought it was an adventure, but Jeannie knew better.

When Michael had called her mobile, she didn't answer.

After the kids were asleep, she'd phoned him, speaking briefly and telling him the facts.

"We're ok. We're in a motel. I needed a break and I thought the kids needed a treat. We'll see you tomorrow night. Bye."

Ending the call before he could respond, she sat, drained, on the end of the bed, watching her "precious babies" sleeping.

Nothing made sense to her anymore. What should she do, what was next?

The following day, sleep-deprived, Jeannie had driven the children to a real estate agency, found a 2-bedroom unit *within coo-ee* of the school and signed up, draining most of her small personal savings' account to pay a 4-week bond for a 6-month lease. The woman in the agency had looked bored, like she'd seen it all before; a single Mum, 2 kids, needing accommodation quickly.

It was just lucky someone had broken a lease the day before and a place was available. Small but clean and quiet, with some furniture. Perfect!

Jeannie had not cared! She had signed, taken the keys and moved in, without even viewing the property. She seemed to be functioning *on automatic* – she acted, she moved, she spoke – without thought, as if pausing to think would bring it all crashing down.

Michael had rung again, upset of course, so she did something she never did – she left Bree in charge at the unit and went to see him.

Jeannie had taken one look at his confused face and had nearly changed her mind, but she knew she couldn't weaken.

She had to act, to change things, to talk – so she had talked.

About how it was always up to her, all the time.

About how he was distant, didn't seem to care about her or the children any more.

About how he never talked to her about what was important.

About how she couldn't do it all anymore.

Michael had tried to understand, but he just seemed to become more confused.

Where was has "constant" Jeannie on whom he relied?

He loved her, so if this was what she wanted maybe he needed to let her do it. She always seemed to understand these things better than he did.

So, he had stayed silent, beaten, unsure and unable to reach out to the woman he loved.

And then, he had let her go. He had let them all go.

Until eventually, they went even further away. Further than the next suburb, further than the edge of the city; to an old farmhouse, a quiet green place, a place to recover and regroup.

Now, here he was across the old wooden table, unsure again about what to do, what to say, even why he had come after so long; vulnerable, looking like a lost little boy.

And here she was, unsure too, wondering about her choices, her broken reactions.

But strangely Jeannie felt ready, finally, to talk to Michael in a way that had seemed so impossible for so long.

CHAPTER 5

COMMUNICATION
A TIME TO BUILD UP

Suddenly they both spoke at once.

Jeannie burst out, wary but wanting him to know.

"I'm really glad you're here. We need to talk."

At the same time, Michael ventured "I missed you Jeannie, you and the children." It was his first admission that his life was diminished without them.

They both stopped as soon as that first sentence was out there, awkward after such a long, mutual silence, feeling their way.

Unexpectedly, it was Michael who broke the new silence, eyes downcast and his voice breaking.

"Jeannie, I'm so sorry I didn't call you before I came here. I just needed to see you, all of you. I could not have another empty weekend, I just could not. The house is too quiet, even for me."

He grinned, almost smiled, going quiet.

Something told Jeannie not to leap into the silent space, not to fill it up with her own words as she wanted to, but to leave it for him to continue.

Finally, after what seemed like hours, he did continue, drawing a long breath and raising his eyes to look at her in that very direct way that was uniquely Michael's.

"I don't think I'm any good without you Jeannie. I don't manage anything well." Looking down at his hands he went on.

"What I mean is, I live day to day. I survive. I work, I run, I eat. Occasionally I laugh. That's it. The spark is gone. You have gone."

He looked up, piercing the distance between them with his brown-eyed gaze.

"I know I'm not very good at this. Is any of it making sense? Can you understand any of this, because I'm struggling Jeannie? *I'm drowning, going down for the last time.*"

Jeannie met his gaze, held it and was about to reply when the front screen door banged.

"Oh, it's Bree – she was getting a lift home with a friend" she began, interrupted by Breanna's voice ringing through the house excitedly "Is Dad here? I saw his car. Oh Dad!"

Bursting through the door Bree came, all emotion and haste, hugging her father, talking, laughing, and crying all at once.

The moment lost, Jeannie and Michael both looked at their daughter, Michael returning her hug with genuine warmth, *drinking in* her near-adult features so changed by the last few months of distance.

Jeannie smiled sadly, strangely buoyed by Michael's last speech, one of the longest she'd heard from him in years!

Silently she vowed to continue the conversation, just as David, the concerned solicitor, had suggested.

Maybe it was a blessing that Bree had interrupted, giving Jeannie time to consider what Michael's words really meant to her now, after so much time had passed.

Today of all days, the day she'd finally made a breakthrough on the road to accepting Matthew's diagnosis.

The irony of that was not lost on Jeannie – maybe God really did have a sense of humour?

That feeling -was it a sense of hope, a spark lit under the cold lump where her warm heart had once been?

Jeannie realised that she wanted to believe in hope, hope for a future for all of them.

Whether that meant the marriage could be saved, be re-invented and re-shaped around the people they had both become, Jeannie wasn't sure.

But hope inspired the confidence to try, at least to *break open new ground*, to set new boundaries, to have confidence to gather the scattered stones of their lives together.

The room had cooled as the late afternoon then moved towards dusk.

Bree and Michael seemed content to catch up, Michael listening to Bree's chatter with a slightly bemused look on his face.

He listened as she described her new life, her new friends, her school, the town, the surf, even the farm.

Sipping her tea, time passed for Jeannie too, until the conversation paused. She turned towards the hallway, stepping half out of the kitchen calling for Matthew to come. She was almost sure he would have had time enough now to adjust to his father's arrival.

Receiving no reply, Jeannie went quietly to his door, not expecting it to be locked. She was ready with words of reassurance if he needed them before meeting his dad again.

"Matty" Jeannie called, pushing open his door.

No reply and no Matthew. Was he hiding under the bed or in the wardrobe?

It wouldn't be the first time.

Jeannie looked for him, expecting to need to comfort Matthew as soon as she found his hidey-hole, but there was no sign of movement, no quiet breathing, nothing.

Frowning, Jeannie returned to the kitchen. Bree and Michael looked up at the same time, and Jeannie was struck in that moment by the likenesses between father and daughter.

"Matthew's not in his room," she said, trying not to sound concerned. Glancing at her watch with a start, she realised that 2 hours had passed since Matthew had arrived home.

Long silences between herself and Michael had slipped by, full of unspoken thoughts and emotional tension. Then Bree had filled some gaps and Jeannie had allowed herself to relax.

Only now she realised that she needed to find her son more than anything else in the world.

Jeannie began to call Matthew's name, but receiving no reply from inside the house she moved towards the back door. Michael's lean frame blocked her way, moving in the same direction.

"Let me go out and look. He's scared because I've arrived without warning. I'll go and find him and talk to him before he has to come back in," he said, reaching out to touch her shoulder before thinking better of it and withdrawing his hand.

"Where will he have gone?" he finished.

Jeannie gazed at him, understanding the need for him to reconnect, but trying to convey a sense of urgency.

"He's got a secret spot in a hollow tree down by the creek. He thinks I don't know about it. You just follow the track at the bottom of the garden. I'm sure he'll be there."

She pointed towards a rusty wire gate that was propped open with a piece of rock.

"Hurry though - he's been out there for hours," her anxiety making her bossy. "And call out to him. He hates to be surprised."

Watching Michael's face, she saw a dawning realisation of Matthew's need to escape, to find a refuge. He did it himself in the form of his office, his refuge in computers and numbers that gave him respite from a world that he struggled to understand.

Matthew was doing the same, and Michael was determined to get this right, to reassure Matthew that his dad understood.

"OK I'm *on it*" Michael threw back over his shoulder as he strode through the door and down 2 stone steps towards the back gate.

"I'll look for him in the house Mum. Don't worry, he'll turn up." Bree disappeared towards the other bedrooms.

Jeannie slowly shook her head. She could hardly remember a time when Michael had been so sure, so determined to act. It was usually her role to lead and his to follow. And Bree offering to help too! *Wonders would never cease!*

〜〜〜〜

Sitting in the kitchen alone, Jeannie was worried. Matthew had been gone a long time – longer than his usual hour or so after school. The afternoon had disappeared in a whirl of emotions and memories, waiting for the past to catch up with the present.

She felt reassured that Matthew always obeyed the rules – that he would not have wandered off, or gone in the creek without her permission.

But today things were unpredictable, different. It felt like anything could happen.

She tried to busy herself getting food ready for an early dinner.

Breanna returned, having found no sign of her brother, and offered to help, setting out 4 places on the old table. She was quiet too, seeming to realise there was a lot more going on here than just her own joy at seeing her father again.

"Is Matty OK Mum?" she asked, but for once Jeannie did not reassure. She decided not to protect her daughter and replied "I'm not sure Bree. He must have gone outside soon after Dad arrived and I haven't seen him since."

Bree stopped and, regarding her mother carefully, she approached Jeannie and put her arms around her shoulders, speaking softly.

"It'll be OK Mum. They need each other you know." Jeannie just stared at her daughter open mouthed. How come Bree knew that?

<hr />

Michael stumbled in the deepening shadows as he emerged from beneath the head-high scrub onto the creek bank.

Quietly he called his son's name, and getting no reply, called again "Matty. It's OK. I'm just here to say hello."

A twig snapped over to his left, and Michael turned just as Matty emerged from behind a wattle tree further along the creek towards the river.

Matthew was taller, his hair a little lighter probably from more time outside than he was used to in the city. He was walking slowly, looking somewhere in the direction of his father's voice. Matthew stopped.

Michael crouched down to be more at his level, realising that Matthew's new height now required him to then look up at his son's face.

Quietly Michael said "It's so great to see you son," opening his arms but expecting nothing. Like Michael, Matthew found hugs difficult.

To Michael's surprise, Matty ran forward the few steps between them, almost tripping over a tree root and landing with a rush in his father's arms.

Both of them laughed at the same time, covering any embarrassment, and peeling away the distance of the last months.

"Hey mate, you're freezing," Michael spluttered as he held Matt even tighter. "Let's get you home," but Matty clung to his dad, mumbling into his shoulder something that sounded like "I love you Dad."

Gob-smacked and choked with unfamiliar emotion, Michael picked up his son and carrying him up the track whispered into his ear "I love you too Matthew, more than you know."

Jeannie looked up as first Matthew then Michael filled the narrow doorway almost simultaneously, acting like a couple of slap-stick comedians getting stuck, as they both tried to come inside at the same time.

They were both red-faced and laughing.

"He beat me by that much," Michael wheezed, as he fell into the nearest chair. Matty pumped a fist in the air, and sat down too.

"We had a race from the gate Mum, and Dad lost!" he began, but his dad stopped him. "Matty go get a jumper and some tracksuit pants. You need to warm up."

Bree and Jeannie looked at each other as Matty smiled and obediently complied. With eyes wide Bree seemed to be saying to her mother "See, I told you!"

Jeannie just smiled as she turned to stir the defrosting beef stew, enough for 4 portions along with 4 rounds of toast. They all needed to eat, to make this seem normal and OK, even though it wasn't.

Soon Matt returned and all 4 sat at the table, almost a family, but unsure of the new dynamics.

Jeannie piled up the plates and as Bree grabbed her fork to start eating, Michael said "Is it OK if I pray? I really want to say thanks for all of this, for today, for all of you."

Jeannie was surprised. Prayer, even a nightly thanks to God for their food, was a distant memory, lost as they drifted from Church youth group to the city so long ago.

"Why not? I'm grateful too," she replied, and they all held hands for long enough for Michael to say a few words of thanks for their time together.

"Amen," they replied as he finished, and "Tuck in" from Matty was the cue to eat. It felt good and right to pray together, and Jeannie hoped that God would be pleased to see it too.

Normally Matty needed lots of persuasion to tackle a stew, that combination of textures and flavours that was so demanding on his sensory system. But tonight, he seemed determined to eat and to ignore his fears, soaking up the excitement of the occasion.

There was laughter as Bree told stories about school and trying to surf "The Highrise."

Jeannie kept them engaged with horror stories about what she had found cleaning caravans after the holiday crowds had left.

Even Matthew tried, telling the others about the ant and the ladybird he'd watched in the afternoon, but he kept quiet about his cold soak in the creek, knowing he'd broken one of Mum's rules, and somehow realising the importance of keeping a happy atmosphere around the dinner table tonight.

After dinner, they sat in the lounge room watching a gardening program, no one was really interested in, but wanting to stay together a little longer.

As the program ended, Michael rose stretching his back, stiff from the long drive and the tension of the day. "I'd better go I suppose. Hope the caravan park has a van free tonight."

"Can't he stay here Mum?" Matthew was first to voice it. "He can have my bed and I'll blow up the airbed."

Jeannie looked at her son, so engaged and animated. "No Matty. Dad can't have your bed. But maybe he could sleep on the couch in this room. What do you think Michael?"

Jeannie wanted to keep this new communication going, so she was willing to compromise a little.

"Alright, that's great. More than I expected. I'll just bring my bag in from the car."

As soon as Michael left the room, both kids looked at their mother expectantly, *unspoken questions all over their faces.* Jeannie only had time for a quick "I don't know what's going on either. We'll talk more tomorrow," before Michael was back carrying a small overnight bag.

Matty's face dropped as he realised his dad was not intending on a long stay.

But as he and Breanna moved towards the bathroom to complete the bedtime routine without protest, both children seemed to realise that their parents needed time to talk.

There were quick hugs all round, but Matthew surprised everyone by asking his father to read just one dinosaur story before sleep. Michael looked at his wife who nodded, happy that Michael was willing.

"Yep mate. Just get your teeth done and pyjamas on and I'll be there in 5 minutes." Matty rushed off, anxious not to miss his dad's deadline!

"Wow," thought Jeannie, "that was too easy!"

Michael returned from the story reading smiling. Jeannie offered his mug of tea and they both returned to the lounge room.

"It usually takes so long for him to settle. Sometimes he's still awake when I go to bed. He must be really tired tonight because of all the excitement," she observed.

Michael sat down regarding her steadily. "He's a great kid Jeannie. He's a credit to you." He shifted position as if uncomfortable and continued.

"I know I've opted out for too long with the kids, especially Matt. I think I was scared he's too much like me."

Jeannie gasped, unable to fully comprehend what Michael had just said. "What do you mean?" she said slowly.

"Well, I'm awkward with people. I don't understand a lot of social situations. He's similar to that isn't he?"

Jeannie sighed. "I don't believe the timing of this."

"What do you mean?" Michael asked.

"Well today I had a long chat with the school principal at Highcrest. And, I have to tell you something. It's a confession of sorts, something I've known for a long time and I couldn't tell you about. Not until now."

Jeannie took a long sip of her tea, the hot liquid fortifying her.

"Michael, this is the time for me to speak, and I hope, this is the time for you to really listen." She shut her eyes as tears threatened, and then felt his hand on hers, lightly holding, reassuring not hurting.

"Speak to me – I'm really listening," Michael said softly "I'm all ears!"

Jeannie sniffed and laughed briefly "Michael that's an idiom! I thought you didn't get that kind of saying!"

Michael smiled too. "I'm trying Jeannie. I'm really trying, for all of us."

Jeannie took another breath. "OK then I will try too."

She looked at her husband across the void of their separation, and began to explain, to recall all the doctor's visits, the psychologist, the paediatrician, the other therapists.

Michael looked surprised. "Of course I remember. But you said that he just had some learning problems and he'd catch up in time." His confusion was evident.

Jeannie couldn't meet his eyes, but she pressed on.

"I didn't tell you everything, and that was wrong Michael. He did get a diagnosis but I couldn't face it, I couldn't face you. I just ignored it and hoped it would all go away. But it hasn't."

She looked up at Michael, dreading the word she had to say.

"Michael, Matty has an Autism Spectrum Disorder. He's high-functioning or what they call "Level 1," but he has Autism."

Michael's face creased with the beginnings of a slow, sad smile. Whatever Jeannie expected him to do, it was NOT to smile at the news.

"Well Jeannie, that would explain an awful lot, wouldn't it?" was all he said.

CHAPTER 6

MORE FAMILY

A TIME TO BE SILENT; A TIME TO SPEAK

"Let's go into the lounge room," Jeannie suggested. This was her house and <u>she</u> *dictated terms.*

Michael followed her down the hallway to the sanctuary of the soft couch and Matt's beanbag.

Red, shaped like a protruding tongue, the beanbag looked vaguely out of place in this old weatherboard farmhouse, but Matthew loved it, loved the way it wrapped around him right from his head and shoulders to his heels (at the tip of the 'tongue'). He liked the quirkiness of it too: Ha! Relaxing on the tongue!!

Michael sat happily in his son's spot, unfolding his legs to stretch down to the tongue tip and onto the carpet square between him and the old leather couch. Jeannie slumped there holding her mug of tea in both hands, expectant.

"Hey! This is actually really comfortable," Michael said, "I reckon I could drift off to sleep right now. It's been a long day."

"No you don't," Jeannie rushed. "This conversation has been a very long time getting started and it's definitely not finished yet. What did you mean 'that would explain an awful lot'?"

Michael wriggled his bottom further into the middle of the tongue, and sipped his tea. The sweet milky liquid always comforted and relaxed him, and tonight was no exception. He looked up at his wife, now pretending to relax with her feet up on the couch, knees bent, hands cupping her own steaming mug.

Michael knew she was waiting for him to begin, giving him space and time to gather his thoughts, but he could also see something else; impatience perhaps, or frustration with him? He wasn't sure, and he knew that now this doorway of communication had opened, he really did not want it to close again. Hard as it might be to tell her, Michael knew it was time, even if it meant tears, recrimination, and frustration. Even if it meant pushing Jeannie away again, he had to tell all and trust that the truth would set them both on a path to a new future.

Secretly, he harboured the hope that that future would be together again, happy, as a family. However, he knew there were no guarantees.

Sipping the cooling liquid, Michael considered where to start.

Stevie had told him to work from his strength- using a system - start explanations at the beginning, then progress through in chronological order, but to try to cut down on the mass of additional, non-essential details he was prone to add.

Stevie said this made people *"switch off"* unless they were as interested it the topic as he was.

Michael knew he was terrible at social conversations – he couldn't do *"small talk!"* He had seen how people's faces changed as he talked at length about his favourite topic; his AFL team Carlton winning in the 1970 Grand Final, and changing forever the way Australian Rules football would be played.

Michael's Dad had been a serious Carlton supporter and had indoctrinated his son from a young age, with Michael becoming a very willing participant!

Die-hard AFL fans might stay with the conversation for a while, but Michael's peer-group were too young to have seen the game played live, and would only know it from old video footage. Even the Carlton "True Believers" *eyes' began to glaze over* when Michael started to recite obscure statistics and describe parts of play in minute detail.

As for his other favourite topic, 19th Century British railways, almost no-one stayed with him once he got into that!

"Michael?" Jeannie spoke softly, warily, not wanting to push too hard and cause Michael to shut own. That had happened too often in the past.

"Sorry, I was *lost in thought,*" he replied quickly.

"Yes, I need to explain. Stevie told me to start at the beginning and go through it, but to leave out the boring details. I can do that but..." he paused, looking at her again to seek guidance about how to manage this difficult conversation.

"I don't mind boring details in this case Michael. In fact," Jeannie paused too, considering. Then she smiled at him encouragingly, "I think we need all the boring details we can get after so little communication for so long."

Michael nodded.

"Well here goes. Stevie said I need to be more open and share more of myself with others." He paused again and gulped the rest of his tea.

Jeannie frowned, wondering who this 'Stevie' was. Someone who had so evidently become a huge part of Michael's life. She bit back the question that hovered on her lips, realising a pang of hot jealousy was spreading in her chest.

Interesting, considering this marriage was apparently over, their separation now legally long enough for a divorce to become just a formality.

A parenting plan, a quick property settlement – Jeannie hadn't wanted any of the property anyway – just a couple of signatures and it was done.

So why was she jealous of 'Stevie', just because she seemed to be giving Michael lots of advice, just because he seemed to be close enough to be telling 'Stevie' things he'd never really shared even with Jeannie back in the days when things were better between them.

Her mind whirred with questions, jealous anger rising, but she pushed it away. She had to focus on what Michael was going to say, for Matty's sake at least.

Michael drew a deep breath and looked at Jeannie's feet, her toes curling inside her thick socks. It was as close to eye-contact as he could manage at the moment.

"Where to begin?" he mumbled. "According to Stevie, I need to begin at the beginning. That's always a good place to start. So here goes..."

Jeannie raised her eye-brows, puzzled, and frowned at the repeat mention of the other woman's name, but her reaction went unnoticed as Michael *ploughed onward*.

"You've known me a long time Jeannie. Since Secondary school, possibly even earlier, I'm not sure. My memory of primary school is very clear and I don't remember you, but you probably remember me?"

He paused for breath, not really needing an answer.

"Back then I was known to everyone, I think. Adults, teachers, they all loved the fact that I was so clever, that I won all the maths competitions, and got top marks in those State-wide tests – you know, the things we had to do every couple of years?" He looked up briefly to check if she was listening.

"Well, they all loved that I brought up the school average every time I did a test! And I loved it too, even though some of the kids made nasty comments in the playground. I guess that didn't worry me, I just focussed on my school work, my reading, and Mum and Dad. I didn't really worry about friends."

"I had one special teacher – Mr Mackenzie – do you remember him?" Michael looked up again, checking Jeannie's face as she nodded.

"Well, Mr Mack was great! I had him in Year 6, the same age as Matty is now. We played all these great maths games and he let me have extra time on the computer when I finished all my work. He brought in computer disks with special educational games and I loved it. I got through them all so fast Mr Mack had to send away to a software company to get me more. I even got Mr Mack to organise for me to spend playtimes in the library so I could read, or use the library computer. Miss Davies in the library let me help her with book returns too. I got so good at it I suggested she change the system a bit to make it more efficient and Miss Davies told me she'd have to *put me on the pay-roll*!"

Michael paused, remembering, "She never did though."

Rubbing tired eyes, he looked across at Jeannie, who smiled encouragingly.

She'd said she wanted details so she'd just have to wait for him to get to the important part. Still, some of what Michael said was interesting, especially as he described his lonely school lunchtimes.

Frowning, she wondered silently how Matthew was managing playtimes at Highcrest Primary.

"Go on Michael, I really want to hear it all," she reassured him.

"Yes I will, thanks. Well, primary school was OK. The kids weren't too bad and I avoided playtimes mostly. Mr Mack seemed to understand me. He even gave me an old camera to take pictures on the weekends. It was great and I loved walking along the bush tracks to find wildflowers or bugs or birds. Something to shoot – with the camera I mean!"

"I know, I've seen all your old photo albums," Jeannie laughed, "You really were obsessed with flowers and bugs – you even labelled them all with the correct scientific names."

Michael smiled too. "I won a photography competition at school with some of those shots at the end of Year 7. I think that particular special interest went on for about 2 years until about halfway through Year 8."

Suddenly, he frowned, a new memory clouding his face.

Jeannie wondered. She remembered a shy boy of whom she had been only slightly aware in the early years of secondary school. She'd known his name even in primary school but he wasn't important in her world of girlfriends, playing netball, and learning to play the piano. She didn't like boys and basically just didn't think about them either way.

Her older sister had begun to talk about boys when Jeannie was in year 6.

Sally was 2 years older, so around Michael's age. She mentioned Michael's name in passing, as the quiet kid who always got top marks and was a bit strange.

Then, as Jeannie moved into Secondary school and the hormones kicked in, boys became people, interesting people!

And Michael was just there, working quietly away in the library or receiving academic awards at school assemblies.

She prompted him for more. "I remember you when I got to Secondary school. You must have been in Year 9 by then. What happened in Year 8 though?"

Michael sighed. "Yes, Year 8. Well, there were 2 Macks in my life. Mr Mackenzie at Primary School who was my friend, who understood me. And then there was the other one – Darren McFarlane, who was in my year."

"I remember that name," said Jeannie.

"My sister Sal thought he was gorgeous for a while, until she found out what he was really like. He *led her on* and asked her to the Year 9 dance. She got all excited and dressed up in a new blue dress Mum made, had her hair done and wore all this makeup. Then when Dad dropped her at the School Hall to meet Darren, he was already there and all over that red-head Renee. He didn't look at Sally at all, just left her standing there until her friends arrived. She was devastated. I remember she rang Dad after only half an hour and he had to go and pick her up early. She cried all night too – I could hear her through the bedroom wall!"

Jeannie frowned, "She didn't go near another boy until she met James at the Church Youth Group in Year 12, and thankfully *the rest is history*!"

Jeannie smiled at Michael.

They both loved Sally's husband Jim, and their twin daughters, but they hadn't seen much of them since they moved to the North Coast.

Jim, then Sally too, had been appointed as Secondary school teachers at a large rural town, where they still lived, their girls now almost through school. James was now Deputy Principal, and Sally ran a thriving business, tutoring students after school. Life seemed good for them, and Jeannie was glad for her sister.

Although far apart due to distance, they spoke often on the phone, and sometimes online, including their parents in a 3-way chat to catch up on family news.

"So how did Darren McFarlane upset you? You've never told me any of this." Jeannie wanted to encourage Michael to keep talking, keep sharing this side of his life that had always been hidden away.

"Darren was always in my year, right through Primary and Secondary school. At Primary he was OK, a bit smaller than me and weedy. He could run really well and mostly won the sprints on Sports Days. We didn't have much in common. I remember quite often I helped him to find books in the library – he wasn't much of a student and I think he had trouble learning to read, so I helped him out a lot."

Michael paused again, then seemed to regather his thoughts and ploughed on with his story.

"By the middle of year 7, Darren had begun to grow really quickly and he raced past all of us until he was around 180 centimetres in Year 8. He was strong too. And he'd forgotten I'd tried to help him. Also, I was *a late bloomer* physically. I was still a *little weed*, skinny and weak in Year 8 and even Year 9. I didn't grow until year 10, I think."

Michael smiled when Jeannie said "It was Year 11. I remember because I noticed!"

He chuckled briefly then continued. "About halfway into Year 8, just before the mid-year holidays, I was pretty upset one day. I was outside the library I think, and someone called me the usual – you know, "Spazz" or "Loony Luckmore.""

He grimaced.

"Then Darren walked up to me. I didn't see him coming. I think I was looking at the ground or something, but I thought he was going to be rude to me too."

Taking a deep breath in, Michael went on. "But he wasn't. He came up and said 'Don't listen to them Luckmore. Come over and sit with us.' I couldn't believe it. Macca McFarlane asking me to sit with his mob of 'Cool Kids'. I suppose I was just beginning to realise about 'cool' and 'nerds' and to wonder about friendships. All that had never really worried me before, but now I suddenly seemed to have a protector, maybe even a friend and a 'cool' friend at that. I couldn't believe my luck."

Michael squirmed to get more comfortable – this was obviously going to be a long story.

"So, for about a week I sat with Darren's gang every lunchtime. I tried to copy their talk, even how they acted and walked. It was pretty sad really, looking back at it. But suddenly I really wanted to fit in somewhere. Anyway, about 2 weeks later – I remember it was the Tuesday, the last week of school that Term – Darren took me aside at recess. He said there was $50 note in Mr Ramsay's desk drawer in our Year 8 home room, under a pile of books. He'd seen Mr Ramsay put it there before recess. Darren said it was his money and Ramsay had taken it from him earlier. He then said if I wanted to stay in his group, I had to go in and take the $50 and give it back to Darren."

Michael paused. "Somehow, I knew it was wrong, but I believed Darren when he said it was his money, so it was OK to get it for him. Plus, I really wanted to stay in his group, and I wanted him to like me. No one else in Year 8 seemed to know I was alive. So I did it! I went into the classroom at the lunch break, and opened the drawer. The money was there under a stack of Maths books Mr Ramsay had been marking. I shoved the note in my pocket and snuck out into the corridor. Of course, just as I was closing the door, Mr Ramsay came back. I think he knew what I'd done as soon as he looked at me. I never have been able to keep a *'poker face'* – is that how you say it?"

Michael looked at Jeannie, who nodded but said nothing.

"Anyway, Ramsay said 'What are you doing inside Michael? The bell hasn't gone yet." Michael again looked ruefully at Jeannie.

"You know what a terrible liar I am. I just said nothing and looked at the ground. Ramsay asked me to turn out my pockets, and of course the money fell on the ground. He just stared at it and asked me if it was mine. Well, I said 'No it's Darren's.' Then, Mr Ramsay looked at me really hard and said 'Who? Darren McFarlane? Are you sure it didn't come out of my desk drawer?'

I just looked at the ground again. I felt so confused because as far as I was concerned the money <u>was</u> Darren's AND it had come from the desk drawer!

I just couldn't work it out so I just said 'Yes'. Then before I knew it, I was in the principal's office, and the Welfare bloke was there too, and Mr Ramsay. They all kept asking me questions at the same time, and I didn't know how to answer. It was like all their voices merged together and didn't make any sense.

I just kept saying it was Darren's money and it was from the desk drawer."

Michael took a last gulp of now-cold tea, and sighed.

"The upshot was that I was suspended for the rest of the term. For 3 days and 4 hours! Mum and Dad were so ashamed of me. Mum picked me up and said something like 'I am really disappointed that you would steal money like that Michael John Luckmore'. I always knew she was really mad with me when she used my full name. And that was the first I knew that I had stolen that money! I suppose the principal, or the welfare bloke, or Mr Ramsay might have used the word, but I had had to block out most of what they said! I just couldn't cope with it."

Taking a deep breath, Michael continued.

"So, I said to my mum 'I didn't steal anything. I was getting Darren's money back for him, that's all'. Somehow, I knew this was not quite the full story, but I also knew I hadn't 'stolen' anything. Stealing was something criminals did with 'the intention to permanently deprive someone of their property'.

I know, because I looked it up in the Macquarie Dictionary the minute I got home!"

Michael again looked up at Jeannie. "I knew I hadn't stolen the money because I was returning it to its owner. Of course, none of the adults involved saw it that way. I did finally explain it all to Mum and Dad and they tried to understand, but the suspension stood. Then at school, all the teachers thought I was either a criminal, or plain stupid to be sucked in by Darren McFarlane."

Again, he paused. "Of course, I found out later that it was NOT his money at all. I was just the *fall-guy* for him all the time."

Jeannie reached out her hand and touched his shoulder, a brief recognition of the pain she saw etched across his face.

"It still hurts, even after all these years?" she asked.

"Yes" was the simple reply.

Michael was OK at telling the facts – that was safe ground – but discussing the emotions, not so. He breathed in another ragged breath and continued.

"I went back to school after those holidays. I sort of hoped that Darren would greet me and pat me on the back for doing what he'd asked me to, and taking the blame. But nothing was ever the same again. Darren and his mates didn't want to know me. He blamed me for telling Mr Ramsay his name and connecting him with the money. And the teachers didn't trust me anymore. I wasn't allowed in the library unless the teachers were there. I had nowhere to go!

I just kept my head down, tried hard to get the academic credits so the teachers would be happy with me. I didn't have any friends and I didn't look for them because I didn't trust anyone. I didn't trust myself either. At some level, I knew I didn't get it – all the social stuff, how to be a friend, working out other people's behaviour, understanding when they were lying to me or kidding me.

So, I just gave up."

"You were lonely though." Jeannie knew she was stating the obvious.

"Yes, in a way. But I just reverted to what I'd always done - school work, my other interests like trains and taking photos. I watched that 1970 Grand Final DVD every weekend for 2 years too!

I tried to disappear as far as everyone else was concerned, except for Mum and Dad of course. They were worried about me, but I think they kept praying I'd find a way as I got older. Dad kept feeding my interests – he found me old videos of Carlton's glory days, and stuff on British trains at the Town Library. I think he organised loans from the State Library too."

"Mum was great – she was upbeat all the time and she always said "God has a positive plan for you Michael." She was just so happy when I met you Jeannie, or should I say when you 'took me under your wing."

Jeannie met his gaze, and this time they both maintained the eye contact.

Jeannie smiled a little sadly. "Your mum told me that Michael. I saw her a lot at church after you went to Uni. You know she wasn't afraid to tell me it was her heart's desire to see us get married; happily ever after she always said! I was a bit embarrassed. I was only about 16 and I was just glad that you'd come to Youth Group when I'd asked you."

"So was I, Jeannie. It was a huge step after all that time by myself, but you were so persistent. I reckon you asked me every lunchtime for 6 months before you *wore me down*!"

Michael's face relaxed. "It made all the difference to me, especially going to Uni the next year. The acceptance I got at Youth Group made it easier in Uni Residences the next year. I seemed to understand a bit more about people, and I actually enjoyed Uni life you know. Mind you, I think it helped that I met a group of people who liked a lot of the same stuff I did."

As Michael paused for breath, Jeannie glanced at the cuckoo clock on the wall. A gift from her parents brought back after a 4-week bus tour of the "Highlights of Old Europe," she had a love-hate relationship with the thing!

It ticked loudly and if she forgot to push up the lever before going to bed, its chiming and music on the hour and half-hour woke her in the middle of the night. Still, her Mum had loved Heidelberg, with its castle and tiny shops selling clockwork everything, and it had been specially shipped to Australia, and kept as an engagement present for Jeannie and Michael.

It was late now, and they both needed sleep, but Jeannie was loath to stop the flood of information Michael was finally sharing with her. Still, she decided to try to push him towards a discussion of the original reason for their talk – Matthew's diagnosis.

"Michael, thank you so much for sharing all this. I know it's not easy for you. What about you have a rest and I'll talk for a while."

He nodded so she went on.

"I know a fair bit about your Uni time, and how you came back home after your parents' accident."

His face clouded briefly but she persisted.

"We got together then so this becomes our story, my story too. And I always knew you'd felt a bit different, a bit of a loner."

She gulped.

"I loved you for that once. For not being like all the rest. For having the guts to be yourself. But let's face it your quirks and routines weren't always easy to live with. I needed an outlet like work, and when the kids came – well, I had their needs to cater for, then their schooling and my part-time work again. You know all this – you were there too!"

She paused, frowning. "But somehow it all got too much for me. You refused to discuss anything with me, especially Matthew's needs. I felt so helpless and then when that psychologist said 'Autism' I think *something just snapped in my brain*!

I just didn't know how to move forward and I couldn't say the words to you Mike."

As Jeannie looked at him, she saw an expression she couldn't interpret.

She hadn't called him 'Mike' since they were newly-weds, when she used to try *pushing his buttons* because he said he didn't like nicknames, even the shorter version of his name, but as they grew to trust each other he had softened, 'Mike' becoming her intimate name for him, a name only Jeannie was allowed to say.

And now, even as she said the word, Jeannie knew the time was right – there was no turning back.

Looking at his face, she spoke softly.

"I could see the same in you Mike. I knew where Matthew got all his quirky nature, his need for routine and order, his obsessions. He's not the same as you but he's like you. Mike, I think you are on the Autism Spectrum too."

Jeannie closed her eyes; there, she'd said it and if all of this talking ended right now with Michael walking out in anger, at least it was finally out there in the open, exposed for all to deal with.

Turning quickly towards her, Michael stretched out his hand. For a split-second Jeannie thought he would strike her, but he said gently "Hold my hand... please?"

She complied, shocked by this reaction, "Michael, I......"

"Shush!" he interrupted, "my turn now. Jeannie, I have something to tell you.

I am on the Spectrum."

Jeannie gasped – "How do you know?" she managed.

"OK, the real reason I came here today. Apart from Stevie telling me I had to that is."

He continued to hold her hand tightly. She realised she was holding her breath, feeling slightly sick as bile rose in her throat at the mention of the 'other woman' who had replaced her in Michael's life.

"After you left, I just kept working as usual for ages and ages. I worked, came home and ate, slept, then worked again. I just kept to the routine – same times as before. I think I believed you would come back! One day I would get home from work and you and the kids would be there and everything would continue as it had been. Even when I saw the children in other places for access visits, I still thought you'd come home at some point. And then you decided to move here!"

He looked around the sparsely furnished room as if seeing it for the first time.

"I *lost the plot* too! My work suffered. Oh, I still went in *like clock-work* and sat at my desk. I looked like I was working but I didn't do anything. I just sat there. After about a week, Ed – you remember Ed, my boss? Well Ed came in, sat in one of the other chairs and said 'Michael, you are not well. You have an appointment with the company's Social Worker today at 11.30am and you are going to attend.' I obviously had no choice, so I went. I didn't even know the company <u>had</u> a Social Worker, but I went down to the 5th floor, and found the right office, and met Stevie."

Jeannie swallowed hard but didn't interrupt. Michael was *on a roll*.

"I went 3 times a week for 4 weeks, and every time Stevie got more out of me. It was like I thawed out a little each time. I shared things I had only ever told you, things about Mum and Dad's deaths, about Uni, even about school. I talked about the kids, and about you."

He looked at her again – that look she could not interpret.

"I talked a lot about me too, the things I like, what I do outside of work. Anyway, on the 12th visit, Stevie looked at me and said "Michael do you know why I'm here, at this company?' I didn't know so I shook my head and Stevie said 'There's an old joke you might have heard. Do you know why Universities always put the Social Work faculty right next to the Computer Science faculty? No, well it's so the Social Workers can teach the Computer Scientists how to socialise!!! Not a very good joke, is it? But the point is Michael, you have told me the story of your life and what's missing, apart from your relationship with Jeannie, is all the social stuff.

You've never learned how to make friends or really be a friend to someone. You really don't know how to have a shared conversation, unless it's about your favourite topics with someone who shares those interests. You struggle to see things from anyone else's perspective. And there's a name for that – it's called 'Theory of Mind' (1). You don't have the ability to think about how others think, and you expect everyone else to know what you are thinking so you don't tell them anything much about your feelings and your deepest longings."

Again, Michael looked at Jeannie.

"I just knew it was true Jeannie. That Stevie had just described me exactly."

He looked away briefly then met her eyes again. "Then it happened! Stevie said "Michael, I think you have an Autism Spectrum Disorder. I think it might be at the high-end of the Spectrum, what we used to call Asperger's Syndrome. These days we just say 'high-functioning' Autism, or Level One." (2)

Stevie went on to tell me that a Social Worker could not diagnose me and I needed to see a Clinical Psychologist or a Psychiatrist who was experienced with Autism. Then that's exactly what I did, Jeannie. I went online and found someone who knew about Autism Spectrum Disorders in adults. I went to see him and it was really hard, but I had to know for sure. Stevie encouraged me every step and sent a long report to the doctor, and ..."

He paused and breathed deeply, looking straight at Jeannie. "I had it confirmed – I am definitely on the spectrum for Autism."

Jeannie met his eyes and kept hold of his hand. "Are you OK?," she asked.

"Yes, yes I am," Michael answered.

"Stevie's been there all of the way, supporting me and giving me information. Stevie ordered me NOT to Google it because there's so much on the Net it's overwhelming! So, I tried not to. I read everything that was recommended by Stevie and the Psychologist though."

"And everyone at work is fine with it. In fact, knowing <u>why</u> I'm quirky or eccentric or whatever way you describe it, it's really helped me. I feel like, after all this time, I've finally found myself."

Jeannie's eyes misted over. "Oh Mike. I'm so happy for you. And I suppose you and Stevie will be able to *make a much better go of it* than we ever could, knowing about the Autism?"

Michael looked at her, confusion obvious on his face. "Me and Stevie?"

Jeannie coughed. "Well, the way you've been describing the closeness of your relationship I just assumed that you were a couple."

Michael's frown deepened, and then, to her surprise, he started to laugh.

And he kept laughing and laughing, louder and louder until tears rolled down his face.

Jeannie leaned towards him, "Shhhh! You'll wake the kids!" she began, but suddenly Michael grabbed her face between his hands, and kissed her firmly on the mouth, holding her, maintaining the kiss as all her words were swallowed up in this unexpected moment.

Months rolled back in a few seconds. Michael probed her lips then deepened the kiss as she allowed him more intimacy than they had shared in many years.

For a few long moments, Jeannie's head swam, as old familiar emotions surfaced.

But suddenly they parted, both breathing hard, and Jeannie pushed him away. "Hey, what's going on?" she sputtered, but he gripped her hand and shooshed her with a finger on her lips. He looked at her with his deep, unblinking stare, but she was peaceful, not concerned.

All of a sudden, this felt right.

"Listen *Dream Jeannie*, listen to me," he said, using her nickname for the first time in a decade or more.

"Stevie and I are NOT a couple. In fact, I think his wife and kids would be very upset to hear that you assume that to be the case!"

"Wife and kids!" Jeannie spluttered.

"Yes, Stevie is a bloke. A really great bloke, and a good friend now, as well as our company Social Worker. He knows that Stevie is a little bit feminine, but he's been Stevie since he was a little kid and it's kind of stuck, so he hasn't changed it! He says he has enough positive self-esteem and male hormones to take any teasing that's handed out! He even said he understood some of my experience at being called names because of the whole Stevie-thing!"

"Oh Mike – that's ... that's so funny. I'm so sorry I assumed...I think I need another cup of tea!," Jeannie jumped up and headed for the kitchen, not sure if she was more uncomfortable about her assumption about Stevie, or about that kiss, and her unexpected reaction to it.

CHAPTER 7

MENDING FENCES
A TIME TO HEAL

"Sounds good." Michael followed her into the kitchen, wondering what would happen now.

Already Jeannie was refilling the kettle and lighting the gas stove. He busied himself washing and drying their cups, finding milk and sugar. The teapot full, Jeannie poured 2 cups, then placed the pot carefully on the trivet.

"There's Anzac biscuits if you want them. I bake now," she added. "I have the time with so little work, and Matty loves them."

"Thanks. Will we go back into the lounge?" Michael waited, wanting to let her take the lead.

"Yes, it's warmer and more relaxed." Jeannie didn't know if she meant relaxed or intimate, and certainly wasn't sure if she wanted to risk the latter yet.

It was all too confusing and they needed to make Matty the priority.

"Let's talk about Matthew – now we both know what we're dealing with," she said, re-settling on the couch as Michael again lowered himself into the beanbag.

"Sure. I really want to help," he replied. "What do you think we should do? I mean, what do you want to do?" Michael was trying not to overstep the mark, to assume there was a 'we' anymore.

He felt closer to Jeannie now than at any time in the last few years, after sharing so much tonight, as well as that kiss – but he didn't want to scare her away.

"OK. The school principal gave me a couple of ideas and I really want to follow them up. One was for me – or us – to get more advice. There's a local therapist who has experience with Autism, and I want to call her tomorrow. Oh!" Jeannie noticed the time!

"Make that today! I'll make a time to see her first and then maybe take Matthew later if she suggests that would work. Also, I have the number of a lady called Melinda. She and her husband have a farm just up the road actually, near the turn off from the highway. They have horses and Melinda teaches kids to ride. She has an interest in kids with extra needs, so I thought Matthew might like to try that."

Michael's eyes widened. "That's a great idea. But what's the school going to do?"

"The principal said that she could maybe get some additional funding for an extra support person in Matthew's class, if I could give her the report with the diagnosis."

Michael sat up a bit straighter. "I could follow that up. I could go to the Health Centre when I get back and ask them, maybe fill in the forms or whatever they require to get a copy from their files. It's a couple of years ago but it will be on their computer system somewhere."

"That would be great Michael, that would help me a lot." Jeannie paused deep in thought. "Then I suppose there's the issue of what we tell Matty – I think that will be one of my first questions for this new therapist."

Michael nodded. "Well, if my own experience is anything to go by, I think the sooner the better. He might already be wondering why he doesn't fit in, and why he doesn't have any friends. He might even be relieved to know – that was the way I was."

"Yes, you're probably right. I sometimes feel so guilty that I haven't done anything about this before now, but perhaps you coming at this time and telling me all about what's been happening for you - I just think it's like your Mum used to say "Everything in its season. He has a perfect plan.""

She smiled sadly. "I don't pray much these days Mike, but just lately I've felt the need to just talk to God, even when I'm doing silly things like putting out the washing. And it's helped a lot – I haven't felt so alone. And now you turning up today..."

Still smiling, Jeannie lay back on the couch, more relaxed than she had been for a very long time. Michael too settled back into the red tongue chair, and *time drifted.*

At 7am, Breeanna wandered into the lounge, blearily rubbing one eye with the back of her hand. Matthew padded down the hallway behind her, stopping short as she opened the lounge door.

"Shhh! They're both still asleep!" Stifling her giggles, she let Matthew have a quick look at his sleeping parents, Mum curled up on the couch her head on a cushion, and Dad stretched out on the 'Tongue', his mouth slightly open as he snored quietly.

Matty laughed too as Bree quietly closed the door. "They must have talked until really late," he said.

The 2 children decided on a plan to surprise their parents. Half an hour later, Bree gently shook her mother's shoulder, and whispered in her ear "Brekky's ready."

"What?" Jeannie sat bolt upright ready to react, but quickly relaxed when she realised it was only Bree.

Michael also roused, momentarily unsure where he was, then stretched out as the realisation dawned that he had slept in his family's home for the first time in months, even if it was on a strange red beanbag!

"I'm hungry Bree! What's for brekky? Lead the way," he said as he clambered to his feet. Jeannie too was standing now, leaning slightly on her daughter's shoulder as she stretched out the kinks of her stiff back. Sleeping on the couch was OK, but she definitely preferred her bed!

"Where's Matty?" she asked. Bree laughed. "You'll see! Come on. Get your shoes on you two," she encouraged, half pushing her mum through the kitchen and out onto the back verandah.

Shoes shoved onto sleepy feet, they all made their way towards the creek. Skirting the big tree, Jeannie and Michael both caught their breath at the same time; there was Matthew, the camping table all set up complete with tablecloth, ready for breakfast on the creek bank.

"*Take a seat*" Bree ordered. Matty grinned "No, don't take those seats anywhere! Sit down. I've got orange juice to start." Jeannie and Michael looked at each other acknowledging their precious but oh-so-literal son, and sat. Jeannie noticed Matthew had his 'usual' Weetbix, already softening in their OJ, ready for him to eat. Their own cereal was in bowls with a carton of milk waiting for use.

Michael looked across the table at her and raised his juice glass. "I propose a toast to ... a time for new experiences, like brekky by the creek... and for lots of laughter." Everyone raised their glasses and joined in the fun. Jeannie smiled, wondering if this might just be the start of a new time of healing and *mending the broken fences* of their lives.

The weekend raced by too quickly. Breanna and Matthew wanted to show their dad their new town, and all their new hangouts. Matthew took Michael on a long hike along the river bank and into the bush, showing off all manner of bugs and birds. Michael snapped away with his digital camera, showing Matty each shot and discussing the correct names of all the insects and feathered friends. Matthew already knew so much about his new environment and kept up with Michael in identifying the creatures. "That's a Spotted Pardalote, and I reckon you can hear a Whipbird over on the other bank somewhere."

While father and son enjoyed their bonding time, Jeannie and Bree had some time to catch up too.

Breanna was itching to ask her mother lots and lots of questions, about Dad and Matthew and what was going on! Jeannie decided it was time to be open with her daughter about Matthew's diagnosis, but didn't expect Bree's response.

"Oh Mum! I knew that."

Jeannie was so shocked, she gasped "How did you know?"

Bree was very matter of fact. "We've got a boy in our year who has Autism and ADHD. He takes medication and sometimes the teachers ask me to walk with him up to the office to get his meds because he gets distracted so easily, so I've talked to him a bit. I've thought for ages that Matty must have ADHD or something, but I didn't know about Autism until I talked to Dane about how it makes him feel, and I suddenly realised that's what it's like for Matty too. But it's good to know for sure. Thanks for telling me, Mum." Bree paused and gave her mum a big hug!

"But what about Dad? Does he have Autism too?" she asked.

Jeannie did another *double-take*! Suddenly she realised how blinded she had been, how unwilling to see what had been *in front of her nose* for so long. Maybe she had just been too close, too involved.

"Yes Bree, he does. But it's only just been properly identified so he's getting some help to understand. He's really relieved to know though."

Breeanna looked down, then back at her mother. "So, what are we going to do now Mum? About Matty I mean? He needs to know too and understand."

Bree frowned. "It might make it easier for him at school don't you think?"

"I do think that, Bree. Dad and I talked about this last night and I'm going to go and talk to a therapist that Matty's school have told me about. I really want to do this soon, but I want to tell Matty the right way, so he understands and doesn't get scared."

Bree was upbeat. "That's a great idea. I promise I won't say anything until you tell me to. And Mum, I'd like to be there when you talk to Matty if that's OK. There's things I'd like to say to him about what he means to me."

Jeannie felt as if she had a lump in her throat the size of a watermelon. "How did I get to have such a wonderful girl?" she gulped as she reached out to hug her daughter. Mother-guilt had swamped her so many times, especially over the last months, as she wondered if she had done the right thing by Breeanna in leaving Michael, then in leaving the city. She was sure that Bree had missed out, that she had not always given Bree the time or attention she had needed as Matthew's needs were more pressing and more immediate.

But perhaps in the face of all the family drama, Breeanna had grown up, had matured and coped, had settled into a new lifestyle and had still had the time to think about her brother.

Jeannie didn't let Breeanna go – she held her close as she told her how proud she was of the mature young lady she was becoming.

"I think I've been selfish sometimes, and distracted too. I know I haven't always been there for you Bree, but I want you to know that you're still my pre...."

"Precious baby" Bree interrupted, "Yes I know Mum. And I reckon it has all been for the best. If Dad and Matty finally get help, then that helps us too!" she finished.

Bree gave her mum another hug and grinned. "I'm going to ring Milly," she grabbed the cordless phone and pushed open the verandah door. "See ya!"

"Good talk!" Jeannie smiled.

All too soon it was Monday. Michael slammed the back of the Pajero shut and turned to hug Matthew hard. "Come back soon Dad" Matthew's voice was muffled by his father's jacket, as he fought back tears.

"Yeah Dad – really soon. I want to show you my surfing!" Bree joined in the hug.

Jeannie held back, letting the 2 children say their goodbyes. When her turn came, she wasn't sure how to say farewell to her husband. What was the protocol with an estranged

—ex who had kissed her so long and intimately not very long before? Just that one kiss, but had it meant something?

Michael solved the problem for her by embracing her in a bear-hug, just like Matthew preferred, and kissing her on the cheek, lingering just a second longer than strictly necessary.

Bree winked at Jeannie over Michael's shoulder, and Jeannie blushed, but returned her husband's warm hug. "Safe travels. That highway's dangerous. Send us a text when you get back."

Michael was going straight to work, with the first item on today's "to do" list being to call the Health Centre and organise a copy of Matthew's diagnostic report. Both parents wanted to get it to the school as soon as they could.

"Yes, I'll do that. And I'll call soon." He looked into her eyes and something passed between them, something that had long been missing – a deeper understanding that they knew had always been there but had been mislaid.

"OK go Dad, or you'll hit peak hour in the city even though you're leaving at *sparrow's*" Bree pulled him towards the car as Jeannie stood very still. Matthew glanced at the sky, but couldn't see any sparrows anywhere, but he was saved from any further confusion about Bree's strange expression, by his father's reply.

"See you" Michael mumbled, then started the car, and before Jeannie realised, he had gone, a brief wave as he trundled up the driveway, then only dust.

Jeannie waved anyway, then turned to hear Matty asking his sister "What's *sparrow's*?" She chuckled and shooed them towards the house, and back into the weekly routine.

As Michael drove away, his mind went to his own return to routine, the routine that had kept him getting out of bed every day for years now. Normally he would be comforted to be going back to the familiar.

But this time, he felt unsettled. He was not at all sure he wanted that life anymore. Maybe, it was time for a change, and maybe, he was ready to handle it!

CHAPTER 8

LOOKING FORWARD
A TIME TO BUILD UP

Breeanna caught the bus about ½ an hour after her father's car disappeared into the morning mist along the river flats.

"OK Matt. Today there are some chores to be done, then we're going to do some jobs in town, followed by lunch. No Maccas though, because you're suspended from school, so no treats. And after that we might visit someone." Jeannie ran through the day so Matthew could think about things ahead of time and get used to the idea of what he needed to do.

"Aww Mum that's not fair, no Maccas', he protested.

He sounds just like any other kid Jeannie thought, but she knew she could use his strong sense of justice to her advantage too.

"Well mate, you did the wrong thing at school. You should have asked to go to the toilet if you needed to adjust your undies – not do it in plain sight of everyone. That's not OK. So even if I do think the school has over-reacted, and not understood completely, you are being punished, so there are 3 chores for today and 3 for tomorrow. That's my rule and I am in charge so I make the rules."

Matthew shrugged; his resistance gone.

"Right, here's a list of the chores for today," Jeannie attached a simple list to the fridge door with a magnet, then read them out to make it a bit easier for Matthew.

"Number 1: Strip all the beds and then put the sheets in the washing machine.

Number 2: Rake up all the leaves in the backyard and put them in the compost bin.

Number 3: Chop up 3 onions and 3 potatoes for dinner."

Ignoring the face Matthew was now pulling, she continued. "Do these by 10.30 then we'll go into town. I need to make some phone calls now. Have fun!" and she grabbed her mobile as she headed out to the verandah.

"OK Mum," Matty mumbled as he slammed the back door closed in a last mild act of defiance.

Jeannie knew he was OK too, and as she dialled the first number she felt strangely at peace with the world.

"Horse Haven, Melinda speaking," a voice jolted her back to reality.

"Oh, that was quick! Sorry, my name is Jeannie Luckmore. I live up the road from you in the old Walters place, and I was given your number by Ms Montgomery at the school," Jeannie said in a rush.

"Yes Jeannie, I've heard about you. You know how small towns are, and Jane told me you might call. Welcome to the area. What can I do for you?" Melinda's warm tone put Jeannie at ease immediately.

"Well, I have a 12-year-old boy, Matthew. He has some extra needs and he finds team sport really difficult. Ms Montgomery thought he might enjoy horse-riding, and he has shown an interest in horses but we couldn't afford to buy one, and I don't know anything about them, so I was wondering if you might be able to teach him..." Jeannie was aware of blathering on, but now her voice trailed off.

Melinda's kind tone was again reassuring as she asked if Matthew had any physical limitations.

Jeannine bit her lip. She needed to begin to trust people with Matthew's needs, so she took a deep breath and replied.

"No, no he's great that way although his hand-writing can be really messy. But otherwise, he's good physically. But Matty has Autism, so he struggles with friendships, and he doesn't get it in games when kids break the rules, and social groups of kids confuse him..." she stopped again.

Seeming to sense Jeannie's awkwardness, Melinda came in "Look that's fine. I do understand and I'd love to meet Matthew. Can you come after school today?"

Jeannie breathed a sigh of relief – she might leave the explanation of the suspension until later, but then remembered one more thing.

"Yes, we can come then. We'll be coming home a bit earlier than usual, around 2 pm if that suited. But Melinda I haven't actually told Matthew his diagnosis yet, so if you could not say anything about that?"

"Oh, that's quite OK. That's all up to you Jeannie. I'll just work with Matthew as I find him and we'll go from there. See you this afternoon then. Bye for now." Melinda was so positive Jeannie felt some burdens lift, but as she pressed the button to end the call, she realised that she hadn't talked about payment.

Shaking her head, she decided to think about that later. If Matthew enjoyed the experience, surely something would work out, somehow. If he didn't like it, then she would need to think again for something that would engage his interest.

As Jeannie put down the phone, Matthew appeared at the open lounge window. "Washing's on Mum. I'm going out the back to rake the leaves now," he told her.

Jeannie nodded as he walked out of earshot, and picked up the phone again.

"Hello this is Meredith Jansen, Counsellor and Psychologist. Please leave me a detailed message and I will return your call as soon as I can. Thanks."

Jeannie left her name and number, preferring to explain more in person when Meredith returned her call.

She was much less *sure of her ground* with this call than the horse-riding one! Horse-riding seemed such a practical, outdoorsy thing, a lot of fun!

Therapy sounded more confronting and so she jumped when her phone rang suddenly only a minute later.

Answering, Jeannie was determined to be strong; this was for Matthew.

"Hello this is Meredith Jansen. I'm sorry I was on another call when you rang. Monday morning is always so busy! Now, how can I help?"

Jeannie felt her heartbeat increase, but this woman too sounded pleasant and helpful.

"Thanks so much for calling me back. I'm Jeannie Luckmore, and I was given your name by Ms Montgomery from Highcrest Primary. I have a 12-year-old son called Matthew, and he has high-functioning Autism." Suddenly Jeannie's voice cracked and she covered the phone.

"Jeannie, are you OK?" Meredith's voice showed her concern.

"Yes, I'm sorry. You see I've known for quite a while about the diagnosis, but I'm only just starting to accept it myself. Matthew doesn't know yet. We need your help!" Jeannie stopped, realising that she had just admitted her own difficulty with owning Matthew's diagnosis, and to a stranger too!

"That's what I'm here for Jeannie. I do have a lot of experience helping with that sort of thing. Would you like to make an appointment to come in and see me by yourself first, so we can talk about how best to move forward and help Matthew? How does Wednesday at 10 am suit you? I'm in Highcrest at

Trawler Place just behind the Tourist Information Centre –
it's number 7."

Jeannie shut her eyes and replied "Yes, yes that's great. I'll
take that time and see you then. Thanks again." She hurried
to ring off before her courage deserted her.

It seemed like she was entering a new world of therapy
and therapists, treatment and long words, a world she had
managed to avoid for too long.

But she realised, that had come at a cost to both Matthew
and his family.

And again, she suddenly realised that she hadn't asked about
the fees Meredith charged. Oh dear, maybe she could ask
Michael for financial help this time.

The sound of the kettle whistling brought her back to the
present, as Matthew's face appeared at the lounge window
again. "Do you want a cup of tea Mum?" he asked. "I've
finished raking and the leaves are in the compost. I'm having
an OJ if you want one, or I can make you a cuppa."

He seemed so grown up, so pleased to be completing his
chores and making tea for her, that Jeannie agreed on the
cuppa!

After that, as they got ready for a trip to town, Jeannie
found herself humming in the kitchen, while Matt finished
his shower. It was turning out to be a beautiful day!

Michael's text arrived just as Jeannie and Matt finished their
shopping.

"Back in the city. At office OK. Will call later. Love to all. M."

Jeannie read it with a smile – typical Michael, to the point – but she appreciated the "love" message more than she expected to.

"Dad's back in the city OK" she told Matthew, who nodded and said "Can we have lunch now?"

Jeannie drove down to the Town Beach, grabbed the picnic basket and rug from the back seat of the ute, and looked at her son. "Picnic time. Let's have lunch on the beach." Matthew looked surprised, but pleased because Mum was organised and happy, and being at the beach meant he could run, roll in the sand and throw rocks into the water.

Jeannie looked at him and smiled. "Lunch first, then running and rolling in the sand Matt." She knew him so well!

"Hmmm!" Jeannie lay back on the picnic rug and considered the blue sky, slightly salty fresh air and the "plop" sound as stones tossed by her son landed in the water.

It all seemed so far from the stress and sadness of the last months, Jeannie could scarcely believe it. She whispered a quiet "Thank you" to the God who had made her, and who also made Matthew who he was. She may have drifted from church, but her faith underpinned her life and she realised how often she had relied on the reassurance of that faith in the darkest hours, and the joy it brought at times like now.

Her wristwatch glittered in the sun. Unlike others who used their phones to tell them the time, Jeannie still wore a watch, a hangover from childhood, when her parents had bought her first watch for her 10th birthday.

"Matt, in 5 minutes we need to pack up and then we'll be leaving."

She knew he needed that warning, just time to think about an approaching change, especially when he was doing something he enjoyed. Sometimes, now he could read, she would write a list or schedule so he could look at it and recheck it if he needed to. She had read that younger children with an Autism Spectrum Disorder needed to see photos or drawings or even actual objects to help them to understand what was coming, to plan their time.

She had also read that people on the Spectrum would always do better if they used "visual supports," even those who were very capable, because they helped to understand more easily and quickly in stressful or difficult situations. Jeannie understood – didn't she use a calendar and a diary, and notes in her phone? Everyone needed some help in remembering and planning their lives.

But for Matthew these things were not "optional," and for him, the written word worked well. His school diary was a great tool too, and Jeannie encouraged Matthew to use it even to write weekend events down too.

Matthew pitched one more flat stone into the water and watched it bounce 4 times on the surface before it sank. "Yes! I got 4 Mum!" he turned and waved at her to show he had heard her warning.

He felt happy and relaxed here at the beach. He didn't mind the sand between his toes or the cold water this time of year. He enjoyed being outside – he was always slightly claustrophobic inside buildings, and needed space around him to be completely calm.

Matt thought about that calm feeling, how his body felt, how his muscles were relaxed then tensed as he threw a rock but not scrunched up in a tight ball like they sometimes felt at school. Sometimes at school, he felt like he had wooden lumps in his stomach or his shoulders weren't part of his body anymore. Often, he felt sick, and always, always there was the fear.

Now he was 12 he could label how he felt, and most of the time he felt afraid, scared, full of fear!

It might be the fear of change, or fear of the unexpected.

It might be the fear of his body's reaction to things like strong smells, unexpected noises or bright lights.

It might be the fear that he would not be able to move enough when he needed to, especially in the classroom at school.

It might be the fear of someone brushing past him, that accidental touch that actually hurt!

It might be the fear of social situations in which he was sure to look stupid. He just always seemed to get them wrong!

It might even be the fear of his family changing again, of Mum or Dad leaving and never coming back. Even if logic told him that it would not happen, he had already had to experience more family breakdown than he could manage.

Sometimes he woke in the night, convinced that Mum had gone, leaving he and Breeanna alone in the dark house. At those times he put on all the lights in his room, stuck headphones on his head and listened to his music, winding his doona around his body so tight he couldn't move, he could barely breathe.

These things helped him to calm, to bring his mind and his body to a quiet place again.

Some other things helped too, like jumping on the trampoline for ages, or going for long walks in the bush, or throwing stones over and over like today.

Other tricks he had learned were taking deep breaths, having a cool drink of water and asking to go to the toilet for a break.

This only worked sometimes at school; some teachers thought he was trying to get out of work if he asked too often, even if he told them he had finished the work and just needed to go.

Miss Spencer was like that. Matty tried to get through all his work even if he felt hotter, and sicker, and sweatier, and itchier and like he needed to move really badly.

Sometimes it was excruciating! Why couldn't she understand that he would work much better, much quicker and concentrate much longer if he could just have a regular break, even if it was only for a few minutes?

Matthew lived in fear of Miss Spencer saying "No" to his toilet breaks, or his trips to Sick Bay. If she did, he thought that he might just boil over and have to hit something, or kick something or run away and not stop until he was a long, long way from those that just didn't understand!

It hadn't happened yet at this school, but it had gone close!

Still, today was great, the weekend had been fun, and he still had the rest of today and all of tomorrow before he had to face school again.

"OK Matty, time to pack up," his Mum called. "Time to go, and on our way, we're stopping at one of our neighbour's places."

While Matthew didn't like meeting new people, he trusted his mother and he thought he could cope if she was there. She put her arm around him as he came up to help with the picnic rug.

"It'll be OK Matty. I'll be there and I feel really certain that you're going to like this lady. Her name is Melinda and she has lots of horses." Jeannie smiled reassuringly.

This was one event she had really wanted to surprise Matthew with, but a little bit of key information – that there would be horses – was helpful to reassure him and help him overcome his first reaction to new things – fear, always fear!

CHAPTER 9

THE HORSES
A TIME TO DANCE!

The early afternoon light was bright and clear, the river sparkling, as Jeannie and Matthew turned off the bitumen and towards home. Indicating right, Jeannie soon turned into a driveway marked by a white post and rail fence and a small sign "Horse Haven."

"Funny, I've never noticed that sign before," Jeannie mused. "Have you Matty?"

Matthew nodded but said nothing, staring out the front windscreen to catch his first glimpse of a horse.

Of course, he had noticed it! Just as he had noticed and remembered every sign, every turn, every detail, every single day!

"Crazy, isn't it? When I pass by here twice a day most days," Jeannie chatted, her nerves a little tight as she hoped Matty would cope with this new experience.

A woman was standing on the edge of a patch of green grass at the front of a long brick house surrounded by a deep bull-nose verandah. In the woman's hand was a lead-rope, and behind her a medium-sized black horse nuzzled her shoulder.

"Hi there," Melinda smiled as Jeannie and Matthew got out of the car and walked slowly towards her. "I'm Melinda and you must be Matthew and Jeannie of course." She stretched out her hand to shake Jeannie's.

"I was just walking Stager to the home paddock. He's been picking at the grass on the front lawn to save me mowing it. Would you like to walk across with me?"

She indicated the direction and led a very compliant Stager across the driveway towards his paddock. Matthew walked calmly beside Melinda, taking frequent glances at Stager over his shoulder.

Jeannie realised that Melinda had set this up so that it would seem natural for Matt to walk alongside a horse as soon as he arrived. He seemed to feel at home with both Melinda and Stager, which she took as a good sign.

"When we get there, I need to put Stager in the paddock then fill up his food bin. Would you mind helping me Matthew? The quicker we get the chores done, the quicker we can have a talk."

Matthew looked at Melinda, and seemed to be considering this idea, before he asked "What do I have to do?"

"I have already brought 2 full buckets from the feed shed. All you have to do is tip them into the food bin in the paddock. I just need to give Stager a brush before we put him inside in the stable."

As they reached the paddock fence, Melinda pointed to 2 blue buckets of horse pellets and chaff. She undid the gate and led Stager towards his food bin as Matty took off at full pace, grabbed 1 bucket in each hand, then very carefully carried them back to Stager's food bin.

"Can you tip them in please Matthew? Do 1 at a time, then give it a bit of a mix with your hand."

Matthew was just tall enough to tip the feed into the bin, then he gave it a good mix. Jeannie stood back to let him finish the task, amazed that he was coping with all these new sensations.

Melinda gave Stager a few strong brushes then let the horse come to the food bin, unclipping his lead rein as she went.

"There you go boy, have your lunch. It's a bit late but that's OK. Thanks for all your help Matthew." She smiled at him as she gave him a compliment.

"Not everyone can do that Matthew, on their first visit. Some children are too scared, or want to stay further away. Have you ever been around horses before?" Melinda addressed her questions at Matthew, showing him that she was pleased that he was mature enough to manage the tasks she had given him.

Matthew shook his head, then said "But I like horses, don't I Mum?"

"Yes Matty, yes you do, although we've never had a chance to get close to them or learn much about them before."

Melinda led the way to the back verandah where a bottle of cold water and some glasses had been set out on a small table.

"Help yourself Jeannie. Matthew and I need to wash our hands," and she led Matthew inside. They both returned minutes later, Melinda carrying a tin of biscuits which she offered first to Jeannie then to Matthew.

"Well, I think we're off to a good start today Matthew," Melinda smiled as Matthew crunched his biscuit. "At Horse Haven we introduce people to horses, show you how to look after them, to care for their gear, and then teach you how to ride properly. We've got 12 horses here that are OK for children to ride. They're all pretty quiet. Do you think you'd like to try learning some more and then having some riding lessons Matthew?"

Again, Melinda addressed her questions to Matthew, and he waited only about 2 seconds before blurting out "Could I ride Stager?"

Melinda smiled. "For sure. I think he would be a good horse for you. He's quiet and sensible, and if you look after him, he'll look after you. But Matthew, before riding, you need to learn all about horses first, just like I said. That's the rules at Horse Haven."

Matthew's next question was also *on the tip of Jeannie's tongue* as she listened to the exchange. "Why is he called Stager?"

Melinda laughed. "That's a great question Matthew. Actually, my husband Bob named him. Stager was born here and when he was a foal he would nuzzle up and demand food from everyone. Bob would always feel sorry for him and give him some. Then as soon as I arrived, he'd do the same to me and I'd give him food too. He tried to trick everyone, and so when we realised what he was doing, my husband said "Hey, *what a stager!*"

He meant that Stager was pretending he was hungry or "staging" like an actor on a stage, when really he's just a big *guts!*"

This time it was Matthew's turn to laugh! Then he jumped as the screen door slammed.

Looking around, Melinda said "Matthew and Jeannie, I want you to meet my husband, Bob. I think you might know him, Matthew?"

Bob walked across and shook hands, first with Jeannie then offered his hand to Matthew, grasping the boy's hand firmly and saying "Hello Matthew. I missed you on the bus this morning. When will you be back on board?"

"Um, Wednesday." Matthew gulped and frowned, confused. It was Mr Maddison, his school bus driver.

Sensing Matthew's confusion, Bob continued "This is where I live Matthew, and Melinda is my wife, Mrs Maddison. I'm just off to pick up the bus and start the afternoon bus run, so I'll see you all later." Bob waved as he walked over to a white sedan parked nearby.

"Well Matty, it was nice to see your bus driver and find out where he lives wasn't it?" Jeannie repeated, knowing it was sometimes confusing for Matthew to meet people away from their "usual" context, like if they met a teacher from school at the shopping centre.

However, he seemed to be adjusting to the new information, and agreed "Yep, Mum. I like Mr Maddison and I think this is a really cool place. Can we come back again please, please, please?"

Jeannie was secretly delighted with Matthew's joy, but she looked at Melinda who nodded and said "What about tomorrow Matthew? I heard you tell Bob that you won't be at school until Wednesday, so why don't you come tomorrow morning and you can help me with a few chores, then I'll give you your first riding lesson. That's if it's OK with your Mum?"

"Yes, that's fine. What time in the morning?" Jeannie frowned, considering that Matthew would still need to do more chores as part of his suspension "punishment," but Melinda answered quickly "I need a hand first thing, so what say you come down at the time you would normally get the school bus? Just wear jeans and boots or strong sports shoes. Once you have tried riding, if you like it, we'll talk about getting more gear. I have riding helmets here, and the rule is that all riders must wear a helmet at all times."

"That's OK. I have to wear one when I ride my bike too." Matthew's face was shining as he looked across to where Stager was finishing the last of his food. "And don't worry Mum, I'll do my chores first thing before we come so they're all finished for you."

Jeannie could scarcely believe it!

First accepting the helmet – which, when Matty had learnt to ride a bike, had taken weeks of short practices before he could tolerate the helmet for a full ride. Now he wore it, but mainly because a police officer had come to Matthew's old school and told all the students that the law said they must wear a helmet if they were riding on their bikes.

Then, offering to complete his chores by 8am!!! It was unheard of! Matthew must be really motivated to ride Stager.

Melinda looked at Jeannie, who nodded, and said "Well we'll get going now. See you tomorrow at 8am?"

"Yes, that'd be perfect. And we'll talk about payment for lessons once Matty decides if riding is for him," she smiled. Somehow, *against the odds*, this was all working out.

Matthew was feeling so excited that he could barely focus on his dinner.

A picky eater at the best of times, he only managed a few mouthfuls before he needed to tell Breanna more about his day. She had already heard everything about Stager, and Melinda, and Bob the bus driver being Melinda's husband, and what Stager ate, and how he was going back in the morning. Luckily Bree was in a good mood too, and tolerated her brother's tea-time chatter.

Jeannie had noticed that this evening, Matty had not needed to disappear to his secret place, or to run around the verandah, or even to wriggle much at the dinner table.

So keen was Matthew to get to sleep and then to wake up ready for action, that he was happy to help with the dishes, have a shower and get into bed. After reading a few chapters of their latest book to calm him, Jeannie left him to rest, knowing that the excitement of the day had tired him out.

She still used the visual timer clock to keep Matty in bed until 6.30am so she knew he would not race out of bed at first light.

Since he was small, Matthew had had difficulty with going to sleep and staying in his own bed. After much perseverance, making clear rules, playing quiet music, using a night light and a timer clock, he had finally developed a better sleeping pattern.

A friend had lent them a weighted blanket, a product made for people with sensory integration disorders. It had helped too, and Jeannie had found a place to purchase one. Matthew loved his "Rocket Ship" blanket, named for the colourful pattern on the fabric. He still used it 5 or 6 years later, saying that it helped his body to "stop" and to feel relaxed. Jeannie was thankful that for Matthew, this particular sensory aid had worked!

Thinking over all these things as she switched off the room light and closed Matthew's door, Jeannie sighed.

She wondered if she and Michael had had more information and help when Matty was younger, and if Matty had received an earlier diagnosis, those difficult early preschool years may not have been so exhausting, and perhaps they would have all coped better.

Still, that was all in the past. It was time to look forward, to be positive about new events and people in their lives.

⸻

Jeannie was right. At first light she stirred, hearing noises and wondering if Matty would go back to sleep. Soon there was silence. She pictured Matty sitting up in bed with his books, itching to get up but obediently following the early morning rules! He was supposed to stay in bed until 6.30am.

She turned over to catch a little more sleep, and the next thing she knew the alarm was urging her out of bed. By the time she showered and dressed, she found Matthew sitting at the kitchen table, almost finished his breakfast.

"Sorry Mum, I woke up early but I stayed in bed. Then I got up at 6.30 and I'm almost finished brekky now. Can I do my chores next?"

Leaning down to give him a firm hug, Jeannie kissed the top of his head. "Finish those Weetbix, then you can get the dirty towels and put them in the washing machine. I'll have brekky with Bree then you can do the dishes. By then, it'll be time to go!"

"Whoo hoo!" Matty shot off his chair and put his empty dish in the sink as he rushed towards the bathroom. Those chores would get finished in record time today!

It seemed no time at all until he was back in the kitchen. Breeanna was slowly eating breakfast, and Jeannie had just finished. While he waited for their dishes, foot tapping impatiently, Matthew frowned.

"Mum, are there any old boots I can wear? I don't want to get my sport shoes covered in mud and horse poo."

Jeannie paused. "There's an old pair of mine in the back of the hallway cupboard. They're a bit small for me, and your feet have been growing so fast they might fit..." but she was *talking to thin air*, as Matthew was already rummaging in the hall cupboard. He re-entered the kitchen in moments, smiling broadly.

"They don't feel that great but they fit OK. I put thick socks on so that's helping" he said, showing her the boots on his feet.

Jeannie nodded. "If you end up enjoying riding, I'll look around for some better ones mate!" she promised.

Matthew grinned. "I reckon you'll have to start saving up Mum. Horse riding boots are pretty expensive!" he said confidently.

"Well, let's wait and see. Now you need to finish those dishes and we'll get going."

Breanna was ready to walk out the door to catch the school bus, and she called over her shoulder "Have a great time

Matt." Matthew's smile spread across his face and Jeannie knew it was going to be a good day.

Then she remembered the discussion she had to have with Mrs Maddison – the discussion about how she intended to pay for the lessons. Jeannie had no idea at the moment, but she did know that she had to make it happen, for Matthew's sake.

—=≈≈≈≈≈—

Breeanna walked to the gate, happy to see her younger brother so excited. Sometimes it had been hard for Bree, trying to make sense of Matthew's strange behaviours, frustrated that he seemed to get so much attention and often it was for doing the weirdest things, or the wrong things!

But she was also fiercely protective of her little brother, and understanding about the autism thing had helped a lot. She had always defended him, both with words and even with fists, when the bullies had picked on him, when people had been mean, or just ignored his needs.

Climbing up the steps, Bree said hello to Mr Maddison, and settled on the bus, placing her heavy bag between her legs. It seemed to get heavier every year, especially now she was in the senior Secondary school.

She was a good student, and could probably aim at any career she wanted, but at the moment she was keen to be a teacher, specialising in teaching children with specific needs. None of her friends talked about their career choices at school but Bree had watched Matthew's journey and she felt like it would be the right choice for her. She already knew something of how hard it could be for these kids, and maybe that would help her to help them – when the time came.

———≈≈≈≈≈———

Matthew positively beamed as he rode Stager across the round yard towards Melinda and his mother.

"He's done so well for his first morning," Melinda told Jeannie. "He's learned really quickly and he hasn't shown any fear either. That surprised me a bit. Most children take a few lessons to be this confident. I'm really impressed with his attitude Jeannie" she finished.

"Well, you teach him the way he learns best," Jeannie wanted to compliment to older woman; she could see how well Matthew had done, but she also knew it was due to Melinda's methods and her patience with him.

"He always does best if you explain things simply, and give him a few rules to follow. He's learned to trust you very quickly which is always the key with Matty."

"Hey Mum, what do you think of me and Stager? Do we look good together?"

In his excitement, Matty spoke loudly, but not loudly enough to scare his horse. He seemed to have a *"sixth sense"* about how to act around horses, like he understood what might scare them.

"Yes mate. You look like a great team."

As Stager approached, Melinda reached out to take the reins.

"OK Matthew. Time to dismount, then we give Stager a brush, and some oats and a drink."

Matthew dismounted carefully and asked "Can I lead him to the stables Melinda?"

"Yes, that's fine. Take him to the first stall and fill up his bucket with water. Your Mum and I will be right there."

As Matthew led Stager away, Melinda turned to Jeannie. "I really think he has a talent here Jeannie. He seems to know how the horse feels and he reacts exactly the right way. What do you think about bringing Matthew here regularly – if he wants to that is?" she asked.

Jeannie bit her bottom lip. "Melinda, I'd absolutely love him to come here and have lessons and help out. I really think he's already in love with Stager, and he does look *like a natural* on horseback."

Jeannie paused then plunged in to the topic that was foremost in her mind.

"The problem is the cost. I just don't think I'll be able to afford the lessons on a regular basis. I looked at your website, and – well, I'm just not getting much work at the caravan park, and ..." she looked at the ground.

"I thought that might have been why you were a bit hesitant. Well, I have had 1 idea," Melinda started.

Jeannie looked up at the woman's kind eyes.

"Jeannie, I heard *on the grapevine* that you're a book-keeper or an accountant by profession. I need help with the books for my business, so maybe we can work something out?" Melinda smiled.

They had reached the stables and Matthew came running out towards them.

"Melinda, I've given Stager his oats and a drink. I brushed him like you showed me," he turned around like a whirlwind and pinned his mother with a hard stare. "Mum, I NEED to come back soon, I NEED to do this. Please Mum. Please."

He was so intense that it was Jeannie who had to break eye-contact, and looked instead at Melinda as she said "OK Matty. Yes, I think we can organise for you to come maybe every week. But you will have to show me you can finish all your homework and do your chores too," she finished as Melinda nodded.

"Yay!" Matty's fist pumped the air and he even danced a little jig on the spot before racing towards the car. "Thanks Melinda and see you soon" he shouted over his shoulder.

"Yes, thanks so much Melinda. Can I call you later tonight to discuss that plan?" Jeannie almost laughed as Matthew's joy spread through her.

"I know we can work something out Jeannie. I'll talk to Bob. Do you want to call me after Matty goes to sleep, if that suits?" Melinda smiled. She felt like joining in Matthew's dance too!

CHAPTER 10

BACK TO THE HARD STUFF
A TIME TO KEEP

"Matthew, Ms Montgomery wants to see you at 9.30 this morning."

Miss Spencer frowned and, to Matthew, her face looked hilarious, but something in her tone of voice warned him not to smile or laugh.

"Finish off your worksheet and go straight up to the office. Don't dawdle on the oval either," she finished, still frowning.

Just like the last time he was called to see Ms M, Matty was feeling hot and sweaty, even though the day was cool and damp, with grey rain clouds scudding across the sky. Head down, he walked slowly towards the office, scuffing his shoes in the dirt beside the pathway, talking to himself under his breath.

"What does she want now? I did my suspension. I haven't done anything else wrong." At least, he didn't think he had.

Arriving at the office, he pushed the heavy glass door and entered.

Mrs Arnold, the Office Manager, smiled kindly at him from behind the reception desk, but Matty looked away, unsure, just as Ms Montgomery emerged from her office.

"Oh good, there you are Matthew. I need to talk with you now you're back at school. Come into my office." Ms M spoke loudly and didn't wait for Matthew's response, striding ahead of him into her inner sanctum.

Matthew, who had been examining her black shiny shoes, shuffled reluctantly after her, his tummy hurting and his head aching.

He felt hot, confused and worried, but he had no idea why.

His body felt like it wanted to run, to be anywhere else but inside this office.

Ms Montgomery turned to face Matthew, but instead of launching into her spiel, looked carefully at the boy in front of her.

"Matthew, come and sit on this chair," she pointed at a comfy –looking armchair, where Matthew settled. She sat next to him, just far enough away.

"You might feel better if you have a try with these squeezy toys Matthew," she continued in a softer voice, and offered Matthew a choice from a small box which housed a collection of squeezable animals, soft spiky balls, and other fidget toys. Obviously, Ms M had been doing some homework since their last meeting, and was trying to help Matthew's sensory needs and reduce the overload he was feeling.

It worked too! Matthew could feel his tension level reducing, and although he still didn't want to be there, he realised that as he relaxed, he could now listen to the principal.

Ms M waited until Matthew sat more comfortably in his seat, and then spoke quietly and calmly, closely observing the boy's reaction.

"Matthew, I now realise that you have been really confused at times since you arrived at our school. Sometimes it's been hard for you to understand what we wanted you to do and what the rules are.

So, I want you to meet someone who might be able to help you. Her name is Mrs Jansen and she works at our school on Wednesdays. She's going to come in today, in a few minutes, to meet you. Then she'll organise to see you again when she is at school next."

Matthew looked at Ms M's chin and asked the question he had been *dying to* ask "Am I in trouble again?"

"No Matthew. You've done your suspension and I've spoken with your Mum. She told me that she has explained to you that what you did was not the way to handle your problem. Can you tell me what you are going to do next time your clothes are uncomfortable?"

Matthew shrugged – Mum had been all through this so it was very clear in his mind. "Yes, I can."

He waited, but Ms M seemed to want him to say more.

Taking a big breath, the words seemed to tumble out of his mouth. "First I put up my hand and ask to go to the toilet.

Then I wait until Miss Spencer says yes. Then I walk to the toilet and go into a cubicle. Then I fix up my clothes." Matthew let out the rest of his breath and sat back into the armchair.

"Excellent." Ms M smiled. "I know you have a great memory and you'll remember what to do. Mrs Jansen is going to help you to write some stories that you can keep in a special folder." She showed Matthew a blue plastic folder with plastic sleeves that you could put pages into.

Matthew smiled – blue was his favourite colour.

"When things are confusing and you don't understand what to do, Mrs Jansen can help you to write down what to do in a special story. Mum can learn to help you too so you can write stories at home sometimes. And eventually you can learn to write them yourself." Matthew wasn't sure about the stories, but he was sure he liked the blue folder, so he smiled back. Maybe it would be OK.

Just at that moment there was a loud knock on the door and Matthew flinched.

"Matthew, it's OK. That will be Mrs Jansen coming to meet you." Ms M reassured him, but fear of someone new made Matty look down.

He noticed some specks of glitter in the carpet, probably a left-over from some little child's "special work" that they had brought to show Ms M.

She was always giving stickers to kids that did great work in class and were sent to show her in her office.

He concentrated on counting the glitter, as a person entered the room.

He could smell a sharp, tangy smell a bit like oranges, then a pair of brown stripey shoes appeared in his peripheral vision.

"Matthew this is Mrs Jansen that I was telling you about." Matty risked a short glance upwards, where he saw a tall, dark-haired woman, about the same age as his Mum, but lots fatter.

"Oops! Don't say that to her. That's rude!" Matthew thought, looking down at the carpet again.

Then Mrs Jansen squatted down beside him, not close but at his level.

"I'm really happy to meet you, Matthew. Ms M has told be a bit about you, and I hope we can get to be friends. On the days I am here we will sit down in the room next to sick bay and have a talk."

Matthew knew the room she meant – he'd seen it when he had visited Sick Bay, trying to avoid the classroom!

Again, he took a big breath and blurted, "Yep OK. But excuse me, can I go now? You smell really funny and my head is aching. Can I go back to class please?"

He figured he hadn't been rude because he said "Excuse me" and "Please" but glancing up he saw that Ms M was frowning now.

His interruption had stopped Ms M as she was about to speak, but realising that Matthew's sensory system was overloading again, she resisted telling him not to be rude and spoke to Mrs Jansen.

"What about you take Matthew out onto the seats near the staffroom? It's quiet there and there's a breeze so Matty should be more comfortable."

"Yes, that's a good idea. Come on Matthew – have a talk outside for a few minutes then I'll walk you back to class." Mrs Jansen's voice was lower pitched and sounded a bit like music in Matty's ears.

He stood and followed Mrs Jansen out of the office, glancing up at the principal, whose face seemed to be a mixture of happy and confused all at once.

Matthew sighed – this business of understanding people's faces was really hard! However, he suddenly remembered to say "Thank you" as he left the room, which he knew was the correct thing to do.

Mrs Jansen led the way to the white-painted seats outside under a huge plane tree, whose large leaves whispered as they rubbed together in the breeze. Matthew felt the fresh air on his face and took another big breath. He couldn't smell that funny smell now and his head felt instantly better.

"Sit down Matthew," Mrs Jansen said, and waiting for Matthew to sit first, sat next to him but not too close.

"I'm really sorry about that funny smell. I think that it is my perfume. I'm sitting downwind of you now so the smell will blow away from us. I promise that I won't wear that stuff again when I am going to see you."

She smiled and Matthew felt confident enough to look at her chin.

"Matthew, my job is to meet with students at the school and talk about how things are going at school and even at home. They call me the School Counsellor. Have you heard of that before?" Matthew shook his head. He liked listening to Mrs Jansen's musical voice.

"OK, so we can get to know each other a bit today, then maybe I can come to see you again next Wednesday. We are going to learn how to write some special stories – I think Ms Montgomery talked about them with you. Is that OK with you?"

Matty nodded.

"Right. Well, the other thing I wanted to mention is that next term, the school is starting a group at lunchtimes for the students who want to learn to play chess. We might try some other games too? I was thinking that you might like to go along."

Matthew thought about that for a few long seconds – he kind of liked Mrs Jansen but he wasn't quite sure he trusted her yet.

"I do play chess already, 'cause my dad taught me," he said, "But who else will be there?"

"Well just a small group, maybe 2 other Year 6 boys and 1 girl. We might ask a couple of Year 5 boys too, but we will wait and see how the first group works out." Mrs Jansen smiled "I'm really glad you know how to play chess. You might be able to help some of the others learn to play."

Matthew thought quickly. It would be OK to help others learn the game, and maybe that would help him to make a friend. Just one friend would be excellent, just like at the last school where his one friend Benjamin was enough.

They were "colleagues" though, not friends, 'cause Benjamin said that "friends are girls that hold hands and giggle."

He nodded again. "Ok I'll come. Can I go back to class now please?"

Mrs Jansen looked pleased, and replied "Sure thing Matthew. I'll come and get you at 10 o'clock Wednesday for that chat. But remember you can come and see me any time on a Wednesday if you need to talk. If I'm busy you can wait in Sick Bay until I can talk with you. I'll talk to Miss Spencer so she knows that is our arrangement. Off you go back to class now and I'll see you Wednesday."

Matthew walked back to class slowly. He needed to think about these new things that were happening in his school life. Since his suspension, things did seem to be a bit better at school, and he hoped it would continue that way.

———≈≈≈◆≈≈≈———

Jeannie breathed in sharply. Again, she had underestimated the power of small communities. Here was Jeannie's "therapist" Meredith, at Jeannie's very first appointment, telling her that she had already met Matthew in her role as School Counsellor at Highcrest School.

"Yes Mrs Luckmore, I spoke to Matthew about seeing me if he needs to talk. He seemed to be happy with that, but I realise he doesn't know me or trust me yet. In my experience, students on the Autism Spectrum often need longer to get to know a new person, and it's imperative that they trust that person in order to establish a relationship. Once that trust is established with Matthew, I'm sure we'll get on well."

Jeannie felt relief flow through her. "I'm sure Matty will come around. He usually just needs some time."

"Well, we'll take it slowly. In the meantime, I wanted to talk to you about a specific strategy for telling Matthew about his diagnosis. I do think that's the next step. Why don't I get us both a cool drink while you think about that?"

As Meredith Jansen poured 2 glasses of water from a large jug clinking with frozen ice cubes, Jeannie drummed her fingers on her knees and bit her bottom lip.

"I'm not sure – I am really worried that he'll feel different and just get angry when we tell him."

Meredith turned towards her client. Fleetingly she thought of so many other families having to deal with this information. So many children and adults had received a diagnosis of Autism over recent years, more than ever before in her long career. And so many were resistant or upset, at least initially.

"You know Mrs Luckmore" she started, but Jeannie butted in. "Please call me Jeannie," she said smiling.

"Jeannie...." Meredith continued. "I do realise this is a hard diagnosis to hear about, but there are a few things I want to say. Firstly, Matthew already knows he's different to his peers, and at the moment, he has no idea why. He might well be asking himself if there is something "wrong" with him" – she used air-quotation marks then continued – "and he probably does know that he struggles socially and with understanding things like facial expressions, but he can't talk about it. He can't put it into words yet. And he is also very well aware that he gets into trouble but doesn't understand why."

Both women knew that she was referring to the latest incident at the school. Jeannie also remembered all the issues at previous schools, and sighed at the thought.

"Well, he has said he doesn't know why the other kids don't like him" she started. "And his only real "friend" – Jeannie also used air-quotes – "Benjamin, well he was odd too." Jeannie blushed. "His parents never mentioned it but I think Benjamin was also on the Autism Spectrum." She looked at the psychologist across the desk, blinking away a tear that had appeared at the wrong moment.

"It's been so hard to know what to do ..." she trailed off, looking down at her hands.

"You know, I do understand what you're saying. Many parents say the same thing to me. And that's why I have tried this strategy that I'm going to suggest to you, many times and with good success. It's all about helping Matthew to understand who he is, his strengths and the things that he finds hard, and to reassure him that others understand and will be there to help him.

We will make a little book called "Pictures of Me" (1) and get all the people that are important Matthew's life to draw and write down great things about him – what he's good at, what he loves doing, what those people like about him. We can ask all the family members, grandparents, friends, teachers, anyone you can think of. Then we put their pages together and make a book about Matthew for him to read. We include a page about what Autism is and how it makes some things more difficult, but also how it is so amazing that his brain works in a different and special way."

Jeannie interrupted anxiously. "So, you've done this before with lots of other children and they've been OK with it?"

"Yes. Looking back, I think most of the students I've completed this with have really appreciated it. Some say they are glad to finally know why they've felt so different from other kids. One boy was really excited that there were other kids out there like him!" Mrs Jansen paused and looked at Jeannie. "How do you think Matthew might react?"

Jeannie looked away. "I'm not sure. I think he might be happy to understand why he has so much trouble fitting in, but he might be scared too," she added.

"Well, that's why I also offer to follow up with some counselling and a special lunch-time program at the school. We don't call it a social skills group. It focusses on games and activities that give the lunchtime breaks a bit of structure, and also, they're often things the students are good at. I mentioned this to Matthew and he seemed to be really interested, especially in playing chess." She stopped and looked at Jeannie, waiting for her to consider what had been suggested.

"Jeannie, I really do think it's time. I think Matthew will benefit from knowing and understanding what Autism means, don't you?" she finished.

Jeannie sighed. "Yes. I'm sure you're right. I suppose I've just been avoiding the diagnosis for so long but I know it's best for Matty." She gulped, then seemed to gather herself. Looking at Mrs Jansen she said, "How do we start?"

"Well, I'll give you some homework! You and other members of the family need to complete this sheet." She pushed a page across the desk and Jeannie looked at it, frowning. "Who else do you think you could get to make a picture of Matty's strengths? They can draw things or write things down. Some people draw stick figures and just put single words that come to mind."

Jeannie was thinking. "I'm sure his sister Breeanna will want to be involved. She's always asking me why Matty behaves the way he does, so it will be good for her. And his dad too." Jeannie knew Michael was ready to help, but like her, was unsure about what to do. This was something simple and positive to try.

"And my parents – Matty loves his Nanna and Gramps even though they live a long way away."

Meredith agreed. "Definitely. We can email or post their pages and they can send them back so we can include them in the book. Anyone else you can think of?"

"Well since we moved here there's really only been Mrs Maddison who's got to know Matty well. She's Matty's horse-riding teacher and they get on really well. Oh, and her husband Bob – he's Matty's bus driver. Matthew's always talking about Bob."

"OK," Meredith paused. "And I think I'll speak to his teacher as well as the principal at the school. I know Matty has been in some trouble there, but it might help him if they show him the positives they can see in his abilities and his personality."

Jeannie could see that might be helpful too, and she nodded her agreement.

Meredith went on to explain the process of completing Matthew's "Pictures of Me" book, and the way that everyone needed to focus on positives.

"Think about what he is good at, what he knows lots about, what he loves to do, what he adds to your family. All of those wonderful things that make him unique," she added.

"Everyone adds their own positive perspective of Matthew. Then we add a page about what an Autism Spectrum Disorder is and link the positives about Matthew to some of those characteristics. That way he can start to see that he is a unique individual, and Autism is only a part of that whole picture. Usually, the students start to see Autism in a different light – as a positive part of their make-up. They see that they have some skills that are different to other kids and maybe they can do some things that other kids find hard. It also helps us to talk about not using an Autism diagnosis as an excuse for behaviour that is not part of that particular diagnosis."

"Yes, I can see what you mean" Jeannie began. "I think I'll learn a lot too. I was really scared at first and I read a whole lot of stuff online that just scared me more. But that wasn't about Matthew, and this is! I think I'm starting to get excited!" she smiled.

Meredith smiled back. "Well, this strategy was developed by a lady called Carol Gray (3). She's an American Special Education teacher, who's done a great deal of work in this field, and she's used lots of ideas, sometimes those that parents have given to her. She's also written books on using *Social Stories* (2) to help children with Autism to plan their behaviour in certain social situations. They're another thing we can work on to add to your strategies to help Matthew. Anyway, let's get this information together over the next 2 or 3 weeks and then we can put the book together early next term. What do you think?"

Jeannie felt a swell of excitement in her chest. Finally, there seemed to be a way forward that might actually work! And she could get all the family involved, especially Matthew. As she left Mrs Jansen's office, she felt something that she had not felt in a long time – hope!

Matthew's last week of the school term dragged on. Eventually it was Friday.

Dad was arriving tomorrow to stay for a week and tomorrow was also his first trail ride on Stager. Melinda was taking him along the river and up to Bellbird Gap, about a 10-kilometre round trip through the bush. He could hardly wait!

That afternoon he raced off the bus, barely having time to wave to Bob, who just chuckled at Matthew's enthusiasm!

The screen door slammed behind him as he threw his school bag into his room, yelled 'hello' to his mother and ran outside. His insides were churning with excited anticipation and he needed to get to his special place to calm down and think.

Watching him head down the path to the river, Jeannie bit back her usual reminder to be careful. She knew he needed downtime after the stress of school, time to process all that had been happening and all that was to happen over the coming holidays. She now realised that Matthew needed a physical release as well as some mental space, and she was ready to wait for him to get to the place in time when she could speak to him calmly.

She also knew he'd be inside again soon, looking for a snack! *Hollow legs*, that kid!

Michael left the city early, driving down the coast, feeling positive about seeing his family. He missed his children badly, though the strict routines of his work and bachelor existence did dull the pain of the separation a little.

And what he had only recently realised was how much he missed Jeannie too.

For the longest time after she left, Michael had felt confused and numb. Now he knew those feelings were those of hurt and betrayal. Jeannie had always been there and she knew he needed his routines and structure, the familiar patterns of his life. In his mind he didn't need to tell her things – she knew what he thought and even what he felt. Or did she?

When things had changed so much, Michael had been forced to reconsider.

It took a while and a lot of help, but he had broken through! Yes, he still needed those routines but now he knew why. He also knew that other people, even those closest to him, did NOT always know what he was thinking, just as he did NOT understand what they were thinking.

Unless those things were talked about out loud!

That's why they said that communication takes two – a speaker and a listener – who BOTH work hard to give and understand messages.

Michael had needed to be given some strategies and information so he could think about things from not just his own perspective, but from other people's perspectives as well.

Now according to Jeannie, Matthew was going to be given that chance too. She had sounded so excited on the phone when she'd called to tell him about the counsellor's suggestion. She had positively gushed, the words tumbling out!

"Oh Michael I really think this is the right way to tell him. It'll make him feel so much better about himself."

Michael glanced at the plastic folder on the passenger seat. He'd done part of his "homework" – a story about how he had felt when Matthew was born and a few memories of fun times in the past.

He was looking forward to finishing his "picture" of Matthew with Matthew present. That had been another of the Counsellor's suggestions, to have Matthew join in as his dad wrote down positive words and ideas about his son. Michael knew Matty would laugh about the stick figures and the cartoons he had in mind. Michael did not claim to be able to draw! But that would be half the fun!

They'd do it tomorrow. Matty was out on his big trail ride today so he'd be tired and ready for bed tonight when Michael arrived.

Michael smiled as he drove on, lessening the distance between himself and his family, spending the time thinking of some new and fun ways to show Matthew just how special he was to his father.

CHAPTER 11

GETTING IT!
A TIME TO UNDERSTAND

The bush was alive this morning. Melinda had insisted that they make an early start, so Matthew had been up at 5am packing a drink and lunch, with Jeannie's help.

The supplies securely stowed in Melinda's saddlebags, they'd ridden out just before 6am, as first light crept across the distant hills from the east. Matty had barely been able to contain his excitement on the short drive to Horse Haven, and Jeannie had laughed, saying "You've got *ants in your pants*!" as he wriggled around in his seat.

"No Mum. I'm just really excited," Matty had said, frowning. "There's no ants back here." Jeannie had nodded her head and smiled at him in the rear-view mirror! It wasn't the time to explain the idiom, not when he was so focussed on the coming fun!

"Well just take 5 deep breaths and think about what you have to do when we get there," she added. It was always better to keep Matty focussed on the steps in his routine to get Stager ready – that would help him to control his excitement and his anxiety about a long ride into unfamiliar territory.   Still,

Jeannie wasn't concerned. Matty trusted Melinda and he trusted Stager even more. That was enough!

Setting off with Melinda, Matty realised that he was feeling better! The routine of getting Stager saddled, packing the saddle bags, saying goodbye to his Mum, then getting moving down the track at last, had worked! Those *"butterflies in his tummy"* were gone! Matty did know that the butterflies were not real. A "figure of speech" was what his teacher called them! But it did feel like his stomach was chock full of butterflies sometimes. Matty used to imagine they were those Ulysses Blue butterflies, and he'd close his eyes and try to count how many might fit in his stomach!

But now he knew it was just something people said. If Matthew had heard a "figure of speech" before and had had it explained to him, he could remember what it meant and work out what people were talking about when they used that expression. The trouble was there were just so many of those funny expressions, and other people used them all the time!

Thinking now of his tummy full of butterflies, he smiled at the thought of letting go a big fart and a whole lot of blue butterflies shooting out into the sky!!! "Focus Matthew" he told himself, as Stager stumbled slightly on the rough stony track.

"OK Matty, we'll trot this next section before the bush gets a bit thicker further on," Melinda encouraged him. Stager seemed to understand what she had said, and picked up his pace as Matty used his knees to give his horse a message.

Early morning mist lay like a blanket on the still water of the river. Matthew caught sight of a thin grey heron standing on one leg at the edge of the water, waiting for a fish. Another water bird – a black tern - stretched its wings one by one, drying out in the first rays of the morning sun. Small birds chirped, unseen in the leaves around him. Ahead, some noisy rosellas were fighting over nectar in a tall flowering gum. A pair of pink and grey galahs flew by, adding colour and even more sound to the start of this day.

Far from being overwhelmed, Matthew was spellbound at witnessing all the life around him, counting the birds and trying to take it all in. Stager just *took it all in his stride*, walking and trotting on command, unfazed by the bush cacophony.

"This is going to be the best day!" Matty thought, as he felt the warm flanks of his horse between his legs and tried to remember all the lessons Melinda had taught him.

Up ahead, Melinda enjoyed the bush waking up around her. "Best part of the day" she thought, hoping Matty was enjoying it too. She was pleased with his riding progress and his natural confidence on the horse. He'd made a strong connection with Stager, and together they had developed a trust that went beyond simple understanding.

Stager seemed to know when a child needed something extra, something intangible, that he could and did provide. But for Matty it seemed that the horse was going a bit further, that he really did understand that this boy needed to rely on him implicitly, and that's just what was happening. It was very special!

The day meandered towards lunch, the cool of the early morning moving to the still, warm air of midday.

The riders had progressed well, with a couple of short breaks to rest their horses and their own backsides! As the river sparkled to their left, they rounded a bend and Bellbird Gap appeared. The river took a sharp turn to the left and disappeared towards distant hills, the blue-green of the gums merging the rounded peaks dipped to form the Gap ahead.

"That's a ride for another day Matty." Melinda explained as they tied up the horses and prepared to eat lunch. "I can take you right up to the top of the Gap where you can see the whole valley. It's an amazing view!"

"When can I do that?" Matthew's eye rounded as his sore bottom was forgotten in the excitement of the prospect of an even more challenging ride.

"Well, we'd have to camp out overnight, so maybe in a few months, after the cold weather finishes." Matty frowned and looked disappointed as Melinda explained. "It's a long way up there – longer than it looks," and smiling she added "Lunchtime! Stager and Diamond have already started," and she pointed towards the tethered horses, enthusiastically picking at the grass on the river bank.

<hr/>

Matthew lay on his back on the river bank, stretching his sore muscles and *watching the golden orb* move slowly across the sky. The sun warmed him, easing the stiffness in his body – he wasn't yet used to such a long ride.

"Melinda, I want to do this every week. It's fantastic!" he stated, as Stager sniffed his hair. "Hey, watch the hair!" Matty laughed and rolled his head, reaching out to pat Stager's nose. It really was the best day ever!

***

Matthew climbed wearily down from his horse, noticing his Mum approaching from the car.

"Have a good day Matty?" she asked. His face lit up, and he nodded "The best!" He slipped the reins over Stager's head and led him into the stables. "I just have to wash him and brush him down now." Matthew sighed, knowing the routine needed to be completed before he could head home for a hot bath. Melinda was chuckling as she approached. Bob was leading Diamond into the stables too, and Melinda wanted to grab a quick word with Matty's Mum.

"He did so well Jeannie! We've had a great day. He's a real natural!" Melinda's eyes shone. "He's got a real connection with Stager too – it's uncanny!"

"I don't know where he gets that from! Certainly not from me!" Jeannie was amazed and more than pleased to hear that news.

"It's a God-given gift Jeannie! He's just so relaxed it's like he's been doing it all his life," Melinda smiled as Matty returned.

Although his legs felt like jelly and his bottom was numb, Matty remained enthusiastic. "Thanks Melinda. It was the best day ever. Can we go again tomorrow?"

"You've got 3 riding classes this week and I'm busy every other day, but I can maybe do next Saturday." Melinda looked enquiringly at Jeannie.

"Is that all right Mum?" Matty jiggled on the spot and looked full in his mother's face with big *puppy-dog eyes*. Jeannie smiled and ruffled his hair. So intent was Matthew on waiting for her answer that he didn't even flinch at her touch as he usually would. "Go and wait in the car and I'll talk to Melinda mate. We'll see."

Matty was reluctant to leave but realised he should obey his mother, at least in this instance. Jeannie and Melinda watched him wander off towards the car. Jeannie looked at the other woman, a blush rising on her cheeks. She knew that now the hard questions had to be answered.

"Melinda, I'm really happy that he's done so well, but we still haven't worked out a way to pay you for your time. I know the little bit I've been able to give you hasn't covered what you've done, so I owe you." Melinda just smiled knowingly and patted Jeannie's shoulder.

"Let's walk to the car – can't keep Matty waiting too long!" she began, well aware that Matthew needed to stick to his usual routine of in-the-car-and-leave. "You know I mentioned that I had heard you used to be an accountant in your previous life!"

Jeannie nodded – *that grape-vine* really did work overtime around here.

"Yes. As I told you last time we spoke about this, I'm qualified but I can't seem to find work here. Everyone wants people full-time and I need to be home for the kids. That means the cleaning job is all I could find."

"Well, you could do some part-time work for yourself couldn't you?" Melinda queried. "Then you could do my books and GST returns for Horse Haven. My usual accountant retired about 6 months ago so I tried to do them myself, but I'm so behind and I'm really desperate! You'd be really helping me out. I could work out what you owe me and pay you for the rest of your time."

Jeannie couldn't believe it! Doing accounts and BAS returns was *second-nature* to her. And she could work around the kids' hours at school and in school holidays. She didn't even need to think. Thrusting her hand out she nearly shouted for joy!

"That's great! Let's shake on that right now. I can come in after the holidays and do a couple of days looking over your old records and getting things in order. Then it will be pretty easy to keep everything running smoothly."

Melinda shook Jeannie's outstretched hand.

Matthew gazed at them from the back seat, a hopeful expression on his face. He'd seen Mum and Melinda talking and their faces looked pretty serious. Then Mum had smiled – a lot! He didn't really understand, but they had shaken hands so maybe that was a good sign. Handshakes usually meant 2 people agreed on something important, or maybe they had just said goodbye that way.

Matty felt those butterflies fluttering in his tummy again! He hoped that handshake meant he could keep riding as much as he wanted, and that meant all the time.

CHAPTER 12

TIME PASSES

A TIME FOR PEACE

The biting frosty mornings seemed to never end, as the days began with clear skies and thin air. The warmth of wood-fired evenings thawed the limbs at day's end and cosy quilted beds beckoned. Winter was colder here than in the city; the natural elements seemed closer at hand.

Sitting up in bed, Jeannie wrapped her fingers around the old chipped mug, her first cuppa of the day helping to push back the cold start. Winter stretched out its tentacles, and only the joy she felt listening to the children bicker about the use of the bathroom seemed to warm her inside. Still, a few more weeks and spring would arrive, with its longer days gradually lengthening into the golden twilight of summer.

Matthew entered her bedroom from the kitchen, still shovelling toast into his mouth.

Breeanna followed, *chattering like a cockatoo* about an after-school dance class. Giving each child a quick *peck on the cheek* as they ran for the school bus – late again – Jeannie felt the heaviness of silence descend on the house. She'd slept poorly, tossing and turning alone in her big bed, then woken to the dawn chorus of early-rising kookaburras, followed by warbling magpies calling from the tall gumtrees that surrounded the house. As the bush woke to this cold day, Jeannie pulled the covers over her head for a few more precious minutes before accepting that sleep was impossible. So many thoughts were whirring in her mind.

First among these was a profound sense of thankfulness for the way Matthew had coped at school over these last 2 months. Since the school had begun to understand his needs, their assistance had been invaluable.

And the whole family had been able to participate in helping Matthew understand his diagnosis of Autism.

Surprisingly, Matthew had been very matter-of-fact about the information that Jeannie had kept to herself for so long. It was as if he already knew at some deeper, instinctive level and being told he was on the Autism Spectrum merely confirmed his suspicions. Although he did still find it hard to talk about how he felt, Matthew had said "Well, I guess it all makes a bit more sense to me now."

He'd enjoyed it when his family and friends listed off all his special skills and abilities in the form of his book "All about Matthew". He really loved his dad's silly stick people with their speech-bubbles and thought-clouds. Jeannie had decided to add those to her pictures too, but she went one step further and added hearts, writing inside of them words for emotions to show how she was feeling about the things Matty could do.

He'd looked at that book every night for those 2 months and he didn't seem to be sick of it yet. Jeannie had heard him reading aloud some parts to himself after "lights out," using the head- torch Michael had given him. She often heard something she'd written: "I just love that you see the world in a different way to me."

And she'd heard Matthew laughing – maybe at Michael's stick men, or at the crazy picture that Breeanna had drawn of Matthew's head, hinged open at the top with all sorts of random things popping out of Matty's brain. Things like a computer, an iPad and an iPhone, a horse of course! It did look a bit like Stager too. As well, there were musical notes, numbers, chess pieces, long complex words (which Matthew liked to use even when a simpler one would do). This was Bree's picture of those unique "Matty" things, and he loved that page so much.

Matthew had been surprised at the picture that his teacher, Miss Spencer, had drawn. It showed him hard at work concentrating on Maths, with numbers and equations swirling around him. She'd written that she thought Matthew was very capable with numbers, and that he was far ahead of the rest of Year 6. She added that maybe he should start to think of studying mathematics at university someday.

And even Ms M had done a page for his book. She wrote down some great things that she had noticed Matthew doing. She said he was really good at reminding other students of the school rules and that was helpful to her and the teachers. She put in a copy of the photo of Matthew receiving an award for Maths at the weekly assembly; he was very proud of that!

Then, at the end of the process when Mrs Jansen the School Counsellor had asked Matthew if he had any questions, he'd looked first at his mother.

"When did you first find out about this Mum?" he'd frowned.

Jeannie remembered now how she had gulped and had difficulty meeting his eye. Haltingly she had admitted that she'd know for a few years but had not understood what to do and what to say to him. She had asked his forgiveness, and her beautiful son had merely looked at her with that super focussed eye-contact that she knew so well, and said "That's OK Mum. I think this is the right time for me to know. I'm old enough to understand it now."

Jeannie had teared-up right away, grabbing a tissue from her pocket. As she wiped her eyes Matthew threw another "curve-ball" question.

"Is Dad on the Autism Spectrum like me?"

Both Jeannie and Mrs Jansen had looked at him in amazement! For a young man who so often failed to understand social relationships in his peer group and to notice emotional responses in others, this was an amazingly perceptive thing to ask.

Jeannie had paused. She'd wanted Michael to be the one to talk to Matthew about this, but his honest directness deserved an immediate answer.

"Yes Matty, Dad is on the Spectrum too. And he really wants to tell you all about that on the weekend when he comes down."

Matthew simply nodded and looked in the direction of Mrs Jansen's face. "OK. Can I go back to class now please? It's nearly time for Maths." But as he got to the door, he'd turned back towards his mum and looked straight at her. "Thanks Mum. It's OK you know," he'd said, before racing off down the corridor, Mrs Arnold's voice ringing after him "Walking please Matthew."

Meredith Jansen had sighed as the door closed. "He's a very matter-of-fact young man, isn't he? I do think that went really well."

And it had gone well, Jeannie now recalled. Matthew had asked a few more questions at home, and had joined an online group for young teens with an Autism Spectrum Disorder. Jeannie had also made contact with a small group of local parents who also had children on the Autism Spectrum, and she was *on a steep learning curve!*

Being a rural area, some of those parents had much older or younger children than Matthew, but they all had a lot in common, and many had already been through similar issues to those she now faced. Some had good ideas about things to do or not do in the future. They'd recommended some great books and talked to her about funding for any therapy or other support Matthew might need. They had all come such a long way in a short time.

Tea finished, Jeannie snuggled back under the winter-weight doona, musing about Michael's reaction to Matthew's new knowledge.

On the Friday evening after the school meeting, Michael was barely out of his car when Matthew raced down and grabbed his hand. "Come on. You and I need to talk" he'd said, and Michael smiled that funny lop-sided smile of his, tossing his car keys to Jeannie as Matty dragged him around the back of the house towards the river.

An hour later, as Jeannie looked anxiously at the darkening sky, the gloomy shapes of the gumtrees looming out of the murk, a thin beam of torchlight appeared on the path and father and son emerged, walking slowly and looking serious. They both shivered slightly as they came into the warm kitchen, and she handed each a mug of pumpkin soup.

"What else is for tea Mum?" Matthew asked between soupy mouthfuls. Michael looked at her, somehow letting her know that all was well. Whatever had passed between father and son at Matthew's special place, would stay at Matthew's special place, and that was OK.

Now so many weeks later, Jeannie realised that that night had signalled a subtle shift in all the relationships in the family. Michael and Matthew had grown closer, talking more regularly on the phone or on Skype, when the broadband allowed.

Breeanna had asked for and read some articles on Autism that Mrs Jansen supplied, and she and Jeannie had a few discussions over late night hot chocolate, after Matthew had gone to sleep.

Bree had been able to share a few of her frustrations at not understanding why Matthew behaved as he did, but at the end of it all, she was philosophical.

"He's my brother, and I'll always love him. But now I understand him a bit better, and I know there's a reason for his weird behaviour, so I can cope with that OK. Maybe I can even help him a bit more too."

Bree had even told a few close friends about Matthew, and that opened up the opportunity for a couple of them to come for sleep-overs without Bree being worried that Matthew's behaviour might spoil her night.

Strangest of all was the way that the relationship between Jeannie and Michael had shifted.

When they had lived together, Jeannie often felt as if she was the only one thinking about the bigger picture of their lives. Sure, Michael had been good at the details – making sure the bills were paid, getting the car serviced at exactly when the repairer's sticker said it was needed, even mowing the lawn, whipper snipping and doing the edges very carefully!

But it was Jeannie who took on all the "big" decisions, like deciding on which school would suit the children, interviews at parent-teacher nights, what activities the children should be enrolled in after school, and how they were going as a family. Generally, when she tried to talk to Michael about this extra load she carried, he'd shied away and expected her to make the decisions. Jeannie had resented that sometimes, feeling like all the big burdens of the family fell on her shoulders alone.

Now that she understood more about the thinking style of people on the Autism Spectrum, who were detail-oriented and often *could not see the forest from the trees*, she could be more at peace with the past. At Michael's last visit a month ago, Jeannie had decided to try to discuss these new ideas with him. And he had been open, talking about how he had not understood her concern back then, how he could not see her perspective and just needed to stay within the things in his ordered life that he felt he could control.

"But I am really trying to think about other people's perspectives now. It's hard, but I know I need to talk about how I feel about things, especially decisions about the kids. And I need to ask how you feel too. I can't just assume that you know what I'm thinking," he'd said at the time.

But what had really *thrown a cat among the pigeons* was his next statement. He'd looked at her and opened his hands towards her in a gesture of need.

"And I also realised that I never told you enough how much I loved you, and how you were the centre of my life."

And right there was Jeannie's dilemma. Thinking about this again, some weeks *down the track*, Jeannie suddenly pushed the covers off and clambered out of bed. She couldn't go there again – it was just too confusing! Even though she'd admitted to herself that she did still love her husband, what did that mean to her new life, to her and the children and even to Michael? Did he mean that he still felt that way now, or was that love in the past?

Jeannie frowned as she pulled off her PJs and *hit the shower*. Maybe a soak under the hot water would clear her head, but confusion persisted. She wasn't willing to move back to the city, back to the lifestyle she'd left behind. This new life was working, both for her and for the kids. She had a great place to live, she had work, she even knew a few people whom she might call friends! Even though the nights were lonely and long at times, that was outweighed by how well the children were doing.

Breeanna was happy, with some good friends and lots of activities in and outside of secondary school.

And Matthew loved the quiet of the bush, the stars so clear at night and the peacefulness of his new home. He was enjoying school now he had some options at lunchtime, and the social stories she was learning to write with him had already helped him to manage a couple of new situations really well. He was gradually gaining some social confidence. Maybe that would lead to him making a friend – even just one would be great!

Of course, he was already starting to learn about secondary school for next year. Meredith Jansen had organised two transition visits already and next term there would be a full program over 3 or 4 weeks where Matthew got to attend at different parts of the school day and participate in different activities, so he could start to get a picture in his mind of what he would need to do and how he would cope. Meredith also worked 2 days a week at the Secondary school so that was a real blessing – having someone Matthew had grown to trust also in that new place.

There were so many positives here, Jeannie realised. *"Hold that thought!"* she muttered as she pulled on her clothes and headed out to start her day. There had to be a way to sort all this out for the best!

CHAPTER 13

A NEW SEASON
A TIME TO GROW

A warm north-easterly breeze floated down the river valley as Matthew clicked his heels, encouraging Stager to a trot along the bush track. "Wait Melinda. I'm coming" he shouted as she disappeared around the next bend.

Stager broke into a rhythmic trot and Matthew saw Melinda just ahead. She waved him past "You go ahead now Matty. Lead the way!"

"We're going up the hill today, aren't we?" Matthew said, surprised. Over the weeks they had explored the valley floor and gone part the way up the slopes of the range on a couple of occasions, but Melinda always decided to turn around after an hour or so, citing Matthew' inexperience.

"Yes, today's the day Matty. We're going to the top ridge. Not all the way across, but up to where you can see the range. It's warmer today and it'll be light until at least 6pm, so your Mum said it would be OK. Next time, maybe, we'll go out overnight and ride all the way across to Shannon's Cutting."

Melinda smiled to herself as she heard Matthew let out a "whoop" and saw him fist pump. Stager paused momentarily as he trotted along, not sure about this strange behaviour, but like the truly great horse he was, he didn't react further and just kept trotting as Matthew held the reins tighter in anticipation of a new adventure.

Jeannie had been concerned when Melinda had told her they'd be longer than usual on the trail. As she pored over the accounts, Jeannie frowned deeply. Melinda knew it wasn't the quarterly BAS return that had her friend so concerned. "Are you sure he's ready for such a long ride?" Jeannie had asked. Melinda recalled how she had reassured Jeannie.

Matthew WAS ready, and he rode Stager with the confidence of a much more experienced rider. Some of that was down to the horse, who really connected with his young rider and helped him out if Matthew was unsure, but mainly it was due to Matthew's perfectionism and literal way of learning.

Everything she had taught him had been taken in and practiced time and time again. Matthew didn't break the rules; he did what she had told him and did it well. And he listened; even when he didn't appear to be taking anything in, Melinda had learned that he DID hear her advice and remembered everything! In fact, he had been known to quote her words back word-for-word if something she said seemed a little different to the last time she'd given that instruction. Sometimes she had had to clarify or re-explain that the instructions were the same, just worded differently, and Matthew remembered that too.

His memory was amazing!

"We'll go straight up, and have a rest break at the top. Then we'll come back down the same way," she'd reassured Jeannie. "It'll take about 5 hours. I want to start teaching him about the whole area, so when he's ready to ride out alone he'll be familiar with all the trails and where they lead. He'll know the look of the valley and the ridge line from different angles, so he won't get lost. In a few weeks we'll do the overnight ride to the next cutting, over the ridge. That way we can come back down the longer way on the other side of the river, and Matthew can see some really wild country!"

Jeannie had smiled anxiously and looked unsure, but she trusted her friend's judgement and knew that Melinda wouldn't allow Matty to ride out alone without being prepared.

Melinda watched now as he rode confidently ahead of her. She knew that he took in every detail, every bend of the river, every turn in the track, every big tree or unusual bush. For one so young he showed a focus and maturity beyond his years, at least where his strong interest in horses and riding was concerned.

"Up to the right now Matty. This is the turn," she called. "Let Stager take you. He knows what to do as it gets steeper. Just lean a bit further forward and relax."

They were up the steep section quickly and the track became less rocky for a while. Stager was mountain-bred, so Matthew wasn't worried, but he concentrated hard anyway. He wanted Melinda to see that he could manage this!

Another 40 minutes of slow climbing and they were clear of the low vegetation. The valley below began to spread out before them, with the view gradually revealing itself, over to the ocean and back along the escarpment.

They rode along the ridge for about 15 minutes before Melinda called out. "This is the spot for our stop Matty. Tie Stager up and give him a drink. We'll *have a good breather* here before we head down again."

Matthew pulled his horse to a stop and dismounted carefully avoiding the rocks either side. There was a small clearing, under a large spreading gumtree, so he led Stager into the shade. Remembering Melinda's instructions, he pulled a length of baling twine from his pocket, then tied it to Stager's reins, before attaching the twine to a low branch. Next, it was time for some water from the saddle-bags. Stager was thirsty, and so was Matthew, but he needed to ask a question. "What's a *'breather'?'* he turned to Melinda as she dismounted.

"It's just a funny word for a rest. Maybe it comes from saying we need to *catch our breath*, and have a break," she explained. She was used to Matthew's need to understand the odd sayings, like if she used an idiom or a metaphor, or if someone was sarcastic. He'd learnt to ask now without embarrassment. She always explained simply, and Matthew stored that explanation away for the next time he needed to understand that saying.

"I get it – it's a good saying because it says what it means!" Matthew stretched his legs and arms, before sitting next to her on a shady rock. Melinda and Matthew shared some sandwiches and had a long drink of water, as the tethered horses snuffled the grass and chewed softly. Matthew closed his eyes and stopped concentrating for a few minutes. His mind drifted as he imagined being able to catch his own breath in his hands, like the saying said..........

"Matthew" Melinda's voice reached him. He opened his eyes "I really wasn't asleep. I'm not tired" he rushed, wanting to reassure her he was up to this.

"That's OK. I know that. I just wanted to show you something interesting." Melinda had walked closer to the edge of the ridge line, and stood on a rock platform that jutted out over the expanse of nothing. The bush fell away steeply this side, all the way down to the highway, then beyond that as far as the ocean. Kilometres of wild bushland, with only a couple of roofs visible. Somewhere behind them, further to the right and over that small hill, was the town and harbour. Between there and where they now stood was the Luckmores' farm house and Melinda's Horse Haven, but they too were hidden by the hills, nestling at the base of the next valley.

Melinda was pointing to the left and down towards the base of the ridge.

"Look that way. About 3 years ago, a huge bushfire was started by lightning down there. Apparently, the lightning hit an old tree and the fire just took off. It had been a really good spring, and then December was hot, so all that spring growth had dried out. It was a bit like this year actually." Melinda frowned as she remembered. "The fire spread all the way up the ridge – look over that way and you can see where it came to."

Matthew followed her pointing finger and saw a line of tall old-growth trees, still-blackened but some with green shoots and undergrowth that had sprung up since the fire.

"It was a scary time I can tell you. We were just so blessed that a southerly change came through and it rained for the best part of 24 hours. The rain put the fire out thank God. But you can see how close it came to coming over the ridge and into our valley. "

It was Matthew's turn to frown now, as he tried to understand. "If the fire had come over the ridge, what would have happened Melinda?" he asked, looking up at her with his usual intense gaze.

Melinda realised he needed a full explanation. Matthew liked to deal with facts and information in detail. "Well, if the wind had remained strong, the fire would have rushed down the other side. The undergrowth was so dry that the only thing that might have stopped it would have been the river, but it's so wild in parts that the fire might have jumped the river and roared back along the other side."

"And that would mean that our place, and your place, and even the town would have been in danger." Matthew closed his eyes, imagining the path of the fire. "We talked about bushfires at school. A guy from the Volunteer Fire Service came and told us we needed to have a Fire Plan. Mum, Bree and I worked out what we would do." He looked at Melinda again with that intense gaze. "What would you do with the horses?" Matthew's anxiety showed in his voice.

Melinda sighed. "We'd need as much notice as possible Matt. Hopefully someone would see some smoke and let everyone in town know. With the fire moving fast, we'd need at least 1 hour to get the horses out and down onto the river flats where there's that big open area. That's the safest place to go."

"Yep, that's what Mum said. That's where we planned to go too." Matthew looked back at the old fire ground. "Mum said we'd put all our valuables, and our photos and stuff in boxes so we could put them in the car in a hurry, then we'd drive to the river flats and the oval. We wouldn't try to stay and put out any fires at home. Bree got all upset that she'd lose her clothes and shoes and stuff, but Mum said they could all be replaced, but we couldn't."

Melinda put her arm around Matthew's shoulders and gave a firm squeeze. He was not usually one for hugs but he seemed agitated thinking about the fire.

"It's very unlikely that those same conditions could happened again Matty," she reassured him. "Still, it's good to have your Fire Plan prepared." She paused, looking at the sun as it began to dip behind the line of gumtrees to their left.

"Come on Matty. We need to get going again or we'll run out of daylight. And as much as that might sound exciting, it's pretty scary out here in the dark!"

Matthew grinned. "I bet Stager could find his way down OK."

"Yep. He sure could! I think *he could do it blindfolded*! He knows this side of the ridge really well. The other side – well he's only been over there a few times, but I dare say he would be OK. But let's not test that today. Back in the saddle you go young man!" Melinda chuckled. Kids!!! So sure of themselves these days.

Matthew walked quickly to the tree where Stager waited, sniffing the cooler breeze. He undid the baling twine and, removing it from Stager's reins, remounted quickly and turned Stager for home. The track down the mountain was steep, and he had to concentrate hard, often leaning back with his feet firmly in the stirrups as Melinda had shown him on previous descents.

Stager was sure-footed and knew where to slow and where to trot on. They made a good team!

An hour later they were on the flat again and Matthew relaxed back into the saddle to enjoy the last few minutes of this very special day.

Finally back at Horse Haven, Matt fed Stager and brushed him down. He was glad of the familiar routine, although his arms ached and his mind drifted. He was totally *"bushed"* – another of those words with 2 meanings that he was beginning to enjoy using.

"Bushed" meant "done-in" or tired beyond belief, which was EXACTLY how he felt. Tired but also so happy. It had been the best day ever, and Melinda promised an overnight ride soon, if his riding continued to improve. And he would make sure that it did!

As the following Saturday dawned, the mist rose silently from the river. Birds chirped, waking to a warming day. As summer approached fast, the bush browned in the sun, overnight dew evaporating quickly as the temperature climbed.

Melinda and Matt climbed higher along the ridge. Today there were 4 other riders and their horses along with them. Matthew felt uncomfortable with these new arrivals, in spite of Melinda's patient explanation that she needed to include other riding students on the trail rides so that her business could make enough money not only to buy feed for the horses, but also to purchase new equipment, and to pay for upkeep on the stables, yards, fences and paddocks. That equipment, which Melinda called "tack", feed and all the rest were very expensive!

While Matthew was able to understand this logically, he still felt uncomfortable with other riders so close by. He loved his long rides with Melinda, who like him was happy to stay quiet as they rode along, listening only to the repetitive sound of the horses' hooves on the dirt track and the bird songs all around them in the bush.

Today these newcomers seemed to have no appreciation of the joy of silence, the rhythms of the bush and the fluid movements of their mounts. Joe, a boy slightly older than Matthew, had ridden ahead and Melinda was having difficulty keeping the group together. She'd asked Matt to ride at the rear of the group as he knew this path as well as she did by now. While Matt hated to come last in the line, he'd accepted Melinda's instructions, but he didn't have to like what was happening!

The other 3 riders were just plodding, 2 girls aged about 14 and another boy slightly older, who all seemed more interested in chatting to each other, than observing the bush or even enjoying the ride. They completely ignored Matthew.

Veering left, the path opened out to the first open riverside area they had seen since leaving Horse Haven an hour before. Melinda and Joe were nowhere to be seen, but Matt knew that this was the stop for their morning tea break, so he reined in and brought Stager to a halt under a huge river gum.

"Hey you guys, we need to stop here for 20 minutes," he called out to the others who were happily allowing their horses to continue walking along the track away from the river.

"What do you know?" called back the teenaged boy whose name, Matthew remembered, was Kyle. "We're keeping going."

"No!" shouted Matthew, getting agitated. Stager sensed Matthew's discomfort and raised his head, sniffing the air. "No, you can't. Melinda always stops here for 20 minutes to give the horses a rest. You could get lost or something." Matthew yelled, his face getting redder as his stomach churned.

"That's quite right Matthew. Turn those horses around now, and dismount under the gumtree near Matthew." Melinda's commanding voice reminded Matthew of some of his school teachers, and he breathed a sigh of relief to see her trotting into the river clearing, holding tightly to the lead rein of Joe's horse, her face showing an emotion that Matthew thought was somewhere between sadness and anger. Joe's face however, was even more confusing for Matthew. He looked guilty and angry all at once, but then he grinned at his friends who had finally stopped riding and turned their horses around.

Matthew closed his eyes. It was just all too hard with these kids who wouldn't obey the rules, and were spoiling his ride and his whole day.

Melinda spent the next 5 minutes organising the other riders to allow their horses to drink, and to have a drink themselves. Then she came over to where Matthew and Stager were standing in their usual shady spot at the water's edge. She reassured Matthew that he had done the right thing, but she also warned him that disappointment was coming.

"I don't think the others are really concentrating Matthew, and I think we might have to go back straight from here." Although every inclination in Matthew was to shout or scream or run, he did nothing. He knew she was correct because the other kids had broken the rules, but it just wasn't fair that he and Melinda missed out because of them.

Finally, he tuned in again, to hear Melinda asking the other riders "So do you want to keep riding out? The track gets steeper from here and you will have to ride in single file. You'll need to concentrate on riding, and staying together. If you can't do those things, we're going back."

To Matthew, Melinda looked cranky. Her face was red, redder than if she was just getting hotter as the sun moved overhead. She was frowning, her lips were pushed together and there were lines around her mouth that were not usually there. He could only remember Melinda being cranky once before, when a horse had got into the feed bins and knocked them all over, spilling feed everywhere. A new student had forgotten to latch the horse's stall correctly and the hungry animal had gone on a feeding frenzy, eating a week's feed in an hour! Melinda had explained to Matthew that she was not really cranky at the student because he had made a mistake, but that she was really cranky because the horse could get sick from eating so much feed all at once.

Today however, she was cranky with the new trail riders. They had disobeyed the rules and put themselves in some danger. Matt stayed quiet. He desperately wanted to continue the ride, but not with these idiots! He really wanted to tell them just how stupid they were, mucking up a great day and a great ride for everyone. But he decided not to speak.

Just last week at school he'd gotten into trouble again by saying exactly what he thought. It was on an "orientation" visit to the secondary school, with his whole Year 6 class. Matthew was fine until the bell rang for the change of lesson.

Suddenly his group was caught up in a mass of students pushing and pressing along the corridor. Bags banged into him, students jostled him, smelly underarms were too close to his super-sensitive nose.

Matt began to panic and pushed blindly ahead, desperate to get outside into the fresh air, with space to himself. Standing outside on the landing, Matt was taking a deep breath when the Secondary school teacher who was looking after his group opened the glass door and grabbed his shoulder.

"What do you think you're doing pushing people? We don't do that here. I don't know what you were thinking but that behaviour could cause a serious accident," he'd bellowed, his face so close to Matthew's that Matt could smell garlic on his breath.

Matt looked down and muttered "I just need a cattle prod to poke them with and get them out of my way!"

The teacher grabbed Matthew's other shoulder, shaking Matthew and shouting "What did you say? A cattle prod? You're coming with me."

Matthew just looked at the ground, trying to switch off the verbal and physical contact being forced on him, trying to cope with this new and horrible situation. As his mind went blank, he heard a quiet voice behind the teacher saying "Excuse me Mr Rice. Can I be of assistance?" It was Mrs Jansen, his School Counsellor – maybe it would be OK.

"What happened here Matthew?" she had asked, keeping her voice quiet and normal. Mr Rice let Matthew go and turned to her, blustering about Matthew pushing other students and telling him he wanted to electrocute them with a cattle prod!

Matthew knew Mrs Jansen would listen to him so he said "They need to be more polite and not push other people.

They were hitting me with their bags and pushing me out of the way and some of them were acting like idiots and if I had an electric cattle prod, I could have given them a high voltage low current zap and they would have left me alone. Then I just needed to get out so I came out here."

It all seemed so logical to him, and Matthew could not see what he had done wrong, but Mr Rice heard only one thing!

"My students are not idiots young man, and I don't appreciate your tone of voice."

Matthew had no idea what was wrong with his tone of voice (whatever that was), but clearly his explanation had made Mr Rice angrier still. At least he had let go of Matthew's shoulders.

Ms Jansen stepped aside and quietly suggested that they all go in now that the secondary school students had moved into their classes and the corridor was quiet. She gestured for Matthew to come nearer and told him to wait inside the door until she had spoken to Mr Rice by herself. Mr Rice ordered the rest of Matthew's group into an adjoining classroom, but he still looked cranky to Matthew, as he returned to speak to Ms Jansen.

Matthew waited exactly where Ms Jansen had indicated, blocking out the conversation as he stared at his scuffed school shoes.

Mr Rice's voice rose over Ms Jansen's quiet tones, "I still think he was deliberately provocative. He needs to be disciplined, autism or not," then their voices receded again as Matthew closed down. He concentrated on a fascinating stream of light coming through a window, with multi-coloured dust particles swirling around like rainbows.

Soon this horrible day would end and he could get back on the bus to "his" school where he knew all the rules and he had learned to trust the people around him. He was so sick of getting into trouble without even knowing why. Sometimes it wasn't fair, this Autism stuff.

Ms Jansen's voice broke into his bubble. "Matt, I think it would be best if I took you back to the bus now to wait for the others. It's only another 15 minutes and you will be leaving." She guided Matthew down the stairs and soon he was settled into the front seat of the school bus, as usual. Bob the driver leaned over and said "You'll be right Matthew. We'll get you home soon."

Matty began to relax.

Later that afternoon, Mum and Mrs Jansen had had a long conversation all about Matthew making more short visits to the secondary school with Mrs Jansen supervising, so he could meet all the relevant staff and check out the school in a more personalised way. That way, Mrs Jansen assured Jeannie, the transition might be more gradual and not as big a "culture shock" for Matthew. Also, his sensory needs could be better catered for.

What they didn't need was for Matthew to get a reputation around the new secondary school as a "difficult kid", even before he had started there.

Jeannie had felt reassured but Matthew was not so certain. When he said those big kids were idiots, he had meant it! Just like a herd of cattle pushing through a narrow farm gate, with HIM in the middle. No way he wanted to do that again!

And now, watching these older kids being defiant and Melinda getting cranky, what he really wanted to say was "You're all idiots. You're just spoiling this great day out. Just listen to Melinda and do what she says," but he knew he needed to trust Melinda to sort it all out.

She was the adult and she was in charge, not him!

Matt counted slowly to 100 and waited, watching the sparkles reflecting off the rippled surface of the river. Melinda's voice interrupted his self-imposed silence. "Matt we're leaving in 5 minutes. We're going to head home," she said recognising Matt's need for a few minutes' notice of the change in plans.

Matthew turned. The other riders were mounting up again, their faces looking happy to be going back to the stables.

Matthew however, was NOT happy. Why should he miss out just because these "idiots" couldn't follow the rules? He felt his body getting hotter, his face sweaty, and his tummy churning. "It's not fair Melinda. I wanted to take Stager up to the ridge again," he moaned.

"I know Matthew," Melinda replied, choosing her words carefully.

"You're right – it isn't fair on you when others do the wrong thing. But sometimes that happens in life. I'm in charge of ALL of you today and I think this is the best idea because the other riders are not obeying the rules. They need to learn that there are always rules when you are out riding in a group. We all have to return together. I'm sorry but that's my decision."

Matt nodded and started to mount up again. He trusted Melinda so he could accept her decision even if he didn't like it! Melinda trotted up beside him and added quietly "We can go out next Saturday and make it an overnight camp like we've been planning. As long as the weather is OK."

"You bet!" Matthew had almost cheered as he trotted behind her! He was finally going to get that special ride and the all-night camp up on the ridge that he'd been waiting for. He was definitely up for the challenge.

So maybe this day wasn't so bad after all.

"You're home early" Jeannie looked up from the pile of paperwork she'd been poring over. Matt didn't feel like explaining and sat heavily on a chair, as Melinda came into the kitchen behind him.

"Sorry Jeannie. Change of plans I'm afraid. It turned out the group was too inexperienced and we had to turn back."

"Bunch of idiots!" Matthew muttered, and Jeannie pretended not to hear him, as Melinda continued "I thought I'd drop Matt home and ask if it's OK to go on an overnight ride next weekend, weather permitting of course?"

"Please Mum say yes," Matthew begged, before Jeannie had time to respond. She smiled at him, then to Melinda said "If you really think he's ready, that's great!" Matthew fist-pumped then jumped up and ran outside, headed to his special place, to process his excitement.

Jeannie knew the overnight trip up Backridge, down into the river valley on the other side of Shannon's cutting, then back along the other side of the river to the old bridge and home, was Matthew's dream. "Thank you so much Melinda. You and Bob have been such good friends and I really appreciate it – Matthew really appreciates it too even if he forgets to tell you," she finished.

Melinda returned Jeannie's smile. "Well, he didn't have such a good day today with these other riders not doing the right thing. But he's just *like the Sheriff* on horseback, letting them know when they break the rules! And he's right too, they were being difficult. I think he's learning to deal with a bit of disappointment though, so that's all good."

Jeannie breathed a sigh of relief. After the issues at the secondary school, she'd begun to worry if Matty would cope in the bigger school after the long holiday break. She could write some social stories and discuss all the changes, but he had to be ready to try to manage his own responses to situations in which he found himself. Melinda was reassuring her that he <u>could</u> change his behaviour if he was given the right help by a trusted person.

That night, after Matthew happily *hit the sack* ½ hour earlier than usual, Jeannie realised that he'd used up a lot of mental energy coping with the day's events. As she drifted off to sleep herself, she said a silent prayer of thanks that both her children were doing OK.

CHAPTER 14

I CAN DO IT

A TIME TO ENJOY

Matthew's face was a picture of joy as he and Stager trotted the last few metres to the top of Backridge. He loved the view from here, and today he was finally going all the way along the ridge, another 7 kilometres of filtered sea views and long looks along the escarpment and the distant ranges. It was close to what Matt thought of as heaven!

Later, as the sun dipped below the blue-grey hills, Matt felt himself tiring. His legs were wobbly now as he pressed his knee into Stager's flanks, but the horse knew what to do.

"Only another few minutes to where we'll set up camp," Melinda called over her shoulder. Matt was glad. He'd loved the ride but he was ready to stop, to set up his swag and eat some of the stew and damper Melinda had ready to warm up in a billycan on a campfire.

She'd explained to Matt that they could have a campfire this weekend, but next week the Fire Restrictions started for the summer, so they could not have a fire then.

Matt knew all about the fire regulations. He'd spent a lot of time online reading them after a man from the local Volunteer Fire Service had come to school again a couple of weeks ago. He'd explained the rules and why they were needed. The class had discussed what to do if a fire threatened their homes or if they saw a fire burning without anyone in charge of it. Matthew's logical mind had locked away all the facts and instructions, just in case. His family already had a fire plan, but this new information was good to have as well.

Thinking about these things was a long way from Matt's mind as he snuggled down into his swag that night. They'd stopped high on the ridge in a flat clearing which dropped away one side, and opened back towards the escarpment and the river valley beyond, the direction of the next day's ride.

He felt so full of food (Melinda's stew and damper were fantastic after the long ride), and of good, happy feelings. The horses were fed and watered, now tethered nearby for the night. Matt heard all sorts of night noises in the bush around him, but he wasn't scared. Melinda lay just a metre away, her face lit up by the dying embers of their fire.

"Goodnight Matt," she whispered, "Sleep well." But Matt was already asleep, totally exhausted, but relaxed in his swag cocoon.

"Wow! Look at that," Matt breathed out, his breath steaming in the thin, cold mountain air of the dawn. The sun broke through above a thin layer of cloud that blanketed the distant horizon. Above him in the tops of nearby gumtrees, birds called and fluttered as the first light touched their night-time roosting spots. "It's so beautiful!"

Melinda agreed. "It's a special time of day isn't it. God's wakeup call."

They packed up camp and were away by 6.30am after a quick breakfast.

Melinda was keen to show Matt different tracks off the Ridge "just in case." Matt had to ask "In case of what?" so Melinda explained.

There were three different routes up the mountain: the track they'd come up on yesterday, which was challenging but much easier than the other two. It was also much longer as it wound around rocky outcrops and through stands of old growth forest.

The second track ran fairly close to the first, and along the same side of the river, but it was very overgrown with bushes and undergrowth. It was also much steeper and there were lots of loose rocks, so it was dangerous. Melinda explained that, although it was a great deal shorter than the other two ways up or down the mountain, only very experienced riders should try it.

"The track we'll take today goes further north and it's not as steep. We end up at the very top of the river where it begins, up in the gorge just under the highest part of the range. Then we follow the river down. We can cross the river anywhere up there because it's very narrow, before it meets a few other creeks and forms the river itself at the bottom of the next valley. So, we'll cross over and follow the river down and along to cross back at the old stone bridge, then home. How does that sound?"

Melinda smiled over at Matt, who just nodded. He seemed very relaxed and happy to take a new, if much longer way home, enjoying the slow pace and the sun warming his back. Stager too seemed rested and enjoying this long leisurely journey with his young rider.

"He did really well. Didn't complain and was OK with looking after the horses when we got back too." Melinda reassured a slightly anxious Jeannie, who, although she trusted Melinda, had had a restless night thinking about her "baby" Matthew out there in the bush.

Melinda went on to say that they would go again after the fire season, and Jeannie gulped and just nodded. As she tidied Melinda's office desk and packed up the pages of accounts that she had been working on, Jeannie couldn't help the realisation that her "baby" was growing up, taking some small steps to becoming an adult. She was not sure SHE was ready for that just yet!

But she thanked Melinda profusely as she stowed the last of the big folders of bills in the filing cabinet and turned off the computer.

It was inevitable that the kids were growing up. She continued to reflect on that as she drove a yawning Matthew home. Everything seemed to be going well – finally!

Matt was loving his riding and the transition to secondary school was progressing well now Mrs Jansen had taken charge. Even Mr Rice seemed to be coming to understand Matthew's quirks.

Bree was also doing well as school. She'd just made her subject choices for Years 11 and 12. While she wanted to keep her options open, Bree was definitely looking at a career as a teacher. "A double degree in Education and Psychology" she'd told her mother, "So I have to work hard!"

Good on her, Jeannie sighed as she thought about that conversation. Bree seemed happy to complete her homework, often going to friend's homes after school to finish assignments, even spending some weekends at Emily's house or maybe with another friend Bonnie, who had similar interests and wanted to be a psychologist.

Jeannie glanced over at the back seat where Matt was struggling to keep his eyes open, and it was only 5.45pm! It must have been quite a physically challenging ride alright!

She smiled as she thought about her last chat with Michael. They were talking a lot now – every couple of days on the phone or on the internet, if the connection was cooperating. Mostly about the children, what they were up to at school, what she was hoping they would do over the next year.

But sometimes they spoke of other things – their shared memories, good times together before kids, and as a family before it all *"went south."* Jeannie didn't really know what it meant – this getting close to her estranged husband again.

He was saving all his holidays and days he was owed through doing overtime so he could spend all the school holidays at the farm.

Jeannie hadn't fully worked out the logistics of that yet. She'd need another single bed, but Melinda had one she could borrow. She hoped it would squeeze into Matt's room. That might upset his sleeping patterns but it couldn't be helped.

Nanna and Gramps were also coming for Christmas, bringing their little caravan down. So, it would be a big family get together with all the trimmings. She was getting a bit excited about that if she was honest!

Jeannie switched on the car radio just catching the last minutes of the news at 6pm. The newsreader was reading the bushfire warnings.

Bushfires were all everyone in town could talk about lately.

Spring had been unusually dry, and summer was shaping up the same way. For early December, the locals all agreed that the paddocks were as *dry as chips*, and dams were dangerously low.

"Level Two water restrictions are now in place across most areas of the state" the newsreader droned in the background. Jeannie thought about the tanks at the farm. She knew the proximity to the river was a real blessing, as she could top up the water tanks for the house any time, as long as the river was flowing. So far it was OK, but others further away from the river were already buying water, and a few times lately she'd seen the tanker going past her gate and turning up to properties across the road.

Still, she didn't want to think negatively when all seemed to be going so well. She turned off the radio, content to drive the last few kilometres to home in peace.

~~~~~~

As Matthew and Jeannie arrived at their farm gate, an old dirty ute turned around in their entrance, speeding away in a dusty cloud which obscured the car and its driver enough so that Jeannie couldn't see who was driving. Strange to see an unfamiliar car out this far – still it must have been someone who mistook their track for the more travelled public road.

"Who was that Mum?" Matthew asked wearily, as the car sped away.

"I couldn't see Matty, too much dust. Probably someone lost. They'll head back to the main road." Jeannie moved on mentally, thinking about dinner and hoping Bree would have started preparing the vegetables.

"Hi Bree. We're home" Jeannie sang out as the front screen door slammed shut. Bree was nowhere to be seen though, not in her room, not in the lounge tapping her foot to music on her phone, not in the kitchen chopping carrots, getting dinner ready as she often did.

Jeannie frowned. Matthew was already in the shower and would be demanding a meal soon. Jeannie had come to rely on Bree's contribution to family life, especially on these late days when she'd been working on Melinda's books and Matthew had been out riding until dark.

Jeannie mentally pinched herself. She really must start telling Breeanna how much she appreciated her help. But where was she?

Breanna had always been so sensible and reliable. Now at nearly 16, she was becoming a beautiful young woman, her sharp mind and generally happy attitude helping her to enjoy life.

Admittedly she had been spending a lot of time with her friends lately, but Jeannie knew them all – it was a small town after all – and trusted Bree's judgement. She'd never questioned Bree about what she did away from home, just accepted Bree's brief and breezy descriptions of her days with friends. "Oh, we just finished homework then chilled at Janna's place," or "We went for a coffee at Molly's café. Emily and some others were there so we went for a walk to the beach." Bree generally got a lift home with a friend's mum or dad, and she was always home when she had agreed to be there. Well, mostly!

Jeannie realised with a twinge of guilt, that recently Bree had been home later and later, sometimes arriving home after her mother, but she'd just been too busy to ask Bree about it.

Too busy with holding down two jobs, with Matthew's issues at school, with making sure he was coping, with going along to her own therapist, even with thoughts of her relationship with Michael.

Pangs of guilt, even panic, began to rear up inside her as she realised that her relationship with her daughter was slipping sideways, when it should be at its strongest and most protective. Bree was in that awkward time between being a child, and developing into a woman – she was growing up fast and needed independence with guidance.

She needed a Mum to talk to, not a Mum that was too busy to notice if she was OK or not. And certainly not a Mum who was a "mate" and let her do anything she wanted, without any rules or limits!

Jeannie realised with blinding clarity that she had not been connecting with Breeanna for a long time. "Dear God, have I mucked up again?" she mumbled, just as the back door shut quietly.

And there was Bree, face red and eyes redder, looking away from her mother and hurrying past her up the corridor to her room.

CHAPTER 15

WHEN BAD THINGS HAPPEN
A TIME TO WEEP

"Bree" Jeannie quietly knocked at the slammed door. There was no answer, just muffled sobs. Jeannie opened the door, and moved to sit on her daughter's bed, not touching Bree as she tried to respect her space. "Bree" Jeannie repeated "I'm here. Can I give you a hug?" She knew she needed to move carefully so that Bree would not withdraw and *clam up* completely without sharing what was wrong.

There was a small nod, the tiniest of movements, so Jeannie gathered Bree into her arms, tears welling in her own eyes as the quiet crying became full-on sobbing. Jeannie just wanted to make it better, but her mother's sixth-sense made her acutely aware that this was not a bumped knee to be kissed better. This was a serious, grown-up problem. So, Bree needed a serious grown-up Mum! "Do you want to tell me?" Jeannie asked. Again, there was a small nod, and Jeannie just waited.

"I'm so sorry Mum. I've really mucked up, and you're going to find out anyway so I need to tell you," Bree began sobbing again.

A chill of dread ran down Jeannie's spine, but she stayed quiet, just continuing to give Bree the physical contact of the hug. The girl took a long, ragged breath and pulled back slightly from her mother. She looked down at the pink and white striped quilt cover decorating her bed. It seemed a left-over from a more innocent time, a time when Bree was a little girl, not the teenager trying to become a woman that Jeannie sat next to now. "Whatever it is, let her tell me," Jeannie thought, biting her lip as she tried to remain calm.

"Mum, I'm such an idiot. You were so right, as usual, and I'm really, really sorry." Bree's voice caught in her throat as she tried not to cry. Jeannie gulped – the evening air suddenly seemed *as thick as mud* and Jeannie felt panic rising.

What had happened? What had Bree done? "Bree, whatever it is, whatever you've done, I'm here and I can help. I love you," she managed, brushing a stray hair from her daughter's face. "Just tell me…"

Bree sniffed and cleared her throat. "I'm so stupid. And I'm so embarrassed. I know you'll be really angry with me but I have to tell you. You'll hear all about it soon anyway – in this town." This last was said *with some venom*, as if the small town that had embraced them and into which they had seemed to fit so well, had suddenly turned against them.

Finally, Bree looked up at her mother and smiled a tight smile, but there was no joy behind it.

"It's about Jonno." Bree looked away and Jeannie squeezed her hand, willing her to go on. "I've been seeing him after school a lot, and sometimes on weekends when I told you I was at Emily's place, I've been down at the Highrise watching Jonno surf. I wanted him to teach me and I'm getting better, but he said I'm too slow." She winced as Jeannie put her arm around her. "There's more Mum. Sometimes we we've gone to his place when his Mum and Dad aren't there. We hung out and ...."

It all came out in such a rush that Jeannie barely understood the words Bree had said, but the message was clear. Her beautiful, innocent, 16-year-old daughter had been spending time with an 18-year-old man, a man with a reputation around town of being a *"bad boy."*

Jeannie's mind was spinning and she dared not breathe. How the heck was she supposed to respond? This was all new, and she was all by herself – no Michael, no extended family or anyone else to turn to. She bit back the words she wanted to scream at the top of her lungs, and fearing Bree would *clam up* completely if she over-reacted; she whispered "Just tell me what happened."

"Oh Mum, we didn't have sex or anything. I'm not ready for that. I'm sick of him asking me to. I want to wait until I'm really in love. I thought I loved him Mum, but he's been really horrible." Bree's big brown eyes grew rounded as she stared up at her mother. "But we drank lots of beer and we got really close to doing it but I always said 'no', and then today..." Bree stopped and looked away. "Today he got really rough. He pushed me when I said I didn't want to go back to his place. He said I'm *'a player'* and he told me he never wanted to see me again. Oh Mum!" Bree collapsed on the bed, sobbing hard again.

"Oh Bree" Jeannie sighed as she took her first breath in what seemed like hours. Perhaps it wasn't so bad, she was thinking. Although Bree certainly thought it was, this situation had happened 100s of times to 100s of mums and dads – she'd have to think about disciplining Bree for drinking alcohol and lying about where she had been, but they would get through this.

"Well Bree, I'm relieved that you had the sense to say "no" to sex, but I'm really unhappy about the drinking and the lying about where you've been. We will talk about that later after I have a long think about it all. But what's this about Jonno getting rough with you. Are you OK?" she looked at Bree and noticed her very pale face behind the reddened eyes.

Bree sniffed back the tears. In a small voice she answered. "We were at the Highrise today. When the tide dropped and there was no surf, Jonno wanted to go back to his place and I knew he'd pressure me again because his parents are away this weekend."

Bree paused, but then shut her eyes as if remembering. Then the *floodgates* seemed to open. "So, we argued really badly and I slapped his face, and he pushed me right out of the car, and I hit my head on the footpath, and just lay there on the ground crying, and he threw my bag out so it landed on my leg and he took off really fast and squealed the wheels. Then there was this huge crash and I looked up and his car had hit a big light-pole."

The words rushed out *as if a dam had burst its banks*. She started to cry again and gulped. "And the ambulance came and they said he's alright but he's in hospital and his car's a wreck and it's all my fault," she finished as the sobbing began in earnest again.

Jeannie frowned as she patted Bree's back. Maybe it wasn't so simple then.

Bree was obviously devastated, but *relief flowed like a river* through Jeannie as she thought about what could have been. At least Bree was home and safe, with no obvious physical injury, although her adolescent broken heart might take longer to heal.

"OK Bree. Calm down now. I'll call the hospital and check on Jonno. We can go in to visit him if you want. And it wasn't your fault. He's a *hot head* who only wanted your friendship for one purpose. I don't think you did anything wrong and I think you'll see that in time," she tried to reassure the girl.

"But Mum, he'll tell everyone and no one will believe me. No-one will be my friend now because he's Jonno Martin and everyone loves him. I'll be the no-body that caused Jonno to get hurt and *total his car*. That's what Ryan said when he dropped me home. He said it's my fault." Bree wailed.

As Jeannie remembered the ute squealing its tyres in her gateway earlier, the door opened and Matthew stood there, his eyes wide.

"What's wrong with Bree Mum? She's so loud and she's been crying for ages," he said. Jeannie rose and gently steered him out of the room. "One of Bree's friends got hurt in a car accident and she's upset. Would you be able to get us a cup of tea please Matt? And some Anzac biscuits and some chocolate from the fridge. Then we might go into town for pizza in a little while."

Matthew still looked doubtful but the lure of Anzacs and chocolate, not to mention the promise of pizza for dinner, *did the trick*. He wandered off towards the kitchen and Jeannie heard the sound of the kettle being filled at the sink.

Emotions were difficult for Matthew to understand, and even though his concern for his sister was genuine, Jeannie knew he was uncomfortable and might react the wrong way, might even laugh at how odd his sister's face looked. He needed a distraction and something practical to occupy himself with, so she redirected him to the kitchen, praying that she might then have only 1 upset child to deal with instead of 2.

Just as Jeannie turned back into the bedroom, Bree sat up on the edge of the bed and swung her legs over the side, holding her head.

"I don't think I want to go and see him Mum. He hurt me." She moved and Jeannie saw a dark bruised area at the top of Bree's left arm and a swelling over her ear. "I hit my head and I don't feel too good either," Bree said, then lurched forward and vomited copiously on the carpet square next to her bed.

"Oh no!" Jeannie rushed to hold Bree up, calling to Matthew to grab a bucket from the laundry. Very quickly Matt's face appeared again and he shoved the bucket forwards to his mother, putting his hand over his nose and mouth as he turned rapidly away and raced out the door. "That's disgusting Bree," he mumbled.

In spite of herself, Bree gave a little laugh. "He got that right," she slurred as she began to dry retch again. Jeannie grabbed a handful of tissues from the bedside table, and wiped her daughter's mouth. Bree lay back on the pillows, her face the same colour as the white pillowcase.

"OK Bree. I want you to lay down for a couple of minutes. I think we're going to head to the hospital to get you checked out for concussion, just in case." Jeannie thought fast. It might just be shock after the events of the day, but Bree had said she'd hit her head and there was a lump. They couldn't take the risk. She tried to smile, and pretend more confidence than she felt. She was the adult and she was in charge. Bree just nodded and closed her eyes as her mother left the room. Bree's lack of protest was a bad sign, Jeannie worried, grabbing the car keys and her handbag.

Jeannie went quickly to find Matt. He'd have to cope with this without any warning – there just wasn't time.

"Matty, we need to get Bree to hospital," she told the wide-eyed boy who met her at the kitchen door. His mouth was full of biscuit, so he didn't reply. "Grab a few more Anzacs, and we'll get dinner in town. And bring your book too," she instructed, hoping the food and his favourite book would be big enough distractions to get him back into the car without protest.

Thankfully he cooperated, a scared look on his face indicating he knew this was serious. Grabbing 3 Anzacs, he ran ahead of his mother to hold open the front door as she carried a listless Breeanna to the car. Jeannie fought to be calm. The darkening road would be treacherous this time of night with animals gathering. "Please God get us there OK," she prayed under her breath as she turned over the engine. Lights still blazing in the house behind her seemed to mock her as rising panic surfaced.

But the lights weren't important – this was her baby girl and Jeannie was the only one Bree could rely on right now.

The trip into town was fast, dusty and dangerous in the gathering dark, but Jeannie refused to think about kangaroos on the road. Fortunately, none appeared and there was no traffic either. In record time, they pulled up at the Emergency Department of the small hospital, and Jeannie carried Bree into the reception area.

The nurse on duty looked up from his paper-work. What had been a quiet night had just turned into something more, and he rushed to bring a wheelchair so that Jeannie could put her daughter into a more comfortable position. The nurse pressed a button, and a wards-person pushed aside the swinging doors. "OK we'll do the paperwork in a minute. Let's get her to the Doctor on duty first," said the nurse, as Jeannie and Matty half-ran behind the wheelchair.

"She hit her head a couple of hours ago and she's been vomiting," Jeannie explained breathlessly. A doctor appeared from another room, identified by the stethoscope dangling around her neck. "What's her name?" she demanded as the wards-person lifted Bree onto an examining bed. "Bree – Breeanna," Jeannie fought her rising panic as Bree flopped back onto the bed.

"Mum, can we wait outside?" Matthew's small voice entered Jeannie's consciousness. Looking down at him Jeannie realised how scared he was. The doctor did too and said "There's a chair just outside in the corridor. Why don't you wait there? I need to examine Breeanna now and there's not much more you can do. I'll be out to see you directly." With a small smile she turned back to Bree, and the nurse ushered Jeannie and Matty to the seats just outside.

〰〰〰〰〰

Three hours later Jeannie and Matt stumbled slowly from the hospital towards the car. The carpark was nearly empty, the asphalt sparkling in the moonlight after a short shower of rain. In other circumstances Jeannie might have thought it pretty, but with Matthew yawning and sighing as he climbed into the old car, she had other things to focus on. "Will she be OK Mum?" he asked sleepily.

"Yes Matt. The doctor just wants to *keep an eye* on her overnight, just in case she does have concussion. But he's pretty sure it was just the shock of seeing the accident," she explained as she reached across to check Matt's seatbelt, giving his shoulder a strong squeeze.

"What about Jonno?" Matty asked. "I saw you talking to his dad in there." Matthew was tired but he had been so good, and he needed the facts before he let himself relax.

Jeannie tried to focus on the road. It was still wet and a little slippery. Her own tiredness and a lack of proper food were creeping up on her too. The ham sandwich from the hospital vending machine had not really *filled the hole in their stomachs*, but Matthew hadn't complained.

"Well Matt, he's OK. His dad said he was really lucky he had put his seatbelt on and the airbag in the car went off when he hit the light-pole. He only has a few bruises and a break in his arm from the impact, but he could have done a lot more damage if he'd driven out of the carpark. Thank heaven he only got as far as the entrance sign."

Jeannie sighed. "You relax Matt. We can't do any more tonight. We'll go and get Bree before lunch tomorrow." She glanced across at Matt and realised he had already drifted off to sleep. He had an incredible ability to *switch off* once he knew the full story. She wished she could do the same.

Jeannie hung up the phone. She'd spent ½ an hour telling Michael all the details of the past few hours and now she felt overwhelmed by the enormity of being a single Mum – fully responsible, catering for so many needs, from disability to education to emergencies, from relationship advice to cooking, cleaning, nursing and counselling. It all felt too much!

And no matter how concerned Michael had been, he was too far away to do anything useful – it was all up to her!

While her parents too had been willing to jump in the car and come, a trip of over 7 hours, she had gently asked them to wait too, just until they knew if Bree was truly OK. The last thing Bree would want was a huge fuss!

Jeannie fell back onto her bed. Just when she thought things were turning around for the better. Now Bree was hurt in so many ways, and she'd have to *pick up the pieces*. She had told Michael not to come down immediately but to wait until the next weekend. He couldn't do anything and Bree would need a few days before she could face her father. Jeannie was just so tired.

As she turned over, the red light on the answering machine flashed and Jeannie sighed. Someone must have called the landline while she was at the hospital. Surely whatever the message was it would wait until morning? But guilt rose and she knew she would need to listen to the message before she could rest. Reaching across she pressed the button.

CHAPTER 16

BAD TO WORSE
A TIME TO GRIEVE

Jeannie stirred and rolled over, her half-closed eyes having difficulty focussing on the digital read-out. 6:14am shone back at her. She groaned from lack of sleep and the sure knowledge that the few hours she'd spent tossing and turning last night would not be enough to carry her through the days ahead.

Birds sang cheerfully in the gumtrees between the house and the river, greeting the sunrise, but Jeannie didn't notice.

She twisted around, realising she'd fallen asleep fully clothed, lying where she'd collapsed after listening to the devastating news the recorded message contained. There was a still-damp patch under her head where her hours of tears were recorded on the sheets and pillow case.

She stood up, feeling old beyond her years, and suddenly she was crying again, tears coursing down her face. Her shoulders shook as she tried to gulp back the sound before her noise woke Matthew.

Too late! A small sleepy face appeared at her bedroom door. "Mum what's wrong? Is Bree OK?" he asked anxiously.

Opening her arms Jeannie enveloped Matt in a hug, forgetting all thoughts of whether he would accept the physical contact or not. Confused by his mother's behaviour, he accepted the hug and clung onto her.

"Yes Matt. She's OK. The hospital said they would call us if anything changed and they haven't called so she's fine. We'll go in to see her as soon as we have brekky. You go and get ready," she added gently hustling him back out of her room. "I need a shower then we'll have breakfast," she went on.

"But Mum..." Matthew started to ask again, but she pushed him towards his room, unable or unwilling to tell him anything more yet, looking for a delay, a distraction, but knowing that it was only a matter of time before she would have to share the terrible news.

Her mind reeled. She knew she would need to keep things in routine as much as possible, or Matt might *"melt down"* in a major way. She wanted to call. It had been too late when she finally noticed the message last night and she needed to call. But she also needed a shower, a little bit of normality to feel a little better before she faced that call.

The shower won and she stumbled into the bathroom, the hot water soon soothing her, albeit briefly. Washing her dank hair helped to delay the inevitable even longer. But she knew she had to make that call.

"Matt, you can have the shower now," she called to him. "We can't collect Bree until after 10am, so *take your time.*" Matt emerged from the kitchen munching some toast he'd made himself.

Jeannie didn't even pause to wonder why she'd encouraged him to "*take his time*" in the shower. She knew given half a chance he would stand under the hot water all day, literally. He just loved the comforting way the water flowed over his body; watching it run off his feet and around the floor of the shower into the plughole was one of his favourite things in the world to do, but since moving to the farm Jeannie had enforced a strict "5 minute rule" for showers, reminding the children that they were on tank water, and that they needed to conserve the water they did have, even though they could pump water from the river as *a last resort*. But today, there were other priorities.

As soon as Matthew was safely under the shower, Jeannie took the phone onto the verandah, at the farthest point from the bathroom that she could find. Unable to contemplate settling into the cane armchair as she usually would, she paced the old floorboards.

The number connected and rang twice. Despite the early hour, an anxious voice answered "Hello?"

"Laura, it's Jeannie. How is he? How's Benny?" Jeannie couldn't prevent her voice catching, her hands sweating as she grasped the phone tightly.

"Oh Jeannie," Laura wailed as if in pain, and the phone went silent. Jeannie realised Laura had covered the mouthpiece with her hand. It seemed an age until her voice came back on, a little more controlled, but Jeannie could hear the torment in her friend's tone.

"He's in a coma Jeannie. They don't know when he'll wake up again – or even IF he will." Laura broke down again. Jeannie heard noises over the phone as if the handset had been passed through water, then a new voice came on the other end of the line.

"Jeannie? It's Dan." It was Laura's husband, Benjamin's dad. She listened without responding. "I'm afraid he's not too good. He's in the Children's. They won't tell us much, or they can't tell us much." He paused – Jeannie could picture him running his fingers through his thinning hair.

Laura and Dan were old friends, a couple that she and Michael had met through the friendship of their respective sons. They were older than Jeannie and Michael by a good few years, and Benjamin was their much loved and long-awaited only child.

"He just looks so peaceful Jeannie, just lying there. But he won't wake up." Dan stopped speaking and Jeannie realised she needed to respond in some way.

"Oh Dan, that's beyond terrible." Jeannie couldn't understand it. All that the message last night had said was that Benjamin had been bashed by a group of boys and was on life-support, and could they please pray for him. What she couldn't understand was why Benjamin, the beautiful boy who loved computers and numbers as much as Matthew did, a quiet boy who *wouldn't hurt a fly.*

"What happened?" she asked quietly. "Why did the boys hurt him Dan? He wouldn't have done anything to upset them surely?" She knew she was talking too much but she couldn't help it.

Dan had gathered himself enough to reply. "It happened after school on Friday afternoon. He was walking to catch the late bus because he'd been at that Computer Group he goes to, and it seems 4 older boys decided to follow him. They kept after him and were calling him all sorts of things but Benny just ignored them, you know, how we've taught him?"

Jeannie just nodded. She knew Dan couldn't see her, but she was overwhelmed, thinking of the discussions she'd had with Laura about trying to help both Matthew and Benjamin learn to ignore the cruel words of other kids and rise above the teasing. And the Computer Group; that was meant to help Benjamin to meet other kids and make friends, friends that were a lot like him and loved computers. Dan was talking again and she forced herself to listen.

"They must have gotten sick of waiting for him to react, so one of them grabbed his backpack and swung him round. He was nearly at the bus-stop, but there was only an old bloke there. He yelled at the boys but one of them hit Ben as another grabbed his bag. And the worst thing happened. He fell and smacked his head on the curb. So now he has what the doctors call a "closed head injury" and they can't tell us what's going to happen. They've given him strong drugs to keep him in a coma because that's the best way for his brain to heal. And the next 48 hours are crucial – he could wake up and be OK, or he might not wake up at all." Dan's voice broke but he kept talking, just unburdening himself to someone who understood.

"And that Mr Bennett, the Deputy Head at the school; he's part of this too. Do you remember him?" Jeannie did.

Mr Bennett was an old-school teacher, a little like Mr Rice at Highcrest Secondary school. He was always giving detention for what seemed to be the least little thing. He and Matthew had clashed a few times and if it hadn't been for Matthew's teacher Mrs Greenacre explaining Matt's unusual view of the world, Jeannie knew that Matthew would have been labelled a rude and disruptive student.

"Yes, I do remember him. What does Mr Bennett have to do with it?" she asked, and Dan sighed as he explained.

"About 2 weeks ago, Ben was at school walking through the playground at lunch. Ben said a group of boys – you know, the 'cool' kids group? They approached him and got talking to Ben. He said he didn't really know them, but since Matthew left, we think he's been very lonely, and he was a bit desperate to be part of a group – any group."

Again, Jeannie visualised Dan running his hands through his hair. She realised with a jolt how long it had been since the two families had met up, since the boys had seen one another. Matthew had phoned Benjamin a few times since they had left the city, but time had moved on and Matthew had been busy coping with their new home and the new school, just as they all had.

Benjamin had been Matthew's only real friend – not that the boys had used that term. They were "colleagues" of course. And it seemed that Benjamin had not been able to find another "colleague" since Matthew had left.

Jeannie tuned in again to Dan's quiet voice. He confirmed exactly what she had been thinking.

"You know, Ben hasn't made any new friends, apart from online on those game sites. He spends all his time in his room gaming. He says he's winning all the levels or something." There was another pause then Dan cleared his throat. "Sorry Jeannie. It's just that Laura and I have been so worried about him and now this. Where was I?"

Dan drew in a deep breath and continued. "Oh so, in the playground, these boys told Ben they would let him into their group if he went into the toilets and wrote some things on the wall in permanent marker. And Ben being Ben thought "I can do that and they'll be my friends." He didn't think it through Jeannie. He just heard that someone would be his friend and decided to do what they told him to. He didn't even know why he wanted to be their friend. He told us afterwards that everyone wants to be in the "cool" group so he thought he should too! He didn't have a clue what was really going on, and I think he's a bit scared of them."

Dan sighed again then said "Well *to cut this long story short*, Benny went into the toilet block, and wrote some things on the wall. It was rude stuff, and Ben says he didn't even know what the words meant. And Mr Bennett chose that moment to come past on yard duty. He asked Benny what he was doing and Benny being Benny, he couldn't lie. He just said he had written the words on the wall like that boy Jarryd had told him to. And then *the flack really started to fly*." Again, Dan paused and it was Jeannie's turn to sigh.

"Sure enough, Ben had done the wrong thing, but those boys had *set Ben up* knowing he'd *fall for it*. They just walked past laughing. Ben was taken to the principal's office, and *all hell broke loose*. The school suspended Ben for 2 weeks. They were talking about expelling him Jeannie – Ben, quiet Ben who *wouldn't say boo to a goose!* Mr Bennett just kept saying it was a "blatant act of defiance" and that Ben was not sorry at all. But he didn't even realise what he'd done. From what he told us he was obsessed with being friends with this cool group."

Dan went on. "Mr Bennett kept saying Ben was cheeky and that he wasn't sorry because he kept smiling at Mr Bennett. You know what it's like Jeannie? These kids think they have to smile because that was the right thing to do, but it turns out Mr Bennett thought Ben was smirking at him. Thankfully the principal, Mr Franklin, seemed to have a bit more understanding and he asked Ben to explain. So, Ben did. He gave Mr Franklin all the facts you might say."

Jeannie remembered Mr Franklin, the school principal. He was strict too, but always seemed fair and really appeared to like the students and his job.

Dan was coming to the end of his sad story, so Jeannie forced herself to finish listening. "And that's why Ben was bashed up. The other boys were punished too, by Mr Franklin. Jarryd was suspended and because he's been in trouble before, he's on his last chance before being expelled. So, they came after Ben that day. They deliberately targeted him and ...... I just wish I could have protected my boy." Dan's voice choked off.

But he really didn't have to say any more. Jeannie *got the picture* all too clearly. She just stood there, on the verandah, so far from her friends yet willing herself to be right beside them.

Finally, after a few long seconds, Jeannie spoke.

"Dan, you and Laura know that Benjamin and Matthew were best mates because they are so much alike. We all know why. They both have high-functioning Autism. I can't begin to know how you are feeling but you can't blame yourselves. You are great parents and you've both done your very best. Think of all those specialists you took him to before you got the diagnosis: the Occupational Therapist for his sensory issues and fine motor skills, and the Speech Pathologist to help with his speech and his social skills, and the tutor to help him with his schoolwork. Let's just wait and see how the day goes. And we're coming up there. I'll wait to hear from you but we're coming up. I want to be there." She paused. "Please don't give up Dan, I've got some praying friends down here. They're Christians. Is it OK if I ask them to pray for Benny?"

"Of course Jeannie, that's more than OK. Anyway, I need to go. We've got to get back to the ward now. I'll *get in touch* when I know more. Thanks for the call."

As Dan rang off Jeannie slumped into the armchair, just as Matthew appeared towelling his wet hair. Jeannie gazed at her younger child momentarily marvelling at how tall he was getting, how he was suddenly filling out his clothes. He was growing up so fast.

"Matt, we need to talk" she said, even as she wondered how to tell him this latest news, how much to say. Matthew was in such a good place at the moment, and this news would spoil it all, but he had to know.

"Matty, sit down for a moment."

As the sun rose slowly behind the manna gum beside the water tank, Jeannie tried to explain Ben's illness to her son. She told him the facts, with most of the details. Matthew was quiet, then as Jeannie finished her story he said "Can I go and see him Mum?"

"Yes Matt, as soon as Mr and Mr White say it's OK." Jeannie smiled in an attempt to reduce the tension they both felt.

Matthew looked down and shrugged. He scrunched both eyes and clenched his fists, blurting out "I knew this would happen and it's all my fault," before bolting for the doorway back into the house.

Jeannie heard his running footsteps down the central hallway, then the kitchen door slammed. She knew where he was going – to his sanctuary by the river, to yell, to kick things, and to try to process the news of his friend's awful injury. For the first time Jeannie thought, she knew how he felt. She couldn't process the reality either. Why was a nearly

13-year-old boy, bright, capable, with a good family around him, now lying in hospital, maybe never to recover?

Matthew was gone a long time. They needed to leave soon to collect Bree from the hospital. Jeannie had called and spoken to the doctor, who was pleased that Bree was showing no further signs of concussion. "Come and get her anytime. She's impatient to leave," he'd said.

Jeannie stood in the sun on the back step and called to Matthew. After a few minutes he appeared, head down, scuffing his feet in the dirt and stones on the path. He pushed past his mother, and walked quietly to the waiting car, slamming the front door and the door of the ute. Jeannie understood – she didn't challenge him – not yet, not until Bree was home and they could all talk about it together as a family. Well, almost a family. She gulped and realised she missed Michael's quiet strength in a situation like this.

※※※

Again, the old ute turned into the farm's driveway. Matt shut the gate. He and Bree had barely spoken since they left the hospital. Bree had seen Matthew's distress and thought it was due to her own injury, so Jeannie had told her the *bare bones* of what had happened to Ben. The two children had been quiet the whole trip home, Bree loosely holding her brother's hand in the back seat, Matthew allowing the contact as he gazed out of the car window.

Jeannie decided that it was best to get all the information out into the open as soon as they got home. She'd make a cup of tea and sit the children down on the verandah. She might even call Dan again to see if there was any change.

Passing the huge King's Park bottlebrush, the house came into view. There was a blue 4WD parked outside the house, and Michael was leaning on the bonnet, waiting for them.

Jeannie's eyes misted over – she could barely believe he'd come all this way on a Sunday, even in these circumstances. The kids were out of the ute's back door running to their father, even before the car was fully at a standstill.

Jeannie wasn't far behind them, all of the family gathered together in a giant family hug, all 4 in floods of tears, as some of the tension of the last days was released.

CHAPTER 17

WHEN THERE ARE NO WORDS

A TIME TO EMBRACE

"I'll drive you back tomorrow morning and you can use my car. I'll just catch the train to work. Please stay at the house. You know there's room and I can sleep on the air mattress in the lounge." Michael looked at the kids and Jeannie with such a sincere longing that Jeannie almost laughed. Except it wasn't funny at all.

"OK Mike. We'll stay with you for 2 nights. Then we'll have to get back for the kids' school. I appreciate the offer, I really do. Especially the use of the car." Jeannie knew Michael hated public transport – all that close proximity to strangers, all the smells and the noise. It had been one of his best days when he rose high enough in his company to be allocated a work parking space for his own car! He was making such a big effort for her and for the children.

Bree too, had been amazing when they had all discussed Benjamin's situation. She'd quietly commented "It makes my problems seem pretty insignificant," and given Matthew a strong hug. Matthew himself had just listened to the talking, and kept his own thoughts to himself. Jeannie hoped that he would *open up* to her later.

〜〜〜〜〜〜

They were all exhausted. After 2 long, tiring days in the city, many kilometres of driving, and many tears with Laura and Dan, they arrived back at Treetops, all longing for some quiet time. Bree had said it as they drove into Highcrest: "It's good to be home." Even Matthew had smiled!

The small part of Jeannie that was not sleep-deprived and stressed after the emotional roller-coaster of the last few days, responded to Bree's comment with a warm feeling. It really was home, this small coastal town with its welcoming people and pleasant environment. But even as she drove the last few kilometres towards Treetops, she thought of Michael, about how down he'd looked as they'd waved goodbye. How good he'd been to take time off work to be with the children while she'd kept vigil at the hospital. And he'd even volunteered to take the public bus down on Thursday to collect his car.

Benjamin had shown few signs of waking as yet, and visiting him had distressed Matthew, so after their initial visit it was decided that the children would stay with Michael. They'd done a few fun activities to keep them busy, visiting the local Bowling Alley, going to the shopping mall, but neither of the children wanted to do much else and both were relieved when Jeannie decided to head home. Jeannie had quite enjoyed the two evenings with Michael and the family all together again, but Benjamin's illness hung over everything and it was a relief to head down the highway. Assuring Laura and Dan that she would come back any time they asked, she'd given her friends a last long hug, praying for a miracle.

Bree managed the farm gate, with Matthew drowsing in the rear seat. Michael's car was bigger than their Ute and much more comfortable, but Matthew roused himself enough to stumble into the house and fall heavily onto his bed. Soon they were all asleep, bags dumped in the hallway, sleep being more important than unpacking after their long day.

———※※※———

The school term was almost over. End of year events at school had finished and only the Year 6 dance and presentation, a kind of end of Primary School graduation night, were still to come.

This Thursday was the last day, then the Presentation and Dance were that night. Friday meant freedom and school holidays for 6 glorious weeks! And Christmas was only a week away too.

"Do I have to go to the dance?" Matthew was NOT keen.

"Yes, you do Matt. I think you'll enjoy it once we're there. I'm coming. So is Bree, and Dad will be here too, so YES you DO have to go. You know Dad is coming all this way on the bus because we've got his car, so don't complain please!" Jeannie shook her head slightly and tried a smile. "I've bought you a new shirt to wear."

"It's itchy and it smells bad," Matthew continued to complain.

"I'll put it in the wash and use the laundry liquid you like. It'll be washed, dried and ironed by Thursday, and you'll look great in it." Jeannie tried to remain upbeat. She knew that the whole Presentation Night was a huge deal for Matthew, let alone the social issues of the dance afterwards, but it was important.

Not only was he receiving 2 awards for Year 6, Mathematics and Computing, but she felt it was important that he tried to manage at the dance, at least for a little while.

"You can wear those earplugs to the dance if you want. They'll reduce the noise level for you. And I promise we'll leave by 8.30pm." Knowing that ½ hour might be his limit, Jeannie continued to reassure him.

"OK, I guess I can cope with that." Matt shrugged. "But no tie!" Jeannie laughed.

"Deal! New shirt but no tie!"

———

"And the Year 6 prizes for Excellence in Mathematics and Excellence in Computing Science go to.........Matthew Luckmore." Matthew walked forward, keeping his eyes fixed on the stairs in front of him, trying hard not to trip over. Mr Hawser, the Principal of the Secondary school, was presenting the Year 6 awards, and Matthew was worried. He had never met Mr Hawser.

But once on the platform his social script kicked in; >I walk up to Mr Hawser, look at Mr Hawser's chin, stretch out my right hand and shake his right hand, then grab the books in my left hand and walk behind Mr Hawser and go off the stage<

He was acutely aware of his parents clapping and Bree whistling loudly from the 4ᵗʰ row of the seats. Mr Hawser shook Matthew's hand and handed him the book prizes, then Matthew stepped around him and started to leave the stage. A big hand on his shoulder stopped him and suddenly he felt a flush of fear. What had he done wrong this time?

Mr Hawser was speaking into the microphone. Matthew's confused brain heard some words which sounded as if they were coming from a long way away.

"I just want to add that Matthew has also received another award, this one from his classmates." Mr Hawser smiled at Matt and picked up shiny gold medal on a gold ribbon.

"This award is one of 2 special Year 6 awards for Citizenship and it is awarded to Matthew Luckmore for always helping in class, and always being willing to assist other students with Maths and Computing." Mr Hawser looked directly at Matthew and then leaned close, putting the medal around Matthew's neck. He again put out his right hand, so Matthew shook it, and finally was able to step around the principal and off the stage.

Suddenly the worst was over. He was back in his seat in the front row. He'd done it! He'd survived the Presentation Night, and Year 6. Now he just had to manage ½ an hour at the dance and he was *"home free!"*

———≈≈≈≈———

"That's it, Mum. That's ½ an hour." Matt looked at his watch as he let go of his mother's hand and walked off the dance floor.

"Trust him to wear a watch," Jeannie thought, but she nodded. "Yep. That's the deal Matthew. Thanks for the dance. Let's go and get Bree and Dad and head home."

Lightning lit the ranges but no rain fell as a summer storm blew over. Michael drove in the farm gate with Matthew almost asleep in the back seat.

Bree sat quietly alongside her brother humming a tune that the band had played at the dance. She was glad she had decided to go. It had been a big night for her brother, and she was happy she'd been there to see him get his awards, especially the one from his classmates. Sometimes it was really hard to be Matthew's sister, but tonight that was something that made her proud.

Jeannie's mobile rang just as they pulled up at the house. "It's probably just Mum checking how it went tonight" she murmured, watching Michael bend into the back seat and scoop his son up in strong arms. Without pausing to check to caller I.D., she shut the car door and hurried inside after her family and away from the closing lightning storm.

"Hi Mum!' Jeannie answered brightly, only to gasp and stop on the top step, listening intently.

"Oh!" she gasped, tears starting to run freely down her face. Bree looked back and asked "What's wrong Mum?" Even Matthew stirred in Michael's arms as his father unlocked the front door. "What's going on?" he mumbled, rubbing his eyes, and struggling to stand up as he pushed out of his father's embrace.

Jeannie brushed the back of her hand over her face, and spoke into the phone. "Thank you for letting me know. I'll call tomorrow." She pressed the end button on her mobile, then slowly turned to face the questioning looks of her family.

"It's Benjamin," she said, squeezing her eyes tightly closed as if trying to shut out the world.

Matthew's tired brain struggled to compute the words, even as his sister burst into tears, and his father reached out to hug his mother close.

Matthew didn't wait to hear more. Everyone's faces looked odd, and Matt could not understand. He just knew that the worst thing possible MUST have happened. He ran for the sanctuary of his bedroom, and slammed the door.

In spite of her tears, Jeannie went to follow him, but Michael grabbed her arm. "Leave him Jeannie. If you're upset, it will just make him more upset too. Just wait, and explain to us what you know. We can tell Matt tomorrow. It won't change anything now." Jeannie nodded and reached for Michael and Bree.

Much later, with everyone finally settled in bed, Jeannie lay looking into the darkness. She thought she heard a click then some creaking, but she dismissed it as the sounds of the old house and wanderings of a tired mind.

Bree and Matthew had taken a long time to settle, even though she could tell them little more than the bare fact that Ben had *taken a turn for the worse.* The family friend of Laura and Dan who had called her had not been willing to share more, and had asked for their prayers. They would all have to wait until the morning, until the terrible phone call she would need to make to Dan.

As Jeannie set the alarm for 7am she sniffed back more tears, and rolled into a ball. Michael's strong arms wrapped around her providing some comfort. She needed his presence in her bed tonight; at some level he'd known and just followed her there when they finally went to bed, Jeannie under the doona and Michael, still fully clothed, on top of the covers.

Wrapped up in their shared place of sadness they both fell into a fitful sleep.

〰〰〰

The alarm blared through the quiet house. Jeannie woke with a start, rolled over to silence the bell, and jumped as a hand touched her back.

"What time is it?" Michael was still half asleep. Jeannie realised he'd slept on top of the doona all night just holding her when she'd stirred and begun to cry all over again. It felt right that he'd been there.

"It's 7am. I knew you had to get up for the trip back," she replied. It was Michael's turn to roll over and sit on the other side of the bed.

"Let's talk about that after breakfast," he mumbled, still waking from a disturbed night. "I think we'll have to call Dan before we decide what to do."

Breakfast was subdued, Michael picking at some cereal while Bree drank juice but refused anything else. She also looked terrible, with dark circles under her eyes. "Where's Matt?" she asked Jeannie, who shrugged, both hands firmly around her tea cup. Not looking up, Jeannie replied "Probably sleeping in. He was so overwhelmed by last night it probably took him ages to settle. But school's over so it's OK."

Michael looked up. "I might go and wake him. You know how he needs his morning routine. It might upset him even more if he wakes up late and his routine is out." Pushing his chair away from the table, he headed down the corridor to his son's room, as Jeannie quietly marvelled at Michael's new insights into his son's way of thinking. "Matt where are you?" his voice called from the bedroom, then again from the bathroom.

Michael's face appeared at the kitchen door. "Can't find him in the house. Where do you think he could be?"

"Probably just hiding. He was pretty upset so maybe he woke up early and curled up somewhere in the house," Bree said. "I'll go look in his usual spots Dad."

"OK Bree, and I'll go down to the river and check that hidey hole he showed me." As Michael opened the back door a hot northerly wind blew dry leaves and dust into the kitchen.

Jeannie frowned, her concern mounting. She knew Matthew had been upset, but he was so predictable. He'd be OK.

Even as she tried to reassure herself, something niggled in the back of her mind, like a little fish on the end of a line, tantalisingly close but impossible to hook and land.

"No sign of him Mum," Bree re-entered the kitchen. "I checked inside everywhere, and on the verandah, under the verandah, in the back shed and all round the yard."

"He's not in the hole in the tree either," Michael said slamming the screen door in his haste. "I looked around in the bush but there's no sign."

Jeannie gasped. "Oh no, I do remember something. Last night just as I was drifting off to sleep, I thought I heard the back door click." She looked at Michael, her hand covering her mouth. "I thought I'd imagined it, but what if he went out last night? He wouldn't do that would he?"

Michael just stared at her. "So, he could have been out all night by himself?"

<hr />

They all headed outside, calling Matthew's name as the hot orange sun rose over the shed. The northerly wind blew even stronger now. There was no response to their cries.

Bree paused. "I smell something Mum. I think it's smoke." Jeannie and Michael, at opposite ends of the yard, looked at each other, worry etched on both their faces.

"You're right Bree. Probably just a grass fire somewhere. There's no alerts on my phone yet. The northerly's picking up though. I hope the fire's not up in the valley." Jeannie shuddered. But they had other things to focus on just now.

"I think I'll call Melinda. He might have walked up to Horse Haven." Jeannie ran inside. Dread spread to the pit of her stomach and her hand shook as she found her phone and dialled. She had to find her boy, her beautiful, predictable son who seemed to have, very unpredictably, disappeared.

Michael shook his head. It was at least 3 kilometres to Horse Haven. That was quite a walk in the daylight, let alone at night. Everything looked different in the moonlight too. Michael ran his hand through his hair. "Let's get dressed Bree. If he's not at Horse Haven we'll have to phone the police and go looking."

—✳—

Bent low over Stager's neck, Matt rode on. He was right up on the ridge, at least half way along. He was a bit cold, but the morning sun was warming him now that he had cleared the trees, the day promising to be a *scorcher*! Stager slowed and snorted; he wanted a rest and Matt had not let him stop, not for 3 hours at least. They'd climbed the track non-stop after Matt had sneaked quietly into the stables sometime in the early morning hours.

Walking from home in the dark, Matt had not been scared. His measly torchlight had given out about ½ way there so he'd thrown it on the ground, useless thing. The road was faintly lit by the moonlight. The night was not cold, and the distant flashes of lightning lit up the world every so often. Matt realised most of the lightning and storm action was back in the hills, a long way away.

Stager had been asleep in his stall, head low and tail drooping, when Matt arrived. Murmuring quietly to the horse, Matt had approached slowly so Stager would wake and realise who it was. The big horse knew Matt's voice so well that he had just nickered back, probably surprised at the early start to his day, but accepting the saddle and bridle as if midnight rides happened all the time.

Now, as the dawn light turned into morning and the heat of the day really began, Matt dismounted and gave Stager some water, holding his hand under the horse's muzzle as Stager licked the water gratefully.

"Better not have it all at once boy," Matt said, putting the stopper back in his water bottle. Thank heavens Melinda had taught him so well. He'd even remembered his big water bottle in the middle of the night.

Matthew had had no plan, no pre-organised idea, when he ran away from the kitchen door in the pitch black of night, grabbing his torch from the riverside hidey-hole, then setting off in a long circle, first along the river bank, then tacking back to the dirt track. He'd arrived at Horse Haven a couple of hours later, knowing only that he MUST ride, he must go up high so he could breathe, so he could try to escape these hemmed-in feelings of guilt.

All he could think of, over and over, going round and round in his head, was:

"It's all my fault! If I'd been there, it wouldn't have happened. We shouldn't have come here. I shouldn't have come here. Benjamin was my only friend and I should have protected him."

Even though he knew, in his logical brain, that there was nothing he could have done, that it wasn't his fault, that it wasn't his family's fault, and that if he had been there, HE may have been hurt as well, Matthew could not let go of the feelings of guilt and responsibility for his friend.

He did need to ride, to feel free and clear his head – even if it was the middle of the night!

Now, reaching the top clearing at the highest point of the ridge where he and Melinda had spent the night so many weeks ago, Matthew and Stager paused again. Stager snorted, then stamped his foot as if to communicate with the boy.

"What is it Stager? A snake?" Melinda had warned Matt only last week that snakes would be out and about now the weather was warmer. He knew to watch out for the red-bellied blacks and let them slither away if he could. And to avoid the King Browns too; they were the deadliest to both horse and rider!

As Stager sniffed the air, Matt urged him onward, closer to the edge of the clearing where a huge view opened up, panning along the coast for kilometres. Matthew breathed deeply, anticipating the relaxation he so craved. The freshening breeze had become much stronger, and instead of a long draught of fresh air, Matt started coughing, his eyes watering. That was smoke!

Matt put his hand up to shade his forehead and squinted. Suddenly he saw it, a curl of smoke rising lazily from below the ridge about a kilometre away.

"A lightning strike!" Matt thought, watching the smoke curl upwards, white becoming grey then black at the base. Even as he watched, the breeze picked up and flames shot up from the bottom of the smoke plume. Small at first, they grew rapidly, gathering in the dry bush around them, licking up the trees, travelling through the undergrowth and closing the gap between fire and boy.

For long seconds Matt and Stager just stood there, mesmerised by the sight. As the wind seemed to strengthen, the flames grew closer, yellow, orange and red flickering through the fuel-laden bush as the wind grew. *The beast* was gathering momentum, and virtually racing up the hill towards the ridge.

Matthew knew that if it reached the ridge there was nothing to stop it coming down the valley and straight through their farm, through Horse Haven and on to Highcrest township.

"It's OK Stager, it'll cross the range up ahead of us then go down near the track to the head of the river." Matt reassured the horse with more confidence than he felt. Melinda had said that was what the fires usually did. They'd never come all the way into the valley, and just tended to burn onward into the National Park, until they burnt themselves out.

But even as he said the words, Stager snorting again and stamping as if in response, Matt looked again as the flames leaped higher into the lower canopy of the gum trees.

Then he heard it. It sounded like a train or a big plane roaring in the distance, except its distance away had lessened, probably halved in a few minutes and the fire was below them now, maybe 500 metres from where they stood!

Stager whinnied, but stayed put, waiting for Matt to respond.

Matthew gulped and spoke to the horse as if he understood.

"I can't go down the river track, it's coming too close to there. And I can't take the long track home – it'll take too long. We have to get down there and warn everyone. They need time to get out and it's coming fast. We'll have to try that steep track Melinda told me about, if I can find it."

Even as Matt said the words, he turned Stager's head. The horse seemed to understand the urgency and trotted quickly as Matt crossed the ridge-line and looked around, desperately seeking the entrance to the steep, rocky track that Melinda had described as "too dangerous for us to take."

All at once Stager wheeled to the left.

Matt was going to pull him up but then he saw it. Covered by some light undergrowth, the entrance to the track appeared, disguised but just visible. Stager knew where to go and ploughed forward, as Matthew's logical brain screamed "too steep," "too dangerous for me"; but he knew he had to take the chance. The fire was rapidly gaining on them, and in this moment, Matt had to make a decision based NOT on logic and percentages, but purely on trust – trust in his horse and its ability.

"Down there, Stager," he urged the horse onwards, plunging over the edge and down, down, down the other side of the ridge, hooves scattering the stones, flying over the track, Matt *hanging on for dear life*! He leaned back in the saddle, his feet planted firmly in the stirrups, desperately trying to balance and help Stager as much as he could.

The smoke was thickening again as the fire reached the ridge line behind them. Matt thought it might slow a little as it came down the hill, but he knew the bush was tinder-dry, the wind was up, and he could hear that roar as it gathered momentum to race down the valley. The northerly wind had sneaked around and changed direction, which would push the fire further inland, and towards the town!

"C'mon boy. You can do it!" Matthew had to yell to urge Stager onwards. The big horse stumbled but righted himself quickly. His feathered hooves bit into the dirt of the track and they didn't lose any time.

Matt blinked but didn't let go to wipe his eyes – he needed both hands on the reins to hang on tight! He had to trust Stager, to depend on the horse's senses to avoid obstacles.

The track was getting narrower, more overgrown. The bush was reclaiming this route down the mountain, a route rarely used by anyone until today. But he was gaining on the fire, its progress slowing slightly and theirs increasing, as Stager galloped onwards.

"Please God, please God!! Help me and Stager to get down in time to warn everyone," he muttered.

Matthew knew that Melinda and Bob needed at least an hour to get all their horses down onto the river flats. At this rate, Matthew doubted he was ahead of the fire by that much. If the wind grew any stronger, he might not even outride the fire, but he had to try! He couldn't think about any other alternative now!

He remembered the lessons that Mrs Jansen had taught him about IGNORING things – things like people teasing him, silly comments, scary or upsetting thoughts, things she said he did not have to respond to. He could learn to IGNORE them. So right now, Matthew decided to ignore these negative "what-if" thoughts too. He was going to think positive, helpful thoughts all the way down this track and all the way to safety!

As Stager continued to plunge through the bush, closer ever closer to the river, Matthew's heart raced and he held the reins tighter than he ever had before, chanting *under his breath,* "I will make it down," "I will stay calm," "I will make it down."

Suddenly Matt was almost catapulted over Stager's head as the horse screeched to a halt, dust billowing around them and mixing with the smoke to become an almost impenetrable cloud.

As Matt struggled to sit upright again, he spotted a huge brown snake slithering off the track just in front of Stager's right foreleg, making straight for the river away to the right. The snake had no interest in them as it raced towards relative safety and away from the oncoming blaze, but Matt knew that if Stager had stepped on the snake or even very close to it, the frightened reptile may have struck the horse, and that would have been the end of their race against time. He leaned forward to pat Stager's neck, then urged him on.

Matt knew they were still some way from the valley floor, but he thought he had glimpsed the river through the trees when the smoke cleared enough. He took another quick breath and flicked the reins to get Stager moving even faster. The horse took little urging now the snake scare was over, and once again they were soon racing down the track. Visibility was low due to the swirling smoke, and Matt could only see a couple of metres in front of them.

Suddenly, out of nowhere a hot piece of burning ember fell just to the left of them, igniting the surrounding bush immediately. Matt remembered the Emergency Services people telling his class that even if the fire front was quite a way behind them, the risk of embers igniting other fires further down the valley was very real.

"I will get down. I will stay calm," he said again through gritted teeth, his breathing becoming more laboured as the smoke thickened. "Come on boy, you can do it!' he urged his horse on.

Then finally, there it was! A blue strip appeared through the trees. They were about 150 metres away and still coming downwards at a fast rate, but he could see the river! Stager saw it too, as picked up his pace, galloping through the last stand of trees to the river's edge.

But instead of stopping here for a much-needed drink, Stager knew what to do. He trotted through the shallow water, and turned for home, taking off down the river-side track, Matt not even needing to direct him!

The track this end was still overgrown, and Matt hoped they would soon meet up with the well-used part that turned up the mountain earlier than the track they were following. Matt knew that part of the track would allow them to move more quickly, and Stager seemed to know it too.

As he shifted position, Matthew's sweaty palms slipped and he lost his grip on the reins. Suddenly he felt as if he was going to fall and his mind screamed "No." Just as he reached the *point of no return*, Stager shifted again, and Matt grabbed for a handful of Stager's mane, then managed to grasp the pommel and regain his balance.

That was so close, but again Matt couldn't stop to think about his near-fall. Stager whinnied as he galloped on and Matt held tight. He was tiring now; they both were. Lack of sleep, lots of riding, and smoky air were all catching up with them, but horse and boy knew the importance of this ride.

Lives might depend on them, both horse and human!

And there it was – the main track appeared as they burst through a line of small acacia bushes. Normally this point was about ½ an hour from Horse Haven and about 10 minutes from their farm at an easy pace, but today that would have to be so much quicker. Matt risked a glance behind him and could see the flames coming down the mountain. They had almost reached the valley floor. Matt turned back and grabbed Stager's mane with 2 hands, the reins forgotten. He just needed to hang on for another few minutes!

Through the murk Matt could just make out the outline of the farm house. Coming up the river behind the house, he skidded Stager to a halt at the back gate. Matt was down out of the saddle in a second, racing through the gate yelling "Mum! Dad! Bree!" *at the top of his lungs.* Stager stooped and buried his face in an old half-full bucket of water near the fence that Jeannie kept to throw on the roses. Any water was better than nothing after that desperate ride.

Jeannie looked up from where she sat at the table. "Matt you're here!" She shouted back in excitement and grabbed her son into a tight hug, but he pushed back roughly.

"No Mum, no time! The fire's coming. It's only 20 or 30 minutes away. It's coming Mum!"

"No Matt. Calm down. The Emergency Services say it's over the other side of the ridge and not expected to come over this side at all. It's smoky because there's so much bush." She tried to reassure him, but Matt interrupted, his eyes open wide.

He looked wildly around him. "No Mum, it's already down this side. I know because I've just ridden down ahead of it. There's no time. We've got to follow our Fire Plan! Where are Dad and Bree?"

"They're out looking for you Matt. They went into town and they were going to look at all your favourite spots. They're due to call any minute, but I'll ring them." Jeannie grabbed her phone from the table, but Matt snatched it from her.

"What the....?" She just looked at him, but Matt was determined.

"I've got to call Melinda NOW. She needs all the time left to get the horses out." As he found the number for Horse Haven, he bossed his mother.

"Go and get our fire stuff Mum, if it isn't already in the car. You go...I'll ride Stager right behind you."

Jeannie's gulped back her reply, but moved towards the hallway where the fire boxes sat ready. They'd been prepared for a month, with all the things they would really miss if a fire did come. Surprisingly there were mementoes and photos, and important documents, plus a small bag of clothes and toiletries for each of them, but not much else.

Matt had insisted on an old thread-bare knitted monkey that Nanna had made for him long ago, but apart from that everything else seemed unimportant in the face of a serious fire emergency. Even as she started out the door with two of the boxes, she heard Matt yell into the phone "Melinda. Stop talking! The fire's coming."

Melinda, on the Horse Haven end of the phone, was taken aback, but replied "Matt! No, it's OK it's on the other side of the ridge. The Emergency Services just called me. Are you OK? Do you have Stager?"

"Yes, and yes – we're both OK. But Melinda you've got to go NOW. You and the horses. The fire IS on this side. We've just come down the rocky hill track and it was only just behind us. I think you've only got about ½ an hour if this wind keeps picking up. There are already embers falling everywhere. You've got to go NOW." Matthew was almost screaming in his need to get the message across.

To her credit, Melinda was calm. She knew Matt would not lie, especially about this. She paused for 1 millisecond, then replied "OK Matt. I hear you. We're packed up just in case and we'll leave now. I'll call the Emergency Services and explain what you've seen. Then I'll lead all the horses down to the flats and Bob can bring the truck. Get going Matt – we'll see you there." She hung up and Matt shoved his Mum's phone into his pocket.

He raced out of the kitchen in time to thrust the phone into his mother's hands as she pulled up the car near the house yard. Jeannie knew she had to trust her son. "Get to the river flats Matt. I'll see you there mate." She looked pale as she took off in a cloud of dust.

Matt could feel the heat of the fire now. Stager waited by the back fence, shaking his head as if to shake away the smoky air.

"C'mon boy. Let's go!" Matt swung up into the saddle and turned Stager back to the river. They could cut along for about a kilometre then they would have to go back through the bush to the road.

Stager seemed to have a *second wind*, and galloped steadily along the muddy river edge. Matt felt more confident now, but he knew the fire was only a couple of kilometres away. He thought of the people who lived along the river, some of them elderly. He hoped they would be OK. In the distance he thought he heard a siren, and hoped that the Emergency Services were out on the road and letting people know. He knew Melinda would have called them so his job now was to get Stager safely on the other side of the river on the wide river flats.

Matt bent over Stager's neck and urged him on towards safety.

CHAPTER 18

DON'T PANIC!
A TIME TO SEARCH

Jeannie drove down the dusty, smoky track, praying under her breath, thanking God that she knew this track now and could predict where the potholes would be.

She drove as fast as she dared, all the while praying for a miracle that would save their home and the homes of all the people out along the river. Only a wind change would stop the fire reaching right to the outskirts of Highcrest now.

Maybe the firies could back-burn there and stop it in its tracks, but Jeannie knew it would be almost impossible to halt the destruction of properties upstream from the town. They just would not have enough resources, and the fire was burning too hot! *It was a lottery*. Some would burn and some would be spared. No-one knew which!

Suddenly an Emergency Services truck rushed past, its siren screaming. The firies on board waved her towards town and she gave them a quick thumbs up as she kept driving.

Grabbing her phone, she yelled at Siri "Call Michael" as she held the phone in one hand. She knew it added to the danger, but in the old ute there was no such thing as "hands free" and this was an emergency.

"Michael, oh thank God!" she almost wept with relief. Michael's voice sounded strained as he replied, "Where are you, Jeannie?"

"Listen. I'm on my way to town. Matty came back. He rode Stager up the mountain and he spotted the fire! It's coming our way fast. I'm going to the river flats. Michael, can you and Bree get out there?"

"Yes, Bree's nodding. She knows the place. We're just out at the beach, so we're about 10 minutes away Bree? Yep. OK. Jeannie, stay safe and we'll see you there...... and Jeannie ...." There was a pause and Jeannie thought that the call had dropped out, then Michael's voice came back. "Jeannie, look after yourself. I love you so much," and he choked up as he rang off.

Jeannie didn't have time to think about what he'd said. The gates of Horse Haven flashed by and Jeannie spotted the big truck getting ready to leave. Bob saw her and from a distance waved her on towards the river flats and the town. He obviously didn't need any help, so Jeannie turned back to the road and concentrated on getting to safety herself.

⸻ ≈≋≈ ⸻

Matt re-joined the dirt road just before Horse Haven. As he galloped up the driveway Bob pulled the truck over and shouted at him. *"There's a sight for sore eyes!"* Matthew just shook his head. No time to try to work out what that saying meant!

"Bob, are all the horses out?"

Bob frowned back at Matt. "Melinda's taken them all down to the flats. They should be almost there by now. I've got the gear and the feed in case we're there for a while. But Matty," Bob paused, looking concerned. "We couldn't find Rosey. She must have got spooked and run up the paddock towards the bush, but it's too late now. We need to get going."

Rosey was Stager's pony mate, his best friend; and Stager loved Rosey as much as Matt loved Stager!

Bob revved the big truck and put it into gear. "C'mon Matt. Follow me and we'll get to the flats OK." Matt just looked at Bob and nodded. "I'll be right behind you."

Bob frowned but hit the accelerator and took off. As he turned onto the dirt road, he waved at Matty, who had Stager turned that way too.

But as Bob drove away, the big truck slowly gathering momentum, Matty wheeled Stager around.

"We have to find Rosey, boy." Stager seemed to know the little pony's name and trotted towards the stables.

The home yard was where Rosey should be, but as Matt bent down to release the gate, there was no sign of her. Stager sniffed the air. Matthew was unsure but again, he realised he needed to trust Stager. The big horse had got him this far, and Stager would know where Rosey was hiding if anyone would!

Matthew *gave Stager his head*, and they took off up the paddock towards the bushy area to their left. Smoke swirled and visibility was poor. Matthew coughed as the smoke thickened. He tried to call out to Rosey, and Stager whinnied a couple of times as they trotted further back, towards the oncoming flames. Surely, she wouldn't have come all this way?

Then from the corner of his eye, Matthew saw it. A flash of white! Rosey was white, a Welsh Mountain pony, small and stubborn, and she loved to eat. That "white flash" was near a patch of bush where there was an old well, and the grass still grew there, even in a hot summer.

Stager must have spotted her too. They turned towards the well and there she was, standing with her head down, her ears back and the whites of her eyes showing.

Matthew dismounted clumsily, turning his ankle a bit on the edge of a rock. "Ow!!" he said, but he tried to be calm. Rosey didn't know him well and she was already scared. His ankle throbbed, but there were more important things to focus on, so he ignored the pain.

As he approached Rosey to try to grab her halter, he felt hot breath on his shoulder. Stager was coming too, like he knew that his presence would reassure the frightened pony. Matthew spoke softly to the pony, whispering her name even as the wind blew his words away. They had to leave, and they had to leave now, but if Matt panicked there was no way Rosey would come with him.

Seeming to sense a friend, Rosey didn't turn away or try to run. She let Matthew hold her halter and lead her to stand next to Stager. The big horse bent his neck and nibbled Rosey's ear, as Matthew found a length of rope in his saddle bag, and quickly tethered Rosey to his saddle.

"OK, you two. We need to go." Matthew swung himself into the saddle, cringing slightly at the pain in his foot. It was getting worse, but it was the least of his problems right now. Matt grasped the reins and held onto Rosey's rope to make sure she was coming too.

"Let's go Stager. We need to get to the river flats."

———

Jeannie had parked the ute under a gumtree at the far end of the wide, open area that bordered the river. The expanse was over a kilometre wide, with a fair bit of shade courtesy of some ancient river gums near the water's edge. They'd been here for ever, so Jeannie felt safe under their spreading bows. Down here near the river the air was clearer and cooler. But Jeannie couldn't relax. She paced up and down. Where was her family?

Michael and Bree should be here any time, and Matty shouldn't be far away either. He'd cut through the bush so he should have made good time.

Groups of locals had stopped around the flat area, most under the shade of the gumtrees. Some even had their own shelters set up, attached to caravans or 4WDs. There were people setting up temporary paddocks with star pickets and rope. Horses were led into the fenced areas to graze, although most appeared jumpy and on edge. The smoke was lighter here, but still evident in the mid-morning air. Jeannie waved at Melinda who had about 12 horses tethered about 20 metres away. It looked like everyone was just arriving, having been texted or phoned by the Emergency Services people after Matthew's warning spread around town.

She was about to walk over to see Melinda when she heard a toot and there was Michael's car with Bree hanging out of the passenger window. Sending a 'Thank you, God!' heavenwards, she ran to the car as Michael pulled up alongside her ute. "I'm so glad to see you," she gushed, gathering them both into a huge hug.

Just at that moment the rumble of a large truck sounded behind them, and Bob tooted his horn as he pulled up next to them. "Hey, just thought I'd let you know I saw Matthew. He was coming behind me so he shouldn't be too long." Bob gave them a thumbs up before pulling over to the area where Melinda had their horses.

As Michael, Bree and Jeannie held onto each other, they all looked towards the gate, straining to see any sign of Matthew crossing the bridge and coming towards them. Nothing!

"He can't be too far away." Melinda's voice came from the other direction as she walked over to them. "Bob said he was right behind him," she reassured. Seconds ticked by, seeming like hours, and Michael muttered "I'll go and look for him."

"No Michael, you can't," screamed Jeannie. "Look!" She pointed across the bridge to the roadblock, now set up across the river road. Police and Emergency Services personnel had blocked the road with vehicles and bollards, flashing lights bursting through the gloom.

Bob came up behind them. "He was right behind me. I'm sure he turned to come this way...unless?" Bob paused, a look of doubt on his face. "What Bob? What are you thinking?" Melinda asked, grabbing her husband's arm.

"It's just that I told him we couldn't find Rosey." Bob ran his hand through his thinning hair. "I told him to follow me. He wouldn't have disobeyed me and gone back to look for Rosey, would he?" Bob was almost in tears as he searched Melinda's face for reassurance, then looked at Jeannie. "Would he?" he repeated.

Jeannie stood with tears running down her face, making dirty rivulets across her smoke-stained cheeks. "Oh Bob! I just don't know. He's not himself and he's not predictable at all," she wailed, as Michael tried to console her. Melinda said "I'll let the police know he's still out there. There's fire trucks going up the road all the time so hopefully..." Her voice trailed off as she walked quickly away towards the Emergency Services tent.

Jeannie couldn't hold back her sobs. Surely not Matt as well as Ben? That was just too unfair! She slumped in a heap on the ground as Michael knelt beside her and took her in his arms, both of them incapable of any other thought.

But at that moment Bree screamed "Look!! Look over there," and she ran, pointing upstream towards the river. Through the gloom, Jeannie could just see some movement. A flash of white and some red. Had Matty been wearing that red shirt?

"I can see them," Bree yelled, already 50 metres further up the riverbank and running hard. In the gathering dark of the smoky air, Matthew emerged towards them, still perched on Stager's back, walking slowly, not trotting, the big horse's flanks heaving with effort.

And there beside them was a small white pony. "Rosey's with them," shouted Melinda, as they all rushed towards the boy and his horses.

"Stop! You'll scare her," Matthew called out, and they did stop.

Matthew brought the horses close to his family, and Melinda moved to grab Rosey and untie her from Stager's gear. Glancing at her friends, Melinda said "I'll take Rosey and give her a drink," as she led the pony towards her other horses.

"Matthew, let's get you down," said Michael, as he lifted his son from the horse's back. "Watch out Dad!" Matthew grabbed at a large square object he'd been balancing between his knees. Jeannie reached out to take it – whatever it was – as Michael put Matty on the ground, but his leg gave way and he fell in a heap. "Oww! My ankle," Matthew moaned, but he stayed on the ground, totally spent. Jeannie thrust the package at Michael and dropped to her knees at Matthew's side.

Her boy looked up at her. "It's OK Mum. I think I sprained my ankle, but I'll be OK." Jeannie just burst into tears as she hugged her son.

As Bree led Stager to the river for a drink, Matthew watched his "best mate" *like a hawk.* After all they'd been through, he had to make sure the horse was looked after.

"Thanks Bree," he called to his sister, who responded with a wave of her hand, busy holding Stager's lead rein. She sluiced handfuls of water over the horse's flanks, and spoke quietly to him. Bree knew that Stager had played a huge part in saving Matthew and Rosey, and probably the whole town *if the truth was told,* so to her family, he was even more special now than he'd been before the events of today.

Jeannie's arms were still around Matt's shoulders. He was exhausted, and he needed a drink and some food. It was a long time since dinner the night before. Jeannie seemed to realise and she said "Matty let's get you something to eat and drink. We can talk about all of this later. We're just so happy to see you safe." She looked up at Michael and he stooped to pick up his son. They made their way to the ute, where Jeannie had an esky full of food and drinks to share.

As he carried Matt, Michael kept muttering "You're OK Matt. You're OK."

Matt grinned and put his arms around his father's neck. "Yes Dad. I'm OK. Just relax and take a deep breath," he advised.

Jeannie had to smile. Talk about the *pot calling the kettle black!* Matthew giving his father advice like that would be funny if their situation was not so serious!

"Here Matt, have a sandwich" she offered as the two men in her life reached the ute. Matthew grabbed the sandwich and the bottle of water she held out. Finally, finally, he could relax.

———

Only a short time later, a loud-hailer called everyone on the river flats to the Emergency Services tent. There, Greg Dale, the Emergency Services controller, took over.

"Alright everyone. Listen up. We just want to let you know what's happening out there. Then we want everyone to move towards the southern end of the flats, as far away from the bridge as possible."

Greg paused, the stress of the situation written across his face. However, he maintained a calm presence as he continued the briefing.

"At the moment the fire front is still heading down the valley towards the town. The crews are out there back-burning up past the old Walters place, and we've got more crews arriving soon. The highway in and out of town has been blocked off because it's just too dangerous for anyone to leave now. The main message is to keep calm, keep the animals calm, and stay put. The forecast says that the wind will drop around 2pm, so that will help us. And if you're a praying person, we'd appreciate your prayers for a wind-change to blow it all back on itself."

Jeannie had drawn an involuntary breath at the mention of the "old Walters place," which was now the "new Luckmore place." It was home, and she was not ready to let it go!

While the Emergency controller had been speaking, more Emergency Services volunteers had arrived, and the CWA ladies had set up an urn and some tea and coffee under an adjacent awning.

Jeannie could hear the chatter on the 2-way radio as the crews reported in. As much as she wanted to know if her home was OK, she decided to move back to where Matthew and Bree waited, looking after Stager.

Michael grabbed her hand reassuringly. He seemed to understand that she was upset about the house, but he was also anxious for the family to stick together. "Come on, let's get back to our kids," he said, and she just nodded. She looked back up-river towards the ridge, but all she could see was black smoke. Praying was the one thing she could do now.

Melinda and Bob had set up a big tarpaulin, some chairs and tables, and a few rugs, close to their truck. Everyone flopped on the ground or onto a chair, as Melinda offered everyone a can of cold lemonade.

The shade helped with the heat of the sun, but there was no escaping the smoke, which seemed to fill every crevice. Even Stager was tethered under the tarpaulin, enjoying the shade and a bucket of oats. His horsey smell annoyed no-one. Everyone acknowledged that he and Matthew had earned a rest, possibly even a medal, for their mad rush down the mountain to warn the valley's residents, although no-one yet knew what the outcome would be. You could *cut the air with a knife*, so palpable was the tension they all felt.

Matthew was on his second lemonade and third banana.

"Slow down Matt. Try to relax. You're safe. We're all safe," Melinda reassured the boy.

Jeannie leaned over to wipe his sweaty, dirty face with a tea towel she'd dipped in the river. For once, Matthew did not pull away or complain.

Today everything seemed different. Their world had shifted, and with it, Matthew had changed too.

His eyes opened slowly. They seemed to be stuck together with grime and grit. Blinking Matthew rolled over and sat up. "Where is everyone?" he wondered, then he caught sight of a group of people gathered around the Emergency Services tents.

As he stood up a soft nose pushed against his hand. "Ha! Yes, Stager I'm OK. How are you?" Matthew asked as he hobbled around his horse, checking every part of him. The animal seemed OK, still tethered in the shade next to the truck, happy to be resting close to his friend Matthew.

"I'm going over to check this out, then I'll be back." Matthew was anxious to know how the fire was progressing. He didn't know how long he'd been curled up on the rug, asleep. But he did know that the air smelt better, not as choked with smoke. It was only as he left the shelter of the truck that Matt felt it. The wind had changed direction!

A cool southerly wind had sprung up sometime while he was asleep, and now a few drops of rain were threatening. Matt shivered involuntarily as he walked slowly towards the meeting. It wasn't that he was cold. The cool change had yet to fully arrive, but he felt so relieved and grateful that the wind had changed. Surely the fire would burn back on itself now?

"Well folks, it's better news," he heard Greg Dale saying as he approached the command post. "The town and everything south of Horse Haven is fine, now the change has come." There was a smattering of applause as Greg ran his hand across his face, smudging the ash on his forehead.

"As for the homes north of Horse Haven, well, we managed to save all but one." He paused, then went on. "I'm afraid Rawson's place is gone. We just couldn't save it, but I suppose it was a partial ruin so maybe that's not so bad."

Matthew breathed again, realising he'd been holding a breath waiting to hear which house was burnt down. He punched the air and yelled "Yes!" then looked at the ground, suddenly embarrassed as everyone turned to look in his direction.

Greg Dale smiled.

"Yes, you're dead right Matthew. It's a pretty great result, due mainly to us getting an earlier warning than we might have in other circumstances. I think that the town and many of its residents have a lot to thank young Matthew for. I think you'll be hearing more about that in the near future young man!"

Matthew wasn't sure what Mr Dale meant. It was all a mystery, and he didn't like being the centre of attention for the whole town. It felt like hundreds of eyes were on him, and only him.

Suddenly his dad was there, lifting him up and carrying him back to the family camp. He had understood his son's awkwardness and rescued him by leaving all those prying eyes behind.

"We'll be able to go home soon mate, so just rest up for a bit longer."

Melinda approached too. She had something in her hand. She handed Matt a big square object, saying "I think this is yours now Matt."

It was the same big square object he had saved from the study at Horse Haven after everyone else had left. He had remembered it as he and Stager led Rosey back towards the road. He had tied the horses up and run inside just long enough to grab the mysterious object, wrapping it in a throw rug from the lounge.

Matt had been unwilling to risk this special object being burned in the fire, so he had taken extra risks himself to retrieve it and carry it all the way to safety.

Now he smiled as he unwrapped Melinda's gift to him. No wonder it was special! It was a framed photo of Matthew's hero, a very special horse named Stager.

CHAPTER 19

ENDINGS AND BEGINNINGS

A TIME TO GATHER STONES TOGETHER

Jeannie could hardly believe the week she'd just had! Coming on top of the past year, it had been huge, for everyone. Getting back to normal and cleaning up in the aftermath of the bushfire was the least of it.

It was unbelievable how far the grime from the smoke had managed to penetrate, into every closed cupboard, every nook and cranny in the old farmhouse. She and Bree had spent 3 days cleaning, while Matthew was released to help the Maddisons clean up at Horse Haven.

Although they were the first 3 days of the school holidays, Bree didn't complain. She seemed quieter Jeannie thought, as if she'd done a lot of thinking lately, what with her injury, then the fire too. Not to mention Benjamin. She didn't even ask to go into town to meet her friends! She seemed content to help out at home.

Jeannie had decided to finish the house cleaning first then start on the yard. Although the fire had not destroyed anything but the old machinery shed, a corrugated-iron lean-to at the bottom of the home paddock, they had lost the ancient 4-wheeler and a lot of Mr Walters' old tools had been melted beyond recognition. The heat of the fire was unimaginable until you realised that the shapeless blob of metal was once a shovel or a pick.

Walking around the yard, Jeannie observed how incredibly close the fire had come to taking the house. Tree branches on the edge of the yard were browned by the heat, the bush to the northeast blackened to within 10 metres of their fence. Towards the river the bush seemed wilted, borne down by the ash and heat from the fire. Scattered around the yard were numerous small embers, now cold lumps of charcoal, but then, in the midst of the inferno, each one could have started a mini-fire and the house would be no more.

She even found one lump of black at the bottom of the front steps. Thank heaven it had plopped from the sky onto the old concrete path, burning a small black spot but not going any further.

Jeannie said a prayer of thanks both for the house as well as for her family's safety. She realised that the bushfire preparations they had made at Michael's insistence, as a family activity on each of Michael's last 2 weekend visits, had made a huge difference. Everyone had been involved in cleaning out gutters, mowing, cutting back foliage, taking it all out to the rubbish tip, all in spite of Bree's whining and Matt's glowering!

"If you're going to live this close to the bush, we have to prepare. You've got a Fire Plan, but this firebreak is just as important, and I can't relax unless I know we've done all we can to protect you," Michael had bullied, even mowing a 10-metre-wide section around the outside of the house yard and cutting back the closest branches of the grevillea and bottlebrushes in the bush that approached their home.

Jeannie realised how right he'd been, looking at that area which was fringed with black, the fire taking most of the bush but slowing to a halt when it hit the firebreak. It was more evidence that Michael was trying hard, going outside his "comfort zone" to plan ahead for his family. Bree and Matt complained at the time but now, after the event, they both knew that those efforts may have been the difference between having a home to return to and being "homeless" once again.

Jeannie felt a warm glow as she thought of Michael, something that she suddenly realised she hadn't felt for a very long time, years in fact. Was this the beginning of love resurfacing? She knew she now reacted to his presence with happiness not frustration. She loved seeing him with the children, and wondered at his understanding of Matthew, how patient he was at explaining things and anticipating Matthew's lack of understanding, especially of social situations.

This last week, even without the fire, would have been a big one for them all, but especially for Matthew.

Finally, after the horror of the fire, Jeannie and Michael had made the call to Dan and Laura. By the time that call was made, Laura and Dan had more news. Ben's condition had improved, he had come *back from the brink*, and had even started to move his fingers and make some sounds. Matthew had listened as they explained that, while Ben was not *out of the woods yet,* he was showing encouraging signs of recovery.

Matthew had smiled tentatively and asked some questions, especially about going to the city to see his friend. They were all so drained by the weekend's events, but Benjamin was improving and that was the main thing.

Matthew apologised to his parents: "Sorry, I know I should have waited to find out what was happening, but I saw your faces and you were crying and I just thought Ben must have not made it – I thought he was dead!"

Jeannie just about burst into tears all over again. "Matt, I do understand, and I don't blame you. It was an awful time. I'm just glad you're safe, but please don't run off ever again." She managed a smile and put her arm around Matthew's shoulders.

Matthew leaned into his mother's arm. "I'm still upset about Ben – but I did a lot of thinking on my ride; well, before the fire I mean." He sat down heavily next to his dad.

"I know it wasn't my fault. Even if I HAD been there, I couldn't have stopped those bullies without a cattle prod or a taser, and I probably would have got hurt too! But I could have been there as a friend. I could have talked to Ben about those kids before it happened." He looked up at his mother, then sighed. "I'm probably the only one who understands how hard it is for Benjamin because it's like that for me too."

"I could have talked to him, but he might not have listened, so it probably still would have happened. And... and it was just not fair that he hit his head, but...but I couldn't have stopped that either. I just want to see him get back to normal," he hiccupped, fighting back tears.

"We'll go and see him just as soon as we are allowed to Matty." Michael reassured his son. Although it was not the time or the place, an idea was forming in his mind.

———※※※———

Now as Jeannie looked back on this last week, it suddenly hit her how her Matthew had matured almost overnight, from the confused, needy boy who had arrived at Highcrest only some 10 months previously, to this young man sounding *wise beyond his years*, learning to see the world from another person's perspective. It seemed that life's big events could help a person to see things differently, to learn hard lessons and come through, to a time of healing. There was still a long way to go, more talking to be done, maybe more tears, more laughing, many more steps along this journey. Again, Jeannie felt the stirring of hope that over the coming days, weeks and years, they would all make that journey to healing, together.

———※※※———

Christmas Day dawned bright and already threatened to become *a scorcher*.

Gramps and Nanna had arrived and were enjoying a short sleep in, having taken over Matthew's room for the week.

Matt and Bree, thrown together in one room for a brief time, had surprisingly not complained. It seemed a truce had been called in brother-sister hostilities, perhaps both of them realising the blessing that their sibling was, especially after recent events.

Michael stretched out and yawned, woken by the kookaburra chorus, and rose stiffly from the couch. Presents wrapped in useful outer coverings like tea-towels, scarves and t-shirts spilled from under the gum tree bough which was propped in a bucket of wet sand. Part of the branch was charred and scarred from the fire, but the Aussie Christmas tree served to remind them of what they had survived. The branch was decorated with a few party lights and homemade decorations made with love by the children, in past years at school. It was simple but meant so much.

Michael sneaked quietly into the kitchen to make a start on breakfast, but *stopped in his tracks* as he saw Jeannie had *beaten him to it*. She sat at the table, 2 hands around a steaming mug. As he stepped into the kitchen, she stood and opened her arms to him. "Merry Christmas Mike," she whispered.

"Merry Christmas to you too," he whispered back, then returning her embrace, he took a chance and kissed her firmly on the lips.

"I'm ready Mike" she whispered into his neck, taking a deep breath before returning his kiss, *with interest.* They stayed like this for long seconds, both wondering at this new-found relationship. Mike sensed that Jeannie had more to say and pulled away just a little, looking into her face.

"I'm ready for us to be a family again," Jeannie looked back at him with a smile *playing on her lips.*

"I've been thinking a lot this last week, well probably for a few weeks now. So much has happened, and I've realised what you mean to me. I mean, I knew what you meant to Bree and Matty, but I needed to realise that I have never stopped loving you. I found it really hard there for a long time and I needed to be away from you, but now we've all changed so much. It's time for us to be a family again, all of us. Even if it means coming back to the city, even that." Her voice trailed off as Michael shook his head.

"I've been thinking too," he looked deep into her eyes. "I also realised something. I realised that life can be short. It can be changed in a moment. Benjamin's life was changed by one punch, one fall. Laura's and Dan's lives too. And I realised I could have lost all of you last week. First, I thought Matty might be gone when he disappeared. Then with the fire – I just don't want to think about what would have happened if Matty hadn't been able to get down the mountain so fast to sound the alarm, if Stager had stumbled and Matt had fallen off. I could have lost all of you."

Michael let Jeannie go and indicated for her to sit, as he did the same. Then he took her hands in his and went on. "Jeannie, I want us to be together again too. So, I've done 2 things this week – right outside my *comfort zone* mind you!"

He smiled broadly.

"First, I've listed the city house for sale! Shhh!" He put his finger on her lips as she started to speak. "Let me finish. And second, I've negotiated to do my job differently. I'm going to work 3 weeks from home then have 1 week in the office to consult with the others on my team. It's all do-able Jeannie, I just had to let go of my routines and get my priorities right. Oh, and get the NBN connected as soon as possible! Then I'll have my new routines established *before I know what's hit me!*"

He smiled again and slipped off his chair to kneel on the kitchen floor.

"What do you say? Will you be my wife again, this time for always?" He brought out a blue velvet box, opened to display her engagement and wedding rings, previously hidden away in her sock drawer. He had been busy, searching for those special items she had long-since stopped wearing!

Jeannie laughed. "Get up you crazy person! Of course I will! I don't know how it will work, but yes .... And we will <u>make</u> it work."

"And we will too!" Bree's voice surprised her parents, and turning they found their children holding hands, standing in the doorway with the biggest smiles on their faces! The 2 children had obviously been there for some time, and had overheard most of their parent's conversation, but Jeannie and Mike had been so caught up in their moment that they hadn't noticed.

"Family hug!" said Mike and everyone came together for just that.

Christmas Day that year was unique! After so many changes, so much sadness and drama, the day was a very happy one.

Breakfast was followed by a trip to the early church service at Highcrest, chatting to the Maddisons and other friends after church, then home for an Australian Christmas.

They set up card-tables, folding chairs and beach umbrellas in the back eddy of the creek behind their house, where the water's flow had slowed to summer pace, almost dry in parts but still deep enough in the pools and under the sandy banks for a quick dip when the heat got too much.

"Just like my men – Mike and Matty," Jeannie thought, "*Still waters run deep.*" She and her parents had carried down trays of cold meats, salad, 2 dozen oysters and a bucket of school prawns to go with the sauces already on the tables; lime aioli and cranberry, reflecting both old and new food trends.

"This is a feast," Matthew exclaimed, as he prepared to challenge himself to try some new flavours, as well as to eat in the middle of a river!

"My new idea is '*try it, you might like it,*' he announced to the family as he dipped a peeled prawn into the aioli.

For a change no-one was feeling stressed or cranky. Preparations for the meal had all been done the day before, church had been a blessing, and Gramps had the water, soft drinks, beer and wine cooling in a plastic crate especially dug into the sandy riverbank. Gramps always took charge of hydration!

Michael grabbed Matty's hand, just as the prawn went *down the hatch!*

"Let's say a prayer. We've got so much to be thankful for!" so they all joined hands as the cool water lapped at their toes.

"What was that?" Jeannie roused herself from the couch with difficulty, carefully lifting Mike's arm from where it lay across her chest, still in the same place it had been when they fell into a dreamless post-Christmas-lunch sleep, full of food, drink and good cheer.

Her phone buzzed, echoing loudly through the quiet house, so she quickly stepped out onto the corner of the verandah, hoping not to wake the rest of the sleeping family.

Wondering dully who would be calling at 4 pm on Christmas afternoon, she quietly answered "Hello?"

"Mrs Luckmore? It's Rod Walters – sorry, Rodney, son of Len and Val, your landlord," a voice began. "So sorry to call today but I'm heading off back to the city in about an hour, and I wanted to talk to you about something before I go. Can I have a quick word with you now if it's not too inconvenient?"

Jeannie would normally have delayed, indignant at the interruption on this special day, but something in his voice intrigued her. Then, a mild panic started to build. Surely this bloke could not be calling to throw them out of the house, not on Christmas Day?

"You there Mrs Luckmore?" Rodney was still pressing for an answer.

"Yes, yes I'm here. You just took me by surprise. Go on." Jeannie encouraged him. No matter what, she did need to know what he'd called about.

A sleepy Michael emerged from the lounge room, blearily rubbing one side of his face, and stretching his cramped back. His *face asked the question* "What's going on?" but she put a finger to her lips, trying to listen to Rodney's voice. Quickly she pressed "Speaker" mode on her phone; whatever happened, it was both her AND Mike now, making decisions that affected this family, so he needed to be part of the conversation.

"Again, I'm really sorry to – um – call you on Christmas Day, but I'm only down overnight to visit a friend and I've been thinking about the old property," Rodney went on.

"Uh oh! Here it comes!" Jeannie thought.

"Well, *the bottom line is* that I need to get it sold. I won't be coming back here to live *in the sticks.*" Rodney paused, realising that he may have just insulted Jeannie and her decision to move to the country, to *the sticks!*

Rodney blustered on, "Oh sorry! But you know how it is? What I mean to say is that I've decided to sell and I want to put it on the market straight away after the Christmas break. I'm going to drop the papers off at the Real Estate office on my way out of town, but I wanted you to be the first to know."

As Rodney went on, Michael grabbed Jeannie's hand as if to reassure her.

"The thing is that Dad and Mum really wanted the place to go to a family, so it could be a family home again. And after the fire I just can't keep worrying about the old place, so I wondered if you would be interested in buying the property? Of course, the price would be a bit lower if we sell it privately." His voice petered out and he cleared his throat.

Jeannie looked at Mike and Mike looked at Jeannie.

He made a small nod of his head. Jeannie plunged into the next question. "What price would you be looking at if we were to buy it?" her words rushed out of her mouth almost before she had time to think.

Rodney mentioned a price that made Jeannie open her mouth in surprise, but no words came out! She was shocked at how cheaply the man would be willing to sell. Even considering the fire risk issues, it would be a bargain.

"Are you sure about that price Rodney?" she squeaked, her voice deserting her in her eagerness. Something that resembled joy was starting to bubble up in her gut. Talk about a *gut reaction!* This felt so right.

Jeannie realised she'd closed her eyes as she thought about the idea of owning their own farm, and as she opened them again, she looked straight at Mike, who was smiling and nodding his head. He mouthed the words "Say "yes"."

Rodney was still speaking, and as Jeannie *tuned in again,* she heard him saying "Of course I know the old place needs a lot of work and the shed burnt down! I'd have to replace all that equipment that was destroyed. And, there's a question of my tax situation." Again, he cleared his throat before continuing. "So yes, that's the price to you."

Jeannie's eyes started to fill with tears. She was beginning to see a plan forming for a future she had never dreamed might happen – but she needed to reply.

In a voice firmer with conviction than she felt inside, she said "OK Rodney, I am interested at that price. If you can email me the details, I'll go to see the bank as soon as I can. I think we can make this happen very quickly." As Mike nodded his head and gave her a huge thumbs-up, Jeannie gave Rodney her email address and rang off.

"Do you believe what just happened?" she looked at her husband. "Do you believe it?" she repeated.

Michael just smiled and took her hands in his. "Yep, I think I'm beginning to believe in lots of things again, starting with the miracle of *second chances!*"

As the two of them jigged around the verandah, four bemused faces appeared at the lounge room door, first Matty, then Bree, and finally Nanna and Gramps too. "What's going on?" grumbled Gramps, who was never very happy after an afternoon nap! Michael spun his wife around one more time, and Jeannie laughed.

"Let's make a cuppa. *Have we got some news for you guys?!*"

CHAPTER 20

NEW THINGS CAN BE GOOD THINGS!
A TIME TO CELEBRATE!

As December raced into January, a new year began. Matthew was having difficulty grasping all the events both of the recent past and the oncoming future.

He decided to make 2 lists, one of the things both good and bad that had already happened, and the other a list of all the things coming up in the next 4 weeks before he started secondary school in early February.

The first list had 11 items, almost all of which he could now stop thinking about as they had already finished. Only a few were continuing on.

He decided to code them as good/happy and bad/sad or confusing, using "emotion" faces that he'd learnt about.

Matthew sat down at his desk, and began.

List 1 – Things that have already happened:

1. Bree broke up with Jonno and hurt her head but she's OK now. ☺

2. Benjamin was bashed up: 😷😵 : now he's getting better and better. ☺

3. Benjamin's mum and dad were so sad: confusing when adults don't cope. ☹

4. Remembering being with Ben : an exceptional colleague. 🙂

5. Ride up the ridge: great, cleared my head ☺, scary on the way down 💀, Stager saved me. ☺☺

6. Bushfire : horrible, frightened 😨 but we were OK in the end. Helped the town by warning them early. ✊

7. Clean-up: yuk but looks good now. Bush is growing back already! 😐

8. Christmas in the river! Fun and different, with Dad and Gramps and Nanna. Great to see them. ☺☺☺

9. The house: we get to stay! ☺☺☺☺

10. Dad moving down for good: soon! ☺☺☺☺

11. Mum and Dad back together: hooray!!! ☺☺☺☺

Finishing the list, Matthew realised that numbers 4,8,9,10 and 11 were OK to keep thinking about. Some of the other stuff he COULD keep thinking about, but it would be better if he decided not to.

The other thing he realised looking at his list was that there were far more happy faces than sad or confused ones.

The second list was trickier. Even though it was shorter than the first, it contained more "unknowns."

Still, this was good to do – to see what was coming and to think about it first. It really did help him to manage his feelings and to be ready for the future, at least as much as he could be.

List 2 - Things that are coming in the future:

1. A new school, and making new friends: hard, sometimes confusing. (I can't do much about this one until school goes back). 🙂

2. Speech on Australia Day: not sure how I feel! 🙁 😟 (Mum says I should be very proud.) 😅 🙂

3. Going to secondary school: harder school work 😟, routines again 🙂, meeting new people 😟🙂🙂, learning new things. 🙂🙂

4. Helping Ben in the future: how??? 🙂 🙂

Matthew decided that he needed to concentrate on numbers 2 and 4. He couldn't do much about the others until he went back to school, so they could be IGNORED. Mrs Jansen had been teaching him about choosing what to focus his thinking on, and about ignoring things he didn't like or didn't need to think about much.

The great stuff that was continuing on – buying the house, Dad and Mum being back together, and Dad moving down to Highcrest permanently – they were easy!

Dad had said that with the sale of the city house already happening, they could afford to renovate the farm house, and best of all, they would be connecting the NBN, so Matthew would always be able to log-on.

He had found some chat sites that talked about Autism Spectrum Disorder, and Mum and Dad had given him permission to go on those sites if one of them was around. Matthew thought that was silly! He would never do or say anything stupid on these sites, but that was the rule that Mum and Dad agreed on so that was what he would do. He also knew that "cyber bullying" was a real thing, so maybe Mum and Dad were right to be a bit cautious about what he looked at.

The Australia Day speech was another matter entirely.

Since Mr Dale from the Emergency Services had asked Matthew to attend the Highcrest Australia Day ceremony on 26th January, and to make a short speech, Matthew had been worrying about what to say. He knew he didn't have to say very much but he wanted to say something worthwhile, something people would remember.

He and Dad had discussed an idea, an idea that had started to form even as Matt and Stager had galloped up the ridge that crazy day, with Matthew trying to outrun the overwhelming sense of guilt and loss that he felt about Benjamin. Apparently, his father had had a similar idea too!

Dad had said that he could set it up, and with a good internet connection he would help Matthew run it from home. Matt worked with his father, sometimes until very late, setting up the website, making it user friendly and easy to navigate.

There was so much information out there, so links to other sites they had found were limited to those they had checked out really well, and had found useful. As Michael had said

"There's just so much information out there, so we have to make sure people don't get confused. We have to make it easier for them, not harder."

So, when the site went live at the end of the month, Matty hoped it would help a lot of people.

With Australia Day's speech fast approaching, Matthew made a decision. The best approach was to tell his own story, all of it, in his own way, and to hope people understood.

Australia Day, January 26th, was actually on the Public Holiday Monday this year.

As people gathered in the Highcrest Soldiers' Memorial Park, queuing in hungry lines to buy a sausage sandwich from the local Lions Club volunteers, the Luckmore family *took their seats.*

Matty was nervous, and had refused the tempting offer of a sausage, even though the rest of the family had eaten theirs.

"Maybe later..." he'd mumbled to Jeannie as he checked his back pocket for his speech cards, probably for the 50th time since they left the house.

Mr Arnold from the Lions Club, had promised to keep "*a couple of snags*" for Matty in case he felt hungry after his speech!

Jeannie and Bree had only a vague idea of what Matthew intended to say, assuming it would be *short and sweet!* Michael knew Matt had a few *surprises up his sleeve,* having helped him to write part of the speech, and *acting as a sounding board* for Matthew to practice.

However, no-one but Matthew knew the whole of it!

And no-one at all knew how it would be received by the town, most of whom attended the Australia Day ceremony, especially on a clear warm morning like today.

As the formalities got underway, Matthew took some deep breaths.

Now that he knew the signals his body gave him that anxiety was building, he breathed deeply, counted to 100 under his breath and took little sips from his water bottle. His fingers worked overtime squeezing the squishy fidget ball in his pocket. He excused himself and went to the toilet, waiting in the shade near the amenities block for a few extra minutes, letting his fast-beating heart slow a little, regaining some control.

On his way back to his seat, Matthew heard Wally Arnold, the local Lions Club President, introducing him, so instead of re-joining his family he veered towards the stage.

Mr Arnold was saying: "Matthew Luckmore is the young man whose heroic ride enabled the town to be warned of the bushfire even earlier than the Emergency Services could warn us! We all owe him a debt of gratitude for his brave ride. Please put your hands together to welcome him to say a few words, our Highcrest Young Australian of the Year, and recipient of the Emergency Services Bravery Award, Matthew Luckmore."

It was *like someone pressed the APPLAUSE button*!

Matthew was too preoccupied checking his back pocket and taking out his speech cards, to really take in what Mr Arnold had said.

There was a lot of noise; clapping, and even a few high-pitched whistles. Matthew really wanted to put his hands over his ears to block it out, but he knew that was not the right thing to do at this moment. Instead, he stepped up to the microphone, hoping people would stop clapping and listen.

Mr Arnold had his big hand held out towards Matthew!

He realised he was expected to shake hands, so he raised his hand and Mr Arnold shook it briefly, moving Matthew towards the microphone as he did so. Greg Dale, the Emergency Services Controller, moved forward and placed a medal around Matthew's neck, also reaching to shake his hand.

Then Mr Arnold held up a large framed Certificate which he placed next to the microphone, and again reached to shake Matthew's hand.

It was all very confusing. As Wally Arnold repeated "Let's hear it for Matthew Luckmore, Young Australian of the Year recipient," and adjusted the microphone to Matthew's height, Matty cleared his throat and took another quick sip from his water bottle.

Placing the bottle next to the microphone stand, Matthew straightened up and faced the large crowd. He decided to do what someone very wise (his dad) had told him to do; he picked out one person, Mrs Freeman, an elderly lady with a kind face who was sitting right in the front row in his direct eye line.

He started to speak, making his speech as if it was just to her, hoping no-one would notice his intense concentration on just one person. Dad had said that if Matty started to feel more relaxed he could look around more as he went through the speech, but if not, it was OK.

The important thing was to say what he had to say so everyone would hear it, not to make the perfect speech but to get his message across.

"This is it" Matty realised, as he placed his speech cards onto the lectern. Even though he knew the speech *by heart*, it was reassuring to have the cards there, *just in case*!

In the crowd, Jeannie breathed a silent prayer. "Please God, help him to cope with this," and even as she did so, Matthew found his voice and started to speak.

The microphone squeaked once, forcing Matthew to pull back slightly, but it was OK. The social story that he, Mum and Dad had written had included what to do if the equipment malfunctioned, so Matthew took another deep breath and waited *a split second* before starting again. Peace seemed to fall on the gathering; no-one else spoke or coughed, the breeze dropped away and even the birds were silent. You could *hear a pin drop* and in a strong voice, Matthew began.

"I have Autism," he started, looking up from his notes.

"I have an Autism Spectrum Disorder. Those two names mean the same thing. They also mean that I think a bit differently to most people. I take lots of things literally, and sometimes I don't understand the way other kids do. I might get mixed up or I might not realise that you are talking to me. I might not understand how other people feel, and I might get upset by things that happen around me, like different smells or loud noises. Sometimes I need to go somewhere to calm down, especially at school where there are lots of kids and there are so many situations I don't quite understand."

Matt paused. No-one in the audience moved. It seemed that they were all holding their breath, waiting for him to continue.

"What you need to know is that I'm also really good at a lot of things. Like building Lego designs, and doing mathematics, and working with computers. I'm better at those things than most neurotypical kids my age. Yes, 'neurotypical' is what we call you guys!"

There was a smattering of laughter as people reacted to being given a label themselves, a new experience for most of the audience. As the laughter receded, Matthew continued.

"So, I have Autism, but please don't call it a DIS-ability. I call it my DIFF-ability, because I'm great at lots of things that maybe YOU are not. And one of my abilities is riding horses."

Matthew looked up briefly to find Melinda and Bob Maddison, who were standing near to the seats occupied by Matthew's family. Melinda smiled encouragement and Bob gave Matthew a thumbs up. Matty took another big breath, relaxed his shoulders and went on.

"When I learn something, I like to know ALL about it. I like all the details and I like to understand why things happen. So, I ask lots of questions!" *Out of the corner of his eye*, Matthew saw Melinda nodding her head and smiling.

"When I learned about bushfires, I read lots about how they start, how they burn and what we have to do to prepare. I listened carefully to the Emergency Services when they came to speak at my school, and I went online to learn all the details I could find. My family and I live upstream from the old bridge, up near the bush. In spring, we decided to have a good clean up around our house and make a Fire Plan." He looked up again at the crowd, noting that everyone seemed to be listening.

"Everyone needs a Fire Plan to follow. It's a good idea to write it down or even draw some pictures of what to do so the little kids will remember, then put it up on the wall. I know because that's the way I think. If I see pictures, with words or a story about what to do, I remember and I don't panic so much. I can see it in my mind and I can make sense of things even when it's scary. When I was riding down from the ridge in front of the bushfire, I kept seeing pictures of what was in our Fire Plan, and what the Emergency Services had shown us at school. That was really helpful for me."

Matthew paused again and thought "Now for the hard bit!" but after another big breath, he kept talking.

"Last year my friend Benjamin was bashed up after school. He is 12 years old like me. Some boys bullied him and hit him. He fell and hit his head on the concrete, and he was really sick for a long time."

As he heard a few gasps from the quiet crowd, Matt's eyes grew misty so he wiped his hand across his face. Mr Arnold moved forward as if to support Matthew, a concerned look on his face. But as Matthew took another ragged breath, Mr Arnold stopped and moved back to his chair. Matty was OK.

He started to speak again, this time reading from his cards to make sure he said exactly the right words.

"Ben has Autism like me. We were colleagues at my old school. You'd say he was my best friend. Actually, he was my only friend, and I was HIS only friend. No-one else understood us, except for maybe one teacher. So, when I left that school, Ben was on his own."

Take another breath – keep going.

"I felt really guilty when Ben got bashed, as if it was somehow my fault that I wasn't there to protect him or help him. But then I realised it wasn't MY fault."

Matthew looked up at his audience. He forced himself to slowly turn his head to include every person in what he said next.

"It was EVERYONE'S fault. Not just the boys who bashed Ben; they were just idiots! But everyone else who didn't help him to fit in or try to understand what it was like for Ben, how he thought and how he felt."

"So really we are ALL to blame because we did not learn what it means to have Autism. I am only just starting to learn for myself what it means for me, and I am only ONE person with Autism. Someone once said "If you have met one person with Autism then you have met ONE PERSON with Autism." What that means is that Autism is really different for each person that is diagnosed with it, and each person is a unique individual."

Matthew paused again, thankful that Dad had helped with this part, making it sound really good, and hopefully making people take notice.

His audience was still silent, listening.

"I have only two more things to tell you all," he went on.

"The first is that, if you know anyone with an Autism Spectrum Disorder, learn more about how to help them. Talk to someone who knows, like their parents, or a therapist or a counsellor. And parents, when they are old enough, tell your son or daughter what Autism is. If they don't have Autism, it might help them to help someone they meet at school or somewhere else they go. If they DO have Autism, they need to know why they feel different and act differently to other people, because they already know they do it, they just don't know why."

Looking up again, Matthew said "You'll know when it's the right time, when they start to ask questions! Or if you don't know, go and get some good advice."

Matthew paused again, and took a quick sip from his water bottle, glancing again at his speech cards. He really wanted to get the last part right!

"The second thing I need to tell you is that from next Monday there will be a new website called "Ben's Friends." My Dad and I have started it up and you can all join. It's free and you'll find out more about Autism there. There will be links to other good sites to check out. But the main reason for "Ben's Friends" is so kids like me and Ben can find each other. We can chat online and have friends online, even if no-one at school understands. I really hope that it will help kids with Autism not to feel so alone. In honour of my friend and colleague, Benjamin. Thanks very much for listening."

Matthew finished and reached up to collect all his speech cards. He picked up his framed certificate. Still, no-one had made a sound; maybe he had offended them? He wasn't sure, but Dad had said just finish and walk back to the family, so that's what Matthew did.

As he reached the bottom step though, the clapping started, and in a second everyone was clapping and cheering.

His medal swinging around his neck, Matthew let himself smile, just a little. As the noise grew more deafening Matthew walked slowly away, not towards his family. There was time for them later, as much as he loved each one of them! Now he needed to have a quiet time, and the beach was just a few steps away.

Jeannie rose from her seat, blinking back tears, and went to follow her son to see if he was OK. Michael put out his hand, gently touching her arm.

"No, let him go. He needs a walk, a bit of peace and quiet," and Jeannie smiled, nodding her answer, knowing that this time she could let Matthew go, just for a while anyway.

He was going to be OK. And maybe, just maybe, they all were!

THE END

(for now!)

LIST OF FIGURATIVE LANGUAGE USED IN "DISCOVERING MATTHEW"

Chapter 1:

Expression	Meaning	Possible Category
...the letters on a page danced like mad fairies with a fire cracker up their backsides.	Matthew found it hard to read the letters because his stress was causing the letters to appear to jump around.	Simile
her long red nails morphing into bird-claws	Matthew saw her nails as looking like a bird's big claws.	Simile
playing with yourself	Putting your hand on your genitals for an extended time.	Idiom
Always on Matt's case	Blake was always being unkind to Matt.	Idiom
always with a word to push Matt's buttons	Blake was always trying to upset Matt and make him react.	Idiom
to take the bait	Matt wanted to try not to react, to respond to Blake's teasing.	Idiom
a big ask	It was a big job or task to teach Year 6 in her first year of teaching.	Idiom
They knew what was good for them.	The students knew that Blake was a bully, so they avoided a confrontation with him.	Idiom

Matt was torn	Matthew wanted to go on the bus, but he did not want to get into more trouble, so he had to decide between the 2 choices.	Idiom

Chapter 2:

Expression	Meaning	Category
Breeze through life	Breeanna has an easy-going personality and doesn't worry much about the things that are happening in her life.	Idiom
My two precious babies	Matt and Bree were Jeannie's children and had been her babies – sometimes parents call their children their "babies" even when they are grown-up.	Idiom
Breeanna had fallen for Jonno	Breeanna really liked a boy called Jonno.	Saying

Chapter 3:

Expression	Meaning	Category
Sunday best	Matthew knew that his Mum was dressing in her best clothes. This is what people used to do on Sundays, particularly to go to church.	Idiom
Out wide	Further out to sea, past sight of land.	Saying (fishing, boating)
Face the music	Accept responsibility for something you have done, and possibly be punished for that.	Idiom

The car had boasted...	The car was equipped with – used for facilities that are special or expensive, so the owner could boast about having them.	Saying, personifi-cation
Mrs Arnold will keep an eye on you	Mrs Arnold would pay attention and make sure Matt was OK while he waited.	Idiom
On the front foot	To take the initiative, to speak confidently. (From the sport of cricket).	Idiom
His take on it	What Matt understood – his version of what happened.	Idiom
To buy some time	To delay, to take some extra time e.g., to work out how to say something difficult.	Idiom
To jump right in	To act quickly.	Saying
In a world of his own	Thinking hard about his own thoughts, not attending to the surroundings.	Saying
An extra pair of hands	Additional help; another person to assist in a task.	Idiom

Chapter 4:

Expression	Meaning	Category
Citified	Someone from the country becoming used to city living, and not wanting to return to the county.	Saying
Take the money and run	The real estate agent meant that Rodney would take his money from the sale of the farm and never return.	Idiom

Set their watches by him	Michael's routine was so rigid that people knew exactly when he would arrive somewhere; to be reliable.	Saying
Gone in a flash	Gone suddenly, quickly, in a very short time.	Idiom
Like diamonds	Very valuable and expensive.	Simile
Headhunted	A company had offered Michael a great job because of his exceptional skills.	Saying
Taken his heart in his hands	Michael had taken a big chance that Jeannie loved him. If she did not, his *heart might be broken* (he would be extremely sad).	Saying
Spur of the moment	Unplanned action or decision	Saying
Crying buckets	Crying a lot because she was so happy – tears of happiness!	Saying
Like a pig in mud	Pigs love to roll in mud, so Michael was extremely happy in his situation.	Simile
In her element	Jeannie was also very happy.	Saying
To juggle (running the kids around)	To manage all the different tasks that needed to be done- multitasking.	Idiom
To keep all the balls in the air	To keep everything going, like a juggler keeps all the juggled balls in the air.	Idiom
What a laugh!	How funny or ironically, it's not funny at all!	Saying/ Sarcasm
Out of the blue	Unexpectedly, apparently from nowhere.	Idiom

Looked as sad as Jeannie felt	Mrs Green's facial expression showed Jeannie that she was very sad and upset by the news she had to tell.	Simile
Within coo-ee	A coo-ee is a call that is made using these sounds, and which can be heard for some way. The distance that it can be heard could be said to be "within coo-ee".	Saying: Australian
Functioning on automatic	She was doing things without thinking much about them.	Saying

Chapter 5:

Expression	Meaning	Category
I'm drowning, going down for the last time	Michael uses an analogy of a person drowning, because he feels that his life is similar – he is unable to cope and struggling to survive without his family.	Analogy
Drinking in	Michael was noticing everything about Breeanna because he had not seen her for so long.	Saying
To break open new ground	To talk about or experience new things, to do things in a different way.	Saying
To be 'on it'/ onto it	To be ready to do what needs to be done, immediately.	Saying
Wonders would never cease	An expression of great surprise.	Saying

Unspoken questions all over their faces	Jeannie could see that the children wanted to ask her about why their Dad had come to visit without letting them know, but they decided not to speak at that time – their questions remained in their heads.	Saying
Matty's face dropped	Matthew looked sad and his face changed, as he realised his father was not staying long.	Saying
I'm all ears	Michael means that he's listening, very hard, to what Jeannie has to say.	Idiom

Chapter 6:

Expression	Meaning	Category
Dictated terms	To tell another person what to do.	Saying
Switch off	To stop paying attention.	Saying
Small talk	Polite conversation about unimportant or uncontroversial matters, especially as engaged in on social occasions.	Saying
Eyes began to glaze over	Eyes become dull and lose all expression, usually because the listener is bored or is thinking about something else.	Saying
Lost in thought	Thinking about something and not paying attention to one's surroundings, including other people.	Saying

Ploughed onwards	To continue doing something although it is difficult or boring.	Saying
Put me on the payroll	To pay someone for their work.	Saying
Led her on	To mislead or deceive someone, especially into believing that one is in love with or attracted to them.	Saying
The rest is history	Used when explaining how something happened, to say that you have reached the part of the story that everyone knows.	Idiom
Late bloomer	Michael is indicating that he was slower than other children to grow. He was still small (a *"little weed"*) for longer than others.	Saying
A poker face	An inscrutable face that reveals no hint of a person's thoughts or feelings.	Idiom
Fall guy	A person to whom blame is deliberately and falsely attributed in order to deflect blame from another person.	Saying
Took me under your wing	To help, teach, or take care of someone who is younger or has less experience or understanding.	Idiom
To wear someone down	To weary and overcome by persistent resistance or pressure.	Idiom

Something just snapped in my brain	Jeannie could not think logically because she was under stress, and so acted like something had gone wrong in her brain.	Saying
Pushing his buttons	To do or say something just to make someone angry or upset, or to tease them.	Saying
Lost the plot	To lose one's ability to understand or cope with what is happening.	Saying
Like clockwork	Very smoothly and easily.	Metaphor
On a roll	Experiencing a prolonged spell of success.	Idiom
Make a (much better) go of it	To succeed in doing something.	Idiom
Dream Jeannie	Michael's nickname for Jeannie, based on a character in a 1960's Sit-Com "I Dream of Jeannie".	Saying

Chapter 7:

Expression	Meaning	Category
Time drifted	Time passed by.	Saying
Take a seat	An invitation to sit down.	Idiom
Mending broken fences	To improve or repair a relationship that has been damaged by an argument or disagreement.	Idiom
Do a double-take	A delayed reaction to a surprising or significant situation after an initial failure to notice anything unusual.	Idiom

In front of her nose	Plain; clearly apparent; obvious.	Idiom
Sparrow's	Early in the morning, at dawn.	Slang saying

Chapter 8:

Expression	Meaning	Category
Sure of her ground	To be sure about how to behave and what to say.	Saying

Chapter 9:

Expression	Meaning	Category
On the tip of (Jeannie's) tongue	You are ready to say something.	Idiom
What a stager!	What an actor, or pretender!	Saying
A big guts	Someone who loves food and eats a lot!	Saying
Against the odds	In spite of difficulties and challenges.	Idiom
Talking to thin air	Talking to no-one. Matthew had raced away to get ready for his ride.	Idiom
A sixth sense	A supposed intuitive faculty giving awareness not explicable in terms of normal perception.	Saying
Like a natural	If you say that someone is a natural, you mean that they do something very well and very easily.	Metaphor
On the grapevine	To hear news from someone who heard the news from someone else.	Saying

Chapter 10:

Expression	Meaning	Category
Dying to	To be extra keen to do something.	Saying
Hollow legs	The person eats so much they must have extra space to put the food into e.g. hollow legs!	Saying

Chapter 11:

Expression	Meaning	Category
Ants in your pants	Be extremely restless, uneasy, impatient, or anxious.	Idiom
Butterflies in your tummy	To be very nervous or excited about something.	Idiom
Took it in his stride	Managed the news or the incident well – like it happened all the time.	Idiom
Watching the golden orb	Watching the sun.	Metaphor
Puppy-dog eyes	Big wide-open eyes, begging like a puppy.	Saying
On the grapevine	Local gossip, the way people spread a story, like a grapevine spreading and growing.	Idiom
It was *second-nature*	Something was easy, instinctive.	Saying

Chapter 12:

Expression	Meaning	Category
Chattering like a cockatoo	Talking a lot, and loudly.	Simile

A peck on the cheek	A little kiss (like a quick peck from a hen).	Saying
Curve-ball question	To ask a question that surprises or shocks; unexpected.	Saying
On a steep learning curve	To be learning a lot, probably in a short time.	Saying
Can't see the forest from the trees	An expression used to describe someone who is too involved in the details of a problem to look at the situation as a whole.	Saying
Thrown a cat among the pigeons	To cause an enormous fight or flap, usually by revealing a controversial fact or secret.	Idiom
Down the track	Further along, in terms of time, or movement.	Saying
Hit the shower	To go and have a shower.	Saying
Hold that thought	Used to tell someone to remember what has just been said and then continue discussing it or thinking about it later.	Saying

Chapter 13:

Expression	Meaning	Category
Have a good breather	To stop what you are doing for a short time and have a rest.	Idiom
Catch our breath	To stop and rest, breathe deeply; to take a break.	Saying
He could do it blindfolded	He knows the way so well, he could find his way even if he could not see easily.	Idiom

He's like the Sheriff	The Sheriff is a policeperson, in charge of law and order in a town, so Matt is compared to someone who tells others to keep the rules/obey the law.	Simile
Hit the sack	To go to bed, to sleep.	Idiom

Chapter 14:

Expression	Meaning	Category
It went south	To become unfavourable; to decrease; to take a turn for the worse.	Idiom
Dry as chips	Very, very dry – comparison to wood chips.	Simile

Chapter 15:

Expression	Meaning	Category
Clam up	To stop talking, become silent due to shyness, embarrassment or reluctance to share information.	Idiom
The air became as thick as mud	In the stress of the moment, it felt like the air was thick and full of tension.	Simile
With some venom	To say something nastily, intending to hurt or offend someone.	Saying
Bad boy	His reputation was that he disobeyed laws and did things that were not conventional.	Idiom
Clam up	To stop speaking, or to shutdown, like a clam closing up tightly.	Saying

I'm a player	Someone who cheats on or disappoints their partner in a relationship; does not want to follow-through on promises they have made (Jonno was trying to get Bree to do something she didn't want to by shaming her and embarrassing her).	Saying
The floodgates opened	Something serving to restrain an outburst opened up - the floodgates of Breeanna's anxiety and sadness.	Saying
As if a dam had burst its banks	See above.	Simile
Relief flowed like a river	Jeannie was very relieved that Bree was OK.	Simile
He's a hot head	He reacts without thinking; becomes easily angry and violent.	Idiom
Total (his car)	Destroy or badly damage a vehicle.	Saying
(It) did the trick	It achieved what you wanted.	Idiom
To keep an eye on something	To keep under careful observation.	Idiom
It filled the hole in his stomach	It filled him up; reduced his hunger.	Saying
To switch off	To stop thinking about something or paying attention.	Idiom
To pick up the pieces	To restore one's life or a situation to a more normal state after a shock or disaster.	idiom

Chapter 16:

Expression	Meaning	Category
To (have a) melt down	To become uncontrollably upset, angry.	Saying
Take your time	To spend as much time as wanted.	Idiom
As a last resort	Something that was possible if everything else had failed e.g. water from the river if the tanks were empty.	Saying
He wouldn't hurt a fly	To be too gentle to want to hurt anyone.	Idiom
To cut this long story short	To reduce the information to essential facts.	Idiom
The flack started to fly	An attack on something that you have done or said.	Saying
They set Ben up	To trick someone in order to make them do something.	Saying
They knew he would fall for it	He would believe them.	Idiom
All hell broke loose	Violent or confused activity suddenly begins.	Idiom
He wouldn't say boo to a goose	He is very quiet, shy and nervous. Timid.	Idiom
She got the picture	She understood the situation.	Idiom
To get in touch	To contact someone by phone, email, text or letter, or by visiting.	Saying
The bare bones	Only the basic parts or details; as little as possible.	Idiom

Chapter 17:

Expression	Meaning	Category
To *open up* to someone	To talk freely about a problem or an issue.	Saying
He was home free	To succeed without difficulties.	Metaphor
Taken a turn for the worse	To suddenly become sicker; condition worsens.	Idiom
A scorcher	A really hot, dry day.	Saying
The beast	The fire seemed to have a life of its own, and was like a beast or monster.	Personification
hanging on for dear life	To hang on to something very tightly, as if one's life depended on it.	Idiom
Under his breath	In a very quiet voice.	Saying
The point of no return	A critical point at which turning back or reversal is not possible.	Idiom
At the top of his lungs	Loudly, using all his breath.	Idiom
A second wind	A new strength or energy to continue something that is an effort.	Idiom

Chapter 18:

Expression	Meaning	Category
It was a lottery	Like a game of chance, it was unsure what the result would be.	*Simile*
There's a sight for sore eyes	A way of saying that you are very pleased to see someone.	Idiom
gave Stager his head	He let the horse go where he wanted to go.	Saying

made good time	To go at a steady, desirable pace and arrive somewhere in a timely manner.	Saying
Watched like a hawk	To watch someone or something very carefully.	Idiom
If the truth be told	Used when you are giving your honest opinion or admitting something.	Saying
The pot calling the kettle black	Used to convey that the criticisms a person is aiming at someone else could equally well apply to themselves.	Idiom
To cut the air with a knife	The atmosphere in a place is extremely tense or unfriendly.	Idiom

Chapter 19:

Expression	Meaning	Category
back from the brink	To come back to a better place, from a place that is close to somewhere that is very bad.	Saying
Out of the woods	Out of difficulties, danger or trouble.	Idiom
Wise beyond his years	Smarter than you should be for your age.	Saying
It's a scorcher	The day is going to be extremely hot and dry.	Saying
He stopped in his tracks	To make someone suddenly stop moving or doing something because they are very surprised.	Idiom
She had beaten him to it	To do something before someone else.	Idiom

She returned his kiss *with interest*	She kissed him back enthusiastically.	Saying
a smile *playing on her lips*	A smile is developing and her lips are moving.	Saying
outside my *comfort zone*	To do something that does not make you feel secure, comfortable, or in control.	Saying
before I know what's hit me	Before I am shocked and surprised.	Idiom
Still waters run deep	People who are quiet or shy are often very intelligent and interesting.	Idiom/ Proverb
Try it, you might like it!	A great saying to encourage picky eaters.	Saying
Down the hatch!	Cheerfully swallow something – like 'Cheers!'	Idiom
His face asked the question	His facial expression showed he was asking what was happening, without using words.	Idiom
The bottom line	The ultimate outcome of a situation.	Saying
To live *in the sticks*	To live out in the country, a long way from any metropolitan area.	Saying
A gut reaction	An instantaneous reaction made without thought.	Idiom
To tune in again	To watch, listen, or become aware of something.	Idiom
Second chances	An opportunity to try something again after failing one time.	Saying

Have we got some news for you?	When one is making a definite and forceful statement that someone does not expect, know about, or agree with.	Saying

Chapter 20:

Expression	Meaning	Category
To take a seat	To sit down.	Idiom
A couple of snags	A few sausages.	Colloquial saying
To be short and sweet	Brief but pleasant or relevant.	Saying
A couple of surprises up his sleeve	To have a secret or surprise plan or solution.	Idiom
A sounding board	Someone who listens as you try out an idea or opinion on him.	Idiom
Like someone pressed the APPLAUSE button	Everyone clapped loudly.	Metaphor
To know by heart	To have learned and remembered something so that notes and reminders are not needed.	Idiom
Just in case	A provision against something happening or being true.	Saying
A split second	A very brief moment of time.	Idiom
Hear a pin drop	There was absolute silence or stillness.	Idiom
Out of the corner of his eye	Looking sideways at something rather than directly.	Idiom

Explanation of Figurative Language:

Term	Definition	Example
Alliteration	The repetition of usually initial consonant sounds in two or more neighbouring words or syllables.	The wild and woolly walrus waits and wonders when we'll walk by
Assonance	A resemblance of sound in words or syllables.	holy & stony and Fleet feet sweep by sleeping geese
Cliche	A word or phrase that has become overly familiar or commonplace.	No pain, no gain
Hyperbole	Big exaggeration, usually with humour.	mile-high ice-cream cones
Idiom	The language peculiar to a group of people.	She sings at the top of her lungs
Metaphor	Comparing two things by using one kind of object or using in place of another to suggest the likeness between them.	Her hair was silk
Onomatopoeia	Naming a thing or an action by imitating the sound associated with it.	buzz, hiss, roar, woof
Personification	Giving something human qualities.	The stuffed bear smiled as the little boy hugged him close
Simile	A figure of speech comparing two unlike things that is often introduced by like or as.	The sun is like a yellow ball of fire in the sky

As well as the above, there are also a number of <u>literary devices</u> which can be used in figurative language as well.

These include <u>mood</u>, <u>irony</u>, <u>paradox</u>, <u>oxymoron</u>, <u>allusion</u>, and <u>euphemism</u>.

So, as you can see, our language can be very confusing and complicated!

APPENDIX

Chapter 6:

Theory of Mind (1)

In <u>psychology</u>, **theory of mind** refers to the mental capacity to <u>understand</u> other people and their behaviour by ascribing mental states to them. These states may be different from one's own states and include <u>beliefs</u>, <u>desires</u>, <u>intentions</u> and <u>emotions</u>. Possessing a functional theory of mind is considered crucial for success in everyday <u>human</u> <u>social interactions</u> and is used when <u>analysing</u>, <u>judging</u>, and <u>inferring</u> others' behaviours.   En.wikipedia.org

Theory of Mind is the ability to attribute subjective mental states to oneself and to others (Baron-Cohen et al. 2000). This ability is crucial to the understanding of one's own and other people's behaviour. Autism Spectrum Disorders (ASD) are strongly associated with impairments of Theory of Mind skills.

("Theory of Mind Training of Children with Autism: A Randomised Controlled Trial". Begeer, Geevers et al, <u>J Autism Dev Disorders.</u> 2011; 41(8): 997–1006.)

Autism Diagnostic Categories DSM5 (2)

Diagnostic and Statistical Manual of Mental Disorders 5 (2013), provides diagnostic criteria to help diagnose Autism Spectrum Disorders.

To meet diagnostic criteria for ASD according to DSM-5, a child must have persistent deficits in each of three areas of social communication and interaction (see A.1. through A.3. below) plus at least two of four types of restricted, repetitive behaviours (see B.1. through B.4. below).

A. Persistent deficits in social communication and social interaction across multiple contexts, as manifested by the following, currently or by history (examples are illustrative, not exhaustive; see text):

1. Deficits in social-emotional reciprocity, ranging, for example, from abnormal social approach and failure of normal back-and-forth conversation; to reduced sharing of interests, emotions, or affect; to failure to initiate or respond to social interactions.

2. Deficits in nonverbal communicative behaviours used for social interaction, ranging, for example, from poorly integrated verbal and nonverbal communication; to abnormalities in eye contact and body language or deficits in understanding and use of gestures; to a total lack of facial expressions and nonverbal communication.

3. Deficits in developing, maintaining, and understand relationships, ranging, for example, from difficulties adjusting behaviour to suit various social contexts; to difficulties in sharing imaginative play or in making friends; to absence of interest in peers.

Severity is based on social communication impairments and restricted, repetitive patterns of behaviour.

B. Restricted, repetitive patterns of behaviour, interests, or activities, as manifested by at least two of the following, currently or by history (examples are illustrative, not exhaustive; see text):

1. Stereotyped or repetitive motor movements, use of objects, or speech (e.g., simple motor stereotypes, lining up toys or flipping objects, echolalia, idiosyncratic phrases).

2. Insistence on sameness, inflexible adherence to routines, or ritualized patterns of verbal or nonverbal behaviour (e.g., extreme distress at small changes, difficulties with transitions, rigid thinking patterns, greeting rituals, need to take same route or eat same food every day).

3. Highly restricted, fixated interests that are abnormal in intensity or focus (e.g., strong attachment to or preoccupation with unusual objects, excessively circumscribed or perseverative interests).

4. Hyper- or hypo-reactivity to sensory input or unusual interest in sensory aspects of the environment (e.g. apparent indifference to pain/temperature, adverse response to specific sounds or textures, excessive smelling or touching of objects, visual fascination with lights or movement).

Severity is based on social communication impairments and restricted, repetitive patterns of behaviour.

C. Symptoms must be present in the early developmental period (but may not become fully manifest until social demands exceed limited capacities, or may be masked by learned strategies in later life).

D. Symptoms cause clinically significant impairment in social, occupational, or other important areas of current functioning.

E. These disturbances are not better explained by intellectual disability (intellectual developmental disorder) or global developmental delay. Intellectual disability and autism spectrum disorder frequently co-occur; to make comorbid diagnoses of autism spectrum disorder and intellectual disability, social communication should be below that expected for general developmental level.

Note: Individuals with a well-established DSM-IV diagnosis of autistic disorder, Asperger's disorder, or pervasive developmental disorder not otherwise specified should be given the diagnosis of autism spectrum disorder. Individuals who have marked deficits in social communication, but whose symptoms do not otherwise meet criteria for autism spectrum disorder, should be evaluated for social (pragmatic) communication disorder.

NOTE: Diagnosis of Autism Spectrum Disorder can be made with or without:

- accompanying intellectual impairment.
- accompanying language impairment
- associated with a known medical or genetic condition or environmental factor
- associated with another neurodevelopmental, mental, or behavioural disorder

Chapter 10:

Pictures of Me (1)

This Social Story was described by Carol Gray in her regular publication "The Morning News" in the 1990's. I have used this strategy to explain ASD to clients and their families ever since I read her original article.

Children really enjoy making a book all about themselves, and learning why they feel and act differently to other children makes a huge difference.

See your therapist or teacher for more information.

Social Stories (2)

Social Stories were devised as a tool to help individuals with ASD better understand the nuances of interpersonal communication so that they could "interact in an effective and appropriate manner". Wikipedia

Carol Gray information (3)

For further information about Social Stories visit Carol Gray's website www.carolgraysocialstories.com

AUTHOR'S NOTES

This is a novel based on many years of working alongside families, children and adults who live on a daily basis with Autism Spectrum Disorders.

While it is a work of fiction, and no one person or situation is in any way real, so many of the events and incidents in this fiction are based on actual events that I have either witnessed or heard about as a result of that work.

I hope that through this work of fiction I can spread some light on the world of Autism, especially that of the "high-functioning" individuals who live and work alongside we "neuro-typicals", and in fact make this world a much better and more diverse place to be.

My years working with people on the Autism Spectrum have taught me to have the utmost respect for these individuals and for their families.

It is a difficult journey, no matter where you are on that Spectrum. And I believe that it is often harder for those who are "high-functioning" as they must engage in the "neuro-typical" world, a world which is often very hard work even for those of us who do <u>not</u> have sensory, social and behavioural challenges.

I have set this story in a rural area as that is where I have practised for the vast majority of my professional life.

In rural and remote areas of Australia, it is sometimes nearly impossible to get an accurate and timely diagnosis for an Autism Spectrum Disorder. Many types of therapy that are so helpful and necessary are often unavailable or lacking in the frequency with which they can be delivered.

Again, I have only the utmost respect for the few professionals who offer their services in these areas, who travel and persevere over many years to assist families to understand their precious sons and daughters.

To these dedicated and unsung heroes and heroines - Paediatricians, Psychologists, Speech Pathologists, Occupational Therapists, Physiotherapists, Teachers and Support Staff– you know who you are – very well done and please, keep up that amazing service to these rural and remote communities.

To the families who persevere in spite of little in the way of services and support, I take my hat off to you!

This is a journey of tears and laughter, of frustration and delight – all the extremes and everything in between. There will always be those who doubt your choices, sometimes within your own family group, but please persevere.

Get good and accurate advice and when you find a good therapist, stick to them like glue!! Developing that mutual trust and open relationship will benefit everyone, most of all the person with an ASD.

In my experience, the best outcomes occur when the following things align:

- **An early and accurate diagnosis.** No matter what the "Level" of autism, the other issues which may co-exist, or the family's and individual's own unique make-up, this is most important. Although good outcomes can still follow a later diagnosis, we are all very aware of the importance of Early Intervention when it can be consistently given.

- **Supportive family that remains positive and gives the child or adult with ASD as positive an outlook as possible.** Acceptance of difference is most important! So is looking ahead to those unusual pathways that can be taken to get to the outcome everyone wants. For example, if regular school is just not working, many try home-schooling, or choose to pursue secondary education through Distance Education, TAFE and then to University.

- **Informed advocacy** – either from parents and/or a supportive therapist or other person who understands the diagnosis, the person and the environment in which they live and work. At every stage the person with an ASD will need support, sometimes in the form of encouragement to keep on, sometimes in attendance at planning meetings, sometimes developing the aids (visual and other) that make life that bit easier. Always the person needs those who "get" him or her, to advocate with those who do not, to engage with the school or workplace to help find the best way forward for that person, even when it is NOT what the school or workplace has "usually" done, and most particularly if it is NOT what has been done before for the others with Autism that have passed that way!

Remember and quote – if you have met/taught/assisted/ worked with ONE person with an Autism Spectrum Disorder, you have met/taught/assisted/worked with ONE person with an Autism Spectrum Disorder!!!!

Every single person with an ASD is unique, and every "Individual Plan" needs to reflect that individual's strengths, needs, likes, interests, dislikes – ALL of them- not just what others think might be the case based on past experience.

Finally, I am amazed by those who daily deal with ASD as a family, and particularly by all those individuals who I have had the absolute pleasure of working with over many years.

Thank you all for informing my practise and making me a better therapist and teacher.

Thank you for always knowing more about your ASD than I do, and for finding ways to bring me into your world.

Viv Freestone